T0198656

Tendrils

Rachel Harville

iUniverse, Inc.
New York Bloomington

TENDRILS

iUniverse books may be ordered through booksellers or by contacting:

iUniverse
1663 Liberty Drive
Bloomington, IN 47403
www.iuniverse.com
1-800-Authors (1-800-288-4677)

ISBN: 978-1-4401-6652-5 (pbk)
ISBN: 978-1-4401-6653-2 (ebk)

Printed in the United States of America

iUniverse rev. date: 11/06/2009

I want to thank Cindy for being my right and left hand during this project. I want to thank Amber for being my teen voice. I want to thank my sister for encouraging my dream and my parents for believing I can accomplish anything I set my mind to.

Chapter One

The sun shined brightly through the large French doors that lined the back corner of Bailey's room. She turned in her sleep, trying to shield the light that would wake her from the dream—the dream that always seemed to take her away from the world she truly lived in, a dream where life was perfect…or at least in Bailey's eyes it was perfect. Bailey had grown so accustomed to the dream that it no longer annoyed her. She would let her mind sink deeper into the fantasy that it had created in order to protect her from the truth. In her dream, she was a priority in her parents' life—spending time with her was a gift instead of a chore, and her parents were attentive and caring the way she had seen other parents act. She was never quite sure why she had been dreaming the same dream since she was five years old. Instead of her nanny playing with her in the dream, her parents were there. It was always a sunny day in the park, with everyone laughing, playing and loving one another. In the beginning, the dream had caused Bailey a great deal of discomfort because she knew it never happened. She hated having to relive a daydream every night that would never come true. Her parents would never love her, and she knew it.

Bailey was not like most eighteen-year-old girls. Her parents were so caught up in their own lives that she had to help keep her sister,

Amber, on track and out of trouble. Bailey's parents had more money than they would ever need. Bailey and Amber both had million-dollar trust funds set up for when they turned twenty-one. Bailey didn't worry about money, but she was not like other girls who had such materialistic parents. She could honestly say she would rather have time with her parents growing up than the stupid trust fund they thought would heal her from a childhood lost to nannies and other household help. They traveled a lot for work and pleasure, leaving her and Amber to be cared for by people who got paid to care. It bothered Bailey that her parents were sometimes gone months at a times. She felt if she didn't have pictures of them around, she would truly forget what they looked like.

She could remember being so excited on her seventh birthday. Her mom had planned this big party and invited all of her schoolmates from her private all-girls school. Her mom rented an entire circus to perform. She was getting ready for the party when her mom walked into the room and handed her a box. Inside were ten hundred-dollar bills. "Mary will take you tomorrow to pick out your birthday presents. Daddy and I both hope you have a wonderful birthday. We'll see you in two months," Joanne said hastily as she walked out the door.

"Where are you going? It's my birthday! I thought you were going to be at my party!" Bailey yelled. Her questions made Joanne angry. She looked at her daughter with a cold expression, all traces of pretending to love her gone.

"Now, Bailey. We paid for everything. We don't have to be there for you to know we care. We have important business to tend to, and you have Mary here with you. Don't misbehave!" Joanne said, her tone harsh. "You have guests waiting." Bailey wiped away the tears and walked out to the backyard to the party. Not one single parent was there with their child. There were nannies and housekeepers to care for her classmates during the party. She went through the motions of a party, pretending to be happy just like she had seen her mother do many times with her friends—the facade of making the outside world think you're okay when inside you are falling apart. That night after the party, she cried herself to sleep with only Mary there to hold her.

Mary was a great nanny. Bailey believed she truly loved her, even though it was her job. It's not the same though as having your mom and dad around, but she still appreciated the fact that Mary was there. Mary was a live-in nanny. She had been there since Bailey was born. She cared for Bailey, and then Amber. She was the one who got up in the middle of the night if they were sick or needed her. She cared for them like a mother should, and in reality she was a mother to both of them. Mary, now thirty-six, was eighteen when she started the job.

When Bailey was alone, she sometimes worried about Mary. She thought about all the years she had wasted her life away working for her parents and wondered if she would ever meet someone and leave. This scared her. At eighteen, the thought of losing the only mother she had ever known scared her. Mary had met someone at church, and they had been dating now for five months. If things progressed, she knew it was only a matter of time before she left to start her own family. The thought of that made her feel alone and trapped.

All Bailey wanted was to break away from her life there, to truly get away from her parents, but her sister was just fifteen and still had two more years of high school left. How could she go away to college in September and leave her sister there, especially if Mary was gone? She would have to take it one day at a time and see how things went. Part of her, the selfish part, hoped Mary would stay until Amber graduated from high school, so she could go on with her life without worrying about her sister. The thought made her cry because Mary deserved to be happy. She thought about the years Mary had already wasted caring for her and Amber. She was not getting any younger.

Bailey still yearned to not have to wait for her parents to want to spend time with her. She hoped one day they would be the ones waiting for her. Bailey would graduate in two short months. Her entire high school experience would be over, and her life would change. She was planning to attend the University of California and major in art. She was starting a volunteer job at the local art museum on Saturday afternoon to refresh and rekindle her love of art. In her eyes, art had no rhyme or reason. It was the feelings and emotions of the artist laid out for the world to see and to take from it whatever it wanted. She was drawn to that—taking what she wanted and not what others wanted from her.

She got to the art museum early to pick up her name tag and vest. She would be walking around helping people find their way if they were lost. This would give her a chance to explore each section. Even though she would be helping people, she would still be able to look at the art and figure out what she saw in it. This would also give her a chance to learn more about the different periods and such.

She noticed him briefly when he walked past her. He moved with such poise and dignity that it was hard not to see him. He had an aura of self confidence but not an arrogant one. His eyes shown a sense of compassion for all those who walked among him. It was as if he held some unknown power over them and could force his will at any moment. Bailey knew her imagination was getting away from her so she tried to refocus on anything other than him, but she couldn't help but notice how handsome the stranger was.

He was ruggedly handsome. He looked like a true cowboy, a real man's man. He was dressed in dark denim jeans, a blue polo shirt and a brown, beat-up leather jacket with boots. He was very hot by all standards. He was lean with muscle and definition. He had green eyes and black, luscious hair that suited him well. He was very attractive and would have looked natural on an Abercrombie & Fitch bag.

Bailey felt an unknown pull toward the stranger. He was more beautiful than anyone she could ever picture herself with, but there was something hidden underneath that he didn't want the world to see. She could feel it there, but she just didn't know what it was. She stopped staring and moved on. He was not her type, and she imagined she was not his type either. She started looking at a few pieces of art while helping people find their way to the next section. When she looked up again, he was gone.

The week passed in a blur—school, soccer practice, homework, art classes, picking her sister up after cheerleading and then coming home to have dinner with Mary. After homework, she would usually spend the evening playing board games with her sister or talking to her BFF Annie. Annie was all kinds of different. Considering that they went to an all-girls school, it was no surprise Annie was a little boy crazy. Any chance she got to break away and hang out with her guy friends, she would drag Bailey along. Bailey went mainly to watch out for her and make sure she didn't do anything stupid. Bailey was not interested in any of the guys Annie seemed to find attractive. Oh they were cute, but they were so immature. She just never felt a connection to any of them. Bailey wished she was normal and wanted to fit in like everyone else, but that never suited her. She chose her own path and knew that she alone would make the choices that would determine where her life would take her.

The park they hung out at was a kiddy park by day and a crazy teenage hangout by night. It was stuck back in a little cove away from the main highway, and most cops never came around past 7:00 PM. They didn't meet up until after 8:00 PM most nights. So far, they had never had a police encounter there. They cleaned up any trash before they left, so no one ever knew they hung out there. They also called it by a code name. During the day, it was Hannigan Park, named after some big official who donated a bunch of money to have it updated. Teenagers just called it "The Hang." It was a place to drink, make out and be a little out of control.

Chapter Two

It was Friday night, and Annie called Bailey to go hang out at the park. She didn't want to go, but Annie was insistent. She wanted to say no to Annie. She wanted to say that she had no desire to hang out with a bunch of guys who thought it was funny to see who could drink the most before they threw up, but she knew Annie was not going to let her get away with not going. She needed a wing man, and Bailey was it. Annie pulled up into Bailey's driveway and texted her that she was there. Bailey told Mary goodbye and that she would try and be home early. When Bailey hopped into the car, the true fun began.

Annie was in love with Kyle. Kyle was all she wanted to talk about day and night. This drove Bailey crazy, but she would let her rant on and on about Kyle. Bailey was always grateful when Annie's mom would pick up the phone and yell for Annie to get off the phone and go to bed. She wanted to be a good friend to Annie, but her boy crazy personality sometimes strained their friendship. She wondered if Annie ever thought of anything else, whether she ever dreamed of being anything. Annie seemed to live her life in the moment, not truly understanding that at some point she would have to decide what future she wanted for herself. Annie had a trust fund set up for her when she turned twenty-one, just like Bailey and Amber. Bailey assumed Annie's life would be about the trust money and all it would get her. She hoped it was enough to care for her for the rest of her life because she had no aspirations to have a career. Annie never talked about college or what she wanted to do when she was an adult. Annie had said something once or twice about taking two years to see the world, but Bailey just wanted to finish her education before she did anything else. It was her passion, so why wait to pursue it?

Kyle, along with his best friend Brice, was hanging in the back seat. Brice gave Bailey a smile that was supposed to be seductive but looked a little scary. Kyle gave Bailey his usual scowling grimace. Kyle and Bailey didn't get along. They were both barely able to tolerate one another, but they knew it was part of the deal to be able to have Annie in their lives. When they got to the park, it was already hopping with teens, and people were everywhere. Bailey wanted to crawl into the back seat of Annie's car and hide out until it was over, but Annie pulled her along as they joined a group of kids that Annie knew. Bailey had never seen them before.

The kids were in a group, sitting on picnic tables. Each one looked like they were drinking or had been drinking. Bailey sighed a long, miserable sigh. Annie looked at her and rolled her eyes. The number of boys to girls looked pretty even, so she knew at some point they would all be hooking up, and one would try to hit on her. She dreaded having to fight off a complete moron, but she would do it and deal. They all seemed to grow less uptight as the influence of alcohol took over. Bailey didn't understand why anyone would drink. If she wanted to have fun, she could. She didn't think it was fun to hang out with people who looked like they didn't know if it was day or night outside.

Bailey tried to remain in the background and not draw attention to herself. Then she noticed the pig giving her the once over. She saw the look on his face and knew there was going to be trouble. He approached her with this bullying attitude, and Bailey automatically went on the defensive. "Hey, I'm Seth, your dream come true," Seth slurred almost inaudibly as the smell of alcohol hit Bailey pungently in the face.

"Excuse me?" Bailey snapped. She thought, *how pathetic a line is that.* Seth was a very large guy. He was 6'3 and at least 225 pounds. He looked like every ounce of his body was muscle. Bailey didn't like the look on his face. He was looking at her like he would get his way whether she wanted him to or not. She smiled and slowly moved away from him.

"Where do you think you're going?" Seth asked aggressively.

"That is none of your business," Bailey snapped. Annie had disappeared about fifteen minutes ago into the woods with Kyle. Bailey knew they were making out. Seth grabbed her arm and pulled her into the woods. No one noticed because they were all too intoxicated. "Let me go!" Bailey screamed, her heart racing as she tried in vain to fight off the big ogre. But he was too strong for her. She tried to remain level-headed but panicked when Seth's massive grip tightened on her arm. "SETH, LET ME GO!" Bailey screamed, her breathing heavy. Seth continued to ignore her with full disregard as he pulled her into the woods. The panic quickly turned into a natural instinct for survival Bailey never knew existed for her, and she began to fight him. She clawed at his arms and was able to draw blood. He didn't seem to notice, so she kicked him but his solid mass ended up hurting her instead. Just as Bailey was about to pass out from the fear of what was about to happen to her, she saw something out of the corner of her eye, but it moved so quickly that she wasn't sure if her eyes were playing tricks on her. When she turned to get a better look, she felt Seth release her arm. By the time she looked back around to see why he decided to let her go, he was gone.

Bailey ran back to the car with a feeling that she was being watched, but she made no attempt to try and see who was watching her. She just wanted to get back to the car and wait for Annie to come out of the woods, so they could go home. Bailey didn't want another run in with Seth, so she slipped past all the teenagers and climbed into the back seat of Annie's car, locking the doors once inside. It was in the safety of the car that she realized how close she came to being hurt, and she couldn't hold back the fear any longer. She began to cry. Annie and Kyle came back to the car about an hour later, and Bailey drove everyone home. Bailey didn't say anything to anyone about that night, and she knew she never would. She was just thankful for whatever took Seth's attention away from her.

When Bailey awoke on Saturday morning, she was sore from the struggle at the park. Had it been a weekday, she would have skipped school. But her Saturdays were devoted to the art museum, and it was sheer passion that pulled her from the bed. Today, Bailey would be going to the art museum for pleasure, just as she did every other Saturday when she was not volunteering. She would be able to lose herself in each piece with no interruptions. She frequently lost track of time while at the museum and often found herself staring at the same piece of art for way past the norm, tracing each delicate stroke in her mind and imagining someday that she would create great works that would blanket these walls. Her friends would never understand her love for art. She had attempted once or twice to lure Annie or Amber there with her, but the only response Bailey ever got from them was an eye roll and a comment about not doing school stuff on weekends, so Bailey never pushed the subject after that.

Bailey was absorbed in a European painting when she glanced up and saw the familiar stranger. He was across the room, focused on the artwork in front of him. She continued around the room, taking in each piece slowly. Suddenly, he was right beside her, swiftly maneuvering his body to avoid a collision. She gasped. "I'm sorry…" he said, clearly embarrassed. "I wasn't paying attention to where I was walking…I didn't mean to frighten you." As he regained his composure, he realized she was the girl he saved last night from the intoxicated Neanderthal at the park—his diner in desperate times. Last night was no different, except that he was able to have dinner and also save a beautiful girl in distress. The boy didn't know what hit him…or bit him rather. He was pulled into the woods as helplessly as the girl had previously been. He deserved to die, but he would be okay and never remember what happened.

When their eyes met, he knew he had found her. He was in shock at first. An eternity of searching and truly believing he was destined to stay a vampire forever, and here she stood before him, oblivious to her ability to save him from immortality. Disbelief, confusion, possible fear flashed one by one across her face as he continued to pierce her soul with his gaze. He pulled his eyes away to avoid frightening her further. He would never hurt her. He struggled to avoid eye contact, but his eyes were drawn like magnets to hers once again. A banding of light tendrils expanded from her and linked themselves to him. The tendrils of light were like golden strands of vines that linked their very essences together. Of course, no one but him could see it. He knew she was his soul mate—the one who could free him from the curse.

"Hi, I'm Ashton," he said, in as normal a tone as he could muster under the circumstances. Bailey was still in a haze of disbelief, not understanding what had just happened.

"I'm sorry…what did you say?" she asked, while shaking her head a little, as if trying to free her brain from a fog.

He repeated, "My name is Ashton. What is your name?"

"Oh…my name is Bailey. It's nice to meet you, Ashton."

He knew he had to find out as much about her as possible without appearing to be a creepy stalker. "I'm sorry I almost plowed into you. I come here every Saturday, so you would think I could act more civilized, especially in the presence of a beautiful woman," he laughed, trying to seem breezy but not knowing whether he was able to pull it off.

"Well, I completely understand. I come here a lot, too. I'm surprised I've never *run* into you before," she laughed, hoping he caught the pun. He laughed along with her. Bailey was still trying to figure out why she was drawn to him and why he was talking to her. She was overwhelmingly flattered by his compliment but tried to restrain her joy to keep from blushing.

"So…you like art?" he asked with extreme interest.

"Yes, so much that I will be majoring in it when I start college in the fall," she said.

"Then you have a passion for it?" he asked.

"Yeah, I guess you could say that," she replied.

He knew she felt the pull, and he didn't want to scare her, so he said, "Well I'm sure I'll see you around."

Bailey told him goodbye and walked around to look at some more paintings. When she turned to watch him walk away, he was gone. *Wow, that was weird. What was that? Why did I feel so funny around him?* she thought. She blew it off to teenage hormones and went on to the next section. Before she even realized it, she had been at the museum for over four hours. It was time to go.

When Ashton saw her leaving, he went invisible and followed her. *So much for not being a creepy stalker*, he thought. He followed her to her car and slid inside when she opened the door. He couldn't just let her leave and risk never seeing her again. He had to at least know where she lived. He could hardly believe his gift of a human life was right beside him. He didn't yet realize that she was his gift of life period, not just a human life. As Bailey pulled her car from the curb, Ashton's mind was lost in thought at how long he had waited for her and how he was different from other vampires.

Chapter Three

Ashton had almost given up on ever being human again. After all, he had been alone for 129 years. He had no reason to believe that would ever change. He had spent all these years searching for her—his one true love, someone to see his true self and not the thing he had become. He could still remember how it felt to be human. He was afraid of losing every single cell of his old life. He thought that was inevitable. After all, not a single vampire in history had ever been released from the curse and become human again.

The witch who cursed him with the life of a vampire didn't realize he was special. He had the ability to hold onto some of his humanity and part of his soul. He had met many vampires over the course of his life, and he found that most were too blood thirsty to even think about finding love. They were more likely to kill the person for blood lust than to fall in love and be released from the curse, but Ashton held on to what he could. He still needed blood in order to live, but he would sway people to his will and take only what he could without harming them. He healed them afterward, leaving no mark or memory of the encounter. He didn't like doing this, but this was what he had to do in order to survive. He knew that if he ever found her that he would be free of the blood lust all together. All he wanted was to be human again.

He had lived so many years just going through the motions. He wanted to do more than just exist. He wanted to truly live, and he knew life would never be the same for him once he found her.

When Bailey pulled into the driveway, Ashton was in awe of her house…or estate rather. He started to wonder what he would ever be able to offer her after a lifetime of privilege. He wasn't poor, but he wasn't rich either. He had spent most of his life working different ranches and was finally able to purchase his own ranch in Texas fifty years ago. Something had brought him to this new place three months ago—a need for change, a need to experience a different life, a need to try one last time to find her. Ranching was a lonely life, very fitting for a vampire. He didn't have to worry about people noticing that he didn't age. He was so strong and fit that he was able to work the ranch all by himself.

So he boarded up the ranch and sold the cattle. And off he went to the big city, where he would search for her one last time before going insane. When Ashton settled on his ranch fifty years ago, he had basically given up on ever finding his true love. He decided to live what life he could as a vampire. It wasn't so bad. The fact that he could exist on red meat for a short period of time made it better. He owned a large herd. The longest he had ever gone without drinking human blood was one month. He usually went as far away from his home as possible to sway a human to let him drink.

Ashton was kind for a vampire. He didn't crave the kill like other vampires did. For them, the blood lust is so intense that it is impossible to control. It is a yearning that can surpass all other desires. There is an infatuation for human blood, just like people have a passion for one another. Vampires cannot resist human blood. It is as natural as a human having to breathe. The blood lust is instinctual. Ashton couldn't resist the blood either, but he didn't kill in order to get human blood. He only took what he could without harming the person. This is what made him special. No other vampire has ever existed that would not give in to the blood lust and drain a human dry before being able to stop. He just wanted to get the blood he needed and not leave any trace behind for the human to know he existed. He never took any blood from the old because most were just too weak to survive a vampire, even what little he took. Also, he preferred the fresh taste of young blood. With age, blood starts to taste bitter. Babies had the sweetest blood, like milk and honey in human terms. It was the richest flavor imaginable. But he preferred the blood of humans in their twenties. He liked to think that he had a refined taste. Their blood was just the right vintage for him. In reality, he preferred their blood because they were the strongest and could recover quickly from the bite. The feeding process took less than five minutes. The hard part was finding the victims and swaying them with no one else around to see it happen.

Bailey pulled her car into the garage. As she opened the car door, Ashton slid quickly out. Bailey felt strange, like someone was watching her. She went into the house while Ashton slipped out the garage door. Vampires cannot enter a home without being invited. He watched Bailey as she walked through the house and into the kitchen. She called out for Mary and Amber, but neither was home. She looked at the time and guessed Mary was taking Amber to some sort of party or sleepover. Sure enough, on the island in the kitchen was a note that said, "Bailey, taking Amber to Caroline's house for a sleepover. Be back soon." Bailey had tried time and time again to teach Mary to text, but she just refused. She thought writing notes or talking on the phone was more personal, and she would not accept any other form of communication with Amber or Bailey. Bailey thought she just wanted to let them know she cared enough to talk to them or leave a note, which is more than she could say for her so-called parents. She had not seen them in four months. They would be coming home for the Fourth of July this year, but only for a week and then off to another exotic location. She walked upstairs to her room.

Ashton floated up to the second floor and landed on the balcony to Bailey's room. Bailey opened the French doors to let in the fresh air. Her room was large and not at all what he expected from a girl her age. He guessed that she was eighteen years old, based upon her comment at the museum that she would be starting college in the fall. He figured there would be posters of hot Hollywood guys on her wall, and lots of girly things. Her room looked more like an art studio than anything else. There were easels holding many different projects in the making. On the back wall was row after row of art supplies, including paint, brushes, pencils and blank canvases. Everything was well organized and labeled, but there was chaos in each canvas that held her work. One of her paintings immediately caught his eye. It was a little girl standing alone on an iceberg. She was holding a black balloon and just drifting. This one made him sad. It made him want to go to her and put his arms around her. He could tell the child was scared and alone. He wondered what kind of life she had lived.

Bailey walked onto the balcony. He was so close that he could smell her citrus shampoo. He resisted the urge to reach out and touch her hair. She sat down in a lounger and closed her eyes, trying to free her mind of all thoughts. Ashton went to the opened French doors to get a better view of her room and the things that made up her world. Her bed was not a teenager's bed. He was expecting a twin bed, but she had a queen cherry sleigh bed with a blue comforter set. He wondered if blue was her favorite color. Several bean bag chairs were arranged in a circle on the floor. Maybe this is where she hung out with her friends. He noticed she didn't have a TV in her room. In fact, she didn't have any electronic equipment other than an iPod and doc station. He didn't even see a computer. From the looks of this house, they probably had a room just for computers.

Bailey's thoughts went to her encounter with Ashton. She wondered if he truly talked to her, or if she was just dazed and confused. He had been thinking about other things and didn't realize it when he heard her think his name. He started listening to her thoughts more closely to see what they would reveal, but other than thinking it was weird she didn't linger on him. Instead, she was thinking about what to do if Mary left before her sister graduated high school. He didn't know who Mary was but wondered why this bothered her so. She also had a few random thoughts of hurt and anger toward her parents. He walked over to watch her. He was only a few feet away when, all of a sudden, she opened her eyes and startled him. For an instant, he thought maybe she could see him. She was looking directly into his eyes. He breathed a sigh of relief when she turned her head and got up to walk downstairs. Some lady was pulling in, and he wondered who this was.

"Hey, Mary. How was your day?"

"Pretty good. I spent the day with Jack. How was your day?" Jack is the church guy. Ashton heard her thoughts of not liking Jack for taking Mary away and decided at this point he should go and give her some space. He would see her again as soon as possible. He heard her say as he started to leave, "I had a good day. My usual Saturday at the museum." Bailey wondered all of a sudden why she felt part of herself had just left the room. She looked around, wondering what was going on with her today. Why did she feel so out of sorts and not herself?

"Are you going anywhere tonight?" Mary asked.

"No, I have work to do in the studio," Bailey said.

"Bailey, it's Saturday night. Go be a teenager. Why don't you call and see if Annie wants to come over. You could go to the new club with the cool bands. It's just for kids your age," Mary said.

Bailey didn't want to hurt Mary's feelings or say too much about where Annie was tonight. She didn't want to say the last place she would ever be is the new club called The Underground with its very different music and people she would never know how to be friends with. Annie had taken her there a few times. Annie could fit into any social situation, no matter that she too came from the right side of the money track. Maybe it was because she would partake in the activities with everyone else, but Bailey just didn't want to do things to numb herself to the world. In a way, she already walked around numb and didn't want to be so numb she would disappear. Plus, it's just not her scene. Annie would be there with Kyle, and she was sure they would get into a fight. Annie resented Bailey for being so protective over her, sometimes more like a mom than a friend. Bailey decided to let Annie do what she wanted from now on. She could no longer try to keep her safe. It was not her job to do that. She knew Kyle would break Annie's heart, and she would have to pick up the pieces. That's what friends do. Besides, who was she to judge? At least Annie was putting herself out there.

Bailey had closed herself off from guys. She decided she was not ready to deal with the emotional drama that came with being in a relationship. She wanted to grow as a person and find out who she was before she lost herself in a relationship. If she was being honest with herself, she knew she didn't want to think about a relationship, because she had seen the relationship between her parents. She didn't want a guy telling her how to live her life. Her mother seemed like her father's puppet, and this drove Bailey insane. She wondered sometimes if her mother truly was her mother. They didn't have anything in common. Her mother's world was filled with superficial activities. Joanne was always focused on playing the right role. Bailey didn't really believe she enjoyed her life. She had seen her mother only one time when her guard was down. This had affected Bailey more than anything her mother had ever done to her. Seeing her mother broken and crying and having no aspiration to find out why or even attempt to comfort her made Bailey think she too had a heart that was made of stone. Her mom was the socialite, and Bailey was the suffering artist type. Bailey didn't need all the hype of being invited to the social events of the year, and she wondered if, deep down, Joanne didn't want to be who she had become.

After seeing Ashton today, Bailey thought she might actually like to find someone to love her for her, but she didn't know if he existed. All the guys she had been set up with over the years were so immature, or focused on getting something from her she was not willing to give. She assumed she would be better off not putting herself out there. It wasn't so bad not having a boyfriend. At least she could look back on her life and say, I went my entire junior and senior years without having to be with a guy. *Who am I kidding? I feel like a loser. Part of being a teenager is dating, first love, crushes and stuff like that.* Mary brought her attention back to the conversation when she asked, "Bailey, are listening to me?"

"Sorry, Mary. Guess I was daydreaming. Annie already has plans. Besides, I'm really tired from spending the day at the museum. I'm inspired to work on some of my art projects tonight," she said.

Bailey grabbed a dinner salad and Dr. Pepper and went upstairs after saying goodnight to Mary. She started working on one of the canvas pieces, a project she had been working on for months. She was surprised when she realized it was complete. She didn't think she would ever complete this one, and now it was done. It was dark, but most of her art was filled with dark emotion. She fell asleep happy that night.

Chapter Four

Sunday was like any other Sunday. Mary went to church, and Amber was always over at Caroline's on Saturday nights, staying until late afternoon on Sundays. Bailey had the day to herself. Sometimes she would go with Mary to church, but today she wanted to do something else. It was beautiful outside. She thought of going to the beach and hanging out. She called to see if Annie wanted to go, but she was too tired from being up all night partying. Bailey decided she would take a few things to keep herself entertained. She got a sketch pad, a poetry book, her iPod, a blanket, a cooler, a salad and a bottle of water and decided to make a day of it. The beach was not very crowded, considering the magnificence of the sunshine and the perfect weather. She got everything set up and started sketching the ocean.

Some people like art but are not artists. Bailey was truly talented. She could draw anything, paint and sculpt. You could say she was a jack of all trades when it came to art. She didn't notice Ashton at first, until the light reflected off his sunglasses. He was sitting a few yards away, strumming a guitar. Back when he was human, he loved to write songs, but that was kind of lost when he lost part of his humanity. Something about finding her brought that passion back to him, and he was singing and writing. She liked this. He was creative, and creative people are attracted to other creative people. He watched her watch him, but she didn't know it. He heard her thoughts of liking the fact he was musical. A thought of thinking he was cute slipped through her mind as well, and this made his heart flutter. Yes, vampires have hearts.

Ashton's mind flooded with all the misconceptions about vampires. Hollywood portrayed vampires as undead monsters who rise up from the grave and stalk innocent girls for the kill. But vampires are not the undead. In a way, vampires are trapped between worlds. They are not human, but they are not truly non-human. They still have all the organs and body parts of a human body, but the curse causes the body to stop in time. The blood becomes cursed and like an elixir of life that keeps the organs and body tissue vital. The organs and body remain vital and continue to work as if they were the age of the person cursed. A person cursed at birth would not transform until he turned sixteen, so he would forever have the internal organs of a sixteen-year-old. Ashton was cursed when he was twenty, so even though he was over a hundred years old, he had the eternal organs and outside appearance of a twenty-year-old.

The body becomes shielded by the curse too. It strengthens the vampire's abilities. Everything they could do as a human becomes supernatural. Instead of being able to see two hundred feet away, a vampire can see fifty miles away. Instead of being able to pick up a hundred pounds, they can pick up fifty times that amount. They can also see through buildings, but they cannot see through metal. They can float and move so fast they cannot be seen by human eyes. The ability to go invisible makes them excellent predators, leaving their prey unaware they are being stalked for the kill.

Ashton's mind moved on to thinking about Bailey. He was wondering how to approach her. He had courted a girl in his human life and really loved her, but she died of scarlet fever and he didn't pursue anyone after that. He figured he would never find anyone like her. She was so beautiful, and her heart was so pure. About a week after she passed, the witch started pursuing him. Perfidia had seen Ashton from a distance and wanted him. She noticed the young girl that he courted and was extremely jealous. Perfidia would not let this human girl get in her way of having him. She set about to form a spell—one that would resemble a human disease—to kill her. Once she was out of the way, Ashton would be hers. As she watched them swoon over one another, Perfidia thought she might even consider loving this one…if she were able to do so.

Ashton wanted to marry Elizabeth and was planning to ask her soon. He loved her. She loved him too. But he was worried he wouldn't be able to provide for her and a family. He had saved up some money, but if he waited a little longer they could purchase their own ranch and start their lives together. He decided he would ask her in a month, just as soon as he could find her the right ring. Perfidia watched as Ashton held Elizabeth's hand and looked at her with eyes filled with love.

Even though Perfidia could not read either of their thoughts, she knew they loved one another, something she hated more than anything. She went to her potion room and started making the spell that would kill Elizabeth. If the spell was cast when the moon was full, she would die in less than twenty-four hours. The next full moon was in two days. Perfidia had everything set. She had gotten some of the girl's essence when she "accidentally" brushed against her in town one day. All she had to do now was mix the essence with the other ingredients and speak the spell, and the girl would be dead in less than twenty-four hours.

Ashton looked into Elizabeth's eyes the night of the full moon and decided right then, ring or not, he would ask her to marry him. "Elizabeth, I have loved you from the moment we met. I don't have a lot to offer you, other than my heart. If you will have me, I will do everything to make you happy. I know I don't have a ring yet, but I will get you one," Ashton said.

"Yes! Yes!" Elizabeth cried. She died that night in her sleep. The doctor said it was scarlet fever but was puzzled that it had taken her so quickly. Nonetheless, she was gone…and Ashton was lost.

A week later, Perfidia showed up at Ashton's door and tried to use her powers to lure him, but her powers didn't work because he was mourning his lost love. She was High Priestess Witch, and this made her angry. In the beginning, she had never failed to persuade them to follow her. She was able to get many to become her human minions, instead of having to curse them into vampires. She drew more power from human pain, so she preferred humans to vampires. Being cursed into a vampire was her punishment for denying her request for servitude. She would keep the humans for about ten years before killing them. On rare occasions, she erased their memory and allowed them to return to their family.

Perfidia visited Ashton every night for a week, trying to lure him from his home to come with her, but he was suffering the loss of Elizabeth, so he didn't see Perfidia. On the eighth night, her anger made flames of fire around her. She commanded him to follow her or suffer the consequences. She told him that he now belonged to her and must follow her instructions. He was scared, but he was a man. Even though he had never seen anything like this before, he knew to follow her would eventually bring death anyway, so he decided to face her and die with dignity.

Perfidia attempted to change his mind by torturing him for hours and then asking him to follow her. Again, he refused. The torture continued, and he refused time and time again. She grew more and more angry, and he grew weaker and weaker from the torture. Had she not been blinded by hatred and the desire to always be in control, she would have taken him back to her house and tried to persuade him over time. She really did want to keep this one, but her past wouldn't let her love, so she cast the spell that would turn him into a vampire.

"Vomica cruor phantom ex lux lucis, vas of obscurum."

Once the words were spoken, she could not stop the transformation. Only a High Priestess Witch or wizard could use such a powerful curse to transform a human into becoming a vampire. Once they were a vampire, they would not be able to deny any request by their maker. Ashton would become a vampire in three days. Perfidia told him what he would become and that he would be blood thirsty and kill human after human.

"Ashton, I'm going to explain the rules of living as a vampire. Do heed my warnings," Perfidia said. "You will be human no more. Your lust for blood will not allow you to live with humans. You will exist in the human world, but you can no longer live in it, for the blood lust will be your new soul. Try not to draw too much attention to any area by killing too many humans in the same place. The only way you will cease to exist is if you are killed by a witch or wizard who is in possession of a wizard's blade. The only way you will die by the hand of a human is if you enter into a home uninvited. This is the one place a human is safe and cannot be hunted. If you enter into a home uninvited, you will burst into flames and disappear from existence. There is no afterlife for a vampire, for you have no soul."

"What do you mean; I will not have a soul?" Ashton asked, panic clear in his shaking voice.

"I mean the transformation from a human to vampire decimates the soul," Perfidia said as she laughed a truly wicked snicker when he cried out in pain. His sorrow fed her thirst for more power. A witch or wizard gains more power from a human's mere misery. Even though he would soon be a vampire, in that moment he was still human and knew he would not be able to stop it. For the last week, all Ashton's thoughts had been about seeing Elizabeth again in the afterlife and now even that had been taken from him. For Ashton, everything went black. When he woke up three days later, he was a vampire. He had a craving for blood, but he didn't realize it because he thought everything was a dream. Ashton realized it was not a dream when he couldn't stand to be around people. He wanted to tear into them, but something about him was fighting against his vampire instinct. He didn't understand what this was, but for some reason, after that first week, the urge to kill was gone and never returned. He assumed this was the life of a vampire. He grew so weak that he slept for days. He finally decided to try human blood.

After the vampire instinct kicked in, it was easy to lure humans away and sway their minds to let him drink. After all, he was beautiful. He also had mind-control powers, so he could lure them away easily. Some would go with him just because of his beauty, others he had to sway with mind control. Most women would have followed him off a cliff if he asked them to. After a while, he learned that his saliva sealed the wound he inflicted, leaving no evidence of the encounter. He traveled miles from home to hunt to avoid the chance of ever running into his victims again. He was afraid they would remember him. Later, he discovered his ability to erase their memory of the event. This allowed him to stay close to home.

Ashton looked up in time to see Bailey smile, so he smiled back. He walked over and said, "Bailey, right?"

"Yes, I'm Bailey. Ashton, right?"

"Yes, so how's my art girl?"

She blushed. *His art girl? I wish!* she thought. He smiled at this.

"What are you sketching?" he asked.

"Just some ocean views," she said.

"Can I take a look at it?" he asked.

"Sure," she said. He was really impressed with her artistic ability.

"It's very good. Do you do self portraits?" he asked.

"I have never done a self portrait, but I do draw random people, and sometimes my sister Amber."

"Would you like to use me as a subject?" He asked. Bailey looked puzzled.

"I mean, would you like to draw me?" he asked. She blushed and thought, *draw him? Kiss him was more like it.* She pushed that thought from her mind. He smiled again.

"Sure. A live subject is always fun to draw," she said.

"With guitar…or without?" he asked, as he held the guitar in position and then let it fall to his side while she made her decision.

"Hmmm…sit down and play me a song. I'll draw you in action," she said with confidence in her voice. They chatted while he strummed. She started sketching him effortlessly, giving her mind an opportunity to wander, *how do I flirt? Do I even know how to flirt? I'm hopeless.* He chuckled at her thoughts. Bailey looked at him with a questioning expression on her face.

"Just thinking about how I've been here for three months and never seen you. Now fate has brought us together two times within twenty-four hours," Ashton said.

"Fate? What makes you think fate brought us together?" she asked with one eyebrow raised.

"What else could it be? Dream girls just don't appear on your front doorsteps," he said. Bailey snorted at that response.

"Where did you pick up that line?" she asked.

"Line? What do you mean?" he asked.

"The pick-up line you just said about me being your dream girl," she said.

"I don't have pick-up lines. You're the first girl I've talked to in a long while," he said while giving her a seductive look. Bailey thought, *don't forget to breathe.*

Bailey composed herself and said, "I find that hard to believe."

"Why?" he asked with a crooked smile. She blushed.

"I just do," she said. He smiled because she was thinking, *you love art, you're musical and you're gorgeous. Don't dwell on it too long. Change the subject quickly before you look like a complete moron.*

He decided to help her change the subject. "Bailey, what are your other interests?" he asked.

She sighed, "Hmm…good question. Let's see. Soccer is my sport. It's a way for me to kick butt. I love reading books. I enjoy anything where I can be creative. I am absolutely *obsessed* with poetry," she said. Bailey's obsession with poetry was just another release for her, just like art. It was a way to liberate the pain, so it didn't engulf her. She could set these emotions free with each stroke of the paint brush or each script of the pen.

"What are you interested in, other than art and playing guitar?" she asked.

"I love horses, nature, doing anything outdoors. I have a great affection for sleeping under the stars by the riverbank. Playing guitar is more of a hobby really. I'm not very good at it," he said.

"I like the way you play, even if it is just for fun," she said, blushing a little at her own comment.

"Thanks," he said, as he smiled at her.

After a while, the getting-to-know-you chatter ceased, but there was no awkward silence. The artist and her subject. The musician and his audience. They were both completely engulfed in the natural beauty of the entire experience. Music and the sound of pencil against paper filled the air, against a backdrop of waves rippling against the shore. Ashton watched as Bailey's hair undulated in the light breeze. He really started to notice the streams of light that connected them again. When they were close enough to each other, the light bound them together like a vine climbing up the side of a fence. This gave him great comfort after so many years of being alone.

Hours passed like minutes and before long the sun looked like a giant orange trying to sneak behind the horizon. Bailey reluctantly said to Ashton, "I need to go home. It's getting late." He went around and sat beside her to see the picture she drew of him. It was perfect. It looked just like him.

"Wow, I'm impressed," he said.

"Thanks," she muttered, a little embarrassed.

As she handed the drawing to him, he said, "Keep it…to remember me by."

How could I ever forget you? she thought. He smiled. Bailey got up to leave. "I guess I'll see you at the museum," she said, a little disappointed that he had not asked for her number.

"I'm sure you will, but do you mind if I get your number? I'm not letting you go that easily," he said.

She froze. *He wants my number? Is this reality?* she thought. Part of her, the cautious part, didn't want to give him the number because she would be crushed if he didn't call. She really liked him, but it seemed that everyone she liked or loved never returned the feeling, aside from her sister and Mary of course. She was tired of being afraid to love, so she tore off a piece of paper and jotted down her cell number before she had time to talk herself out of it. This pleased him.

"I'll call you tomorrow. What time is good for you?" he asked.

She thought, *Yeah, right. I'm sure you will. Guys never do what they say.* Nonetheless, she decided to play along. "I get out of school tomorrow at lunch. It's half day for seniors. Just leave a message if I don't answer, and I'll call you back," she said.

Smart girl, he thought. *She wants me to know she won't be waiting for my call.* He liked her independence, but he didn't like how guarded she was. She was afraid to trust anyone. He wondered what had happened to make her feel that way. He wanted to reach out and hold her right there.

"Bailey, thanks for a fun day. Can't wait to see you again," he said. As Bailey walked away, she was trying to come to terms with the fact that Ashton seemingly liked her. Thoughts raced through her mind. *I should have said this. I should have done that. I wonder if he'll call me. He probably thought I was a dork when I snorted while laughing.* Ashton secretly watched her to make sure she made it to her car safely. He didn't offer to walk her because he wanted to play it cool and not appear too clingy. Besides, he was having too much fun reading her thoughts.

That evening, Bailey was in a more cheerful mood than normal. She hummed Ashton's song while she fixed a bite to eat. Mary and Amber noticed her smiling to herself, as if having a private conversation in her head. She was in a completely different world. Mary and Amber looked at each other strangely and then at Bailey, who was oblivious that they were even in the room. "What is going on with you tonight?" they both asked simultaneously.

"Huh?" Bailey asked as she snapped back to earth.

"Why are you acting so…weird?" Amber asked.

"I'm just happy. I had a good day…that's all," Bailey replied.

"Happy?" Amber asked. "I didn't know you knew what that word was," she laughed.

"Oh, shut up, Amber," Bailey said, as she got up to leave. She walked upstairs to her room and closed the door. A few minutes later, there was a knock at the door.

"It's me," Mary said with a familiar voice that Bailey knew all too well. "Do you want to talk, Bailey? Is something wrong?"

"I'm fine, Mary. I'm just a little tired. Can we talk tomorrow?" Bailey asked.

"Sure," Mary said. "Get some rest. We'll talk tomorrow."

That night, Bailey went to bed for the first time ever with a peace and calmness that she didn't recognize. She slept so well that she didn't hear the alarm clock go off. She had to hurry to get to school on time. She grabbed some jeans and a t-shirt and put her hair in a ponytail. There was no time for makeup, but she hardly ever wore makeup anyway. She was not really into fashion. It's hard to be fashionable when your school dress code is a uniform. She was so grateful, especially today, that seniors didn't have a dress code the last two months of school. It was a stepping stone to their independence. They would no longer be part of a unit. She no longer had to rely solely on her personality to set her apart. What a relief.

When she arrived at school in jeans and a t-shirt, her friends rolled their eyes. They were all dressed in the latest fashion. "Who is going to dress Bailey tomorrow?" Annie asked. Everyone started laughing. Bailey joined in. She dealt with her little clique of friends by not taking their remarks to heart. They were more or less Annie's friends. She really wondered sometimes why Annie was her best friend. After all, they were so different. They had really grown apart over the past year. Annie was focused on being at all the cool parties and spending time with Kyle, while Bailey was more interested in spending time at the museum. Bailey had become a person who didn't really enjoy much of her life. All she wanted was to break away, and all Annie wanted was to live in the moment—the same moment over and over again—as long as her parents would fund it. Annie's parents were around more than Bailey's, so they did seem to truly love her. Maybe her life was different. Maybe she didn't need or want to escape, but Bailey did.

Bailey got through history and Algebra and finally made it to economics. She would be free to leave in less than forty minutes. Annie was in her economics class and usually wanted to text back and forth about Kyle. The only answers Bailey had to reply were *TMI, WTF* and *OMG*. This made it easy for Annie to rant on and on without Bailey truly having to listen. But then Annie really caught Bailey's attention when she texted something about Kyle's cousin Adam wanting to meet her.

"What are you talking about?" Bailey texted.

"Kyle's cousin is really interested in going out with you," Annie replied.

"Why? Kyle hates me. That doesn't make sense," Bailey wrote.

"Kyle may not like you, but Adam thinks you're very attractive!" Annie replied.

Bailey rolled her eyes at Annie. Annie was clueless. Kyle was playing some kind of cruel joke on her. After all, Adam was a sophomore in college and Kyle hated Bailey, so he must have told his cousin everything about her. Kyle thought she was weird for not wanting to drink and have fun, but Adam didn't think so. He was majoring in medicine and wanted a woman with an independent streak who didn't just follow the crowd. From Kyle's description of Bailey, he felt she was perfect for him. He had seen her picture and, although she was no beauty queen, she was real. He thought she was beautiful.

The teacher gave a pop quiz, so the texting stopped. After class, Annie walked over to talk to Bailey. "What are your plans for the rest of the day?" Annie asked.

"Well, I was thinking of going back to the beach. I had a great time there yesterday," Bailey said.

"Really? Why? Did you meet a guy?" Annie asked in a mocking tone.

"Well...actually I did," Bailey said.

Annie squealed, "Tell me everything!" Bailey told her everything, and Annie thought the guy sounded poor and weird.

"If you really want to date now, what about Adam? He's going to be a doctor," Annie said. Bailey sighed with disgust. This is just another example of how Bailey and Annie are different. Bailey couldn't care less about having a future doctor as a boyfriend. She just wanted to find someone to love her for her.

"Kyle's here to pick me up. At least walk with me to his car, so I can tell you more about how wonderful Adam is...pleasssse, " Annie begged. Bailey walked right into the trap. Adam was waiting in the car with Kyle. They planned to force Bailey to go hang out with them. As they approached the car, Adam jumped out.

"Hi, I'm Adam," he said. Bailey was mad. Annie had tricked her, and now she would be forced to wiggle her way out of this situation. Or, she would have to go with the flow for once and see what happened. If she were being honest, she was really hoping Ashton would call. She had thought about him all day. She smiled.

"Hi, Adam. I'm Bailey."

"So...are you going with us to the beach?" he asked. She turned and glared at Annie. Just then, her phone rang. It was a number she didn't know, and her heart stopped.

"I don't know if I can go. Can you give me a minute to take this call?" Bailey asked. She turned and walked a few feet away from them. Ashton had been watching the scene from a distance. He didn't like this Adam guy talking to Bailey. He was jealous. He heard her wish that he would call, so he did.

"Hey, Bailey. It's Ashton."

"Hi," Bailey said, her voice a little shaky.

"I was wondering what your plans are for the rest of the day." Her heart was pounding in her chest. She thought for sure everyone around could hear it. How is it possible she had two guys wanting her attention today? She wanted at least one of them...Ashton. He smiled.

"I don't know. My friend Annie just invited me to go to the beach with her boyfriend and his cousin."

"Someone trying to steal my girl?" he asked.

She laughed. "Oh, I'm your girl am I?" she asked.

"A man can dream, can't he?" he said with longing in his voice. Bailey's face went completely red. Ashton saw this from a distance, and he wanted to kiss her then and there.

"Bailey! COME ON!" Annie yelled. She didn't want to go with them, but how could she get out of this?

"Bailey, I would love to spend time with you today," Ashton said "If you want to…that is. We can meet at the coffee house on the corner of Spring and Fourth and go from there," Ashton said. It took Bailey exactly one second to decide.

"Can you hold on a minute?" she asked.

"Sure," he said.

She walked over to Annie and whispered in her ear, "I didn't know you wanted me to hang out today. I've already got plans, but thanks for asking." She turned toward Adam, "I'm sorry. They didn't tell me about this until ten minutes ago, and I've got to be somewhere." He looked at her, and she could see he was truly wishing she would go.

"Can I at least get your number?" Adam asked. Ashton froze. *Get her number? Hell no, you can't have her number,* he thought, but he didn't say anything. He stood there on the sidewalk…not breathing. He couldn't wait to hear Bailey's response.

"I have to go. I'm running late. Annie can give it to you. I hope you guys have fun."

Ashton sighed and let out a deep breath. He was hoping she wouldn't give him her number. He could tell by the way she shifted the responsibility to her friend that she really didn't want to.

"Bye, everyone," she said, as she walked away in a hurry.

"Are you still there?" she asked.

"Yes, I am. Bailey, how many times a day do guys ask for your number?" He chuckled. She blushed.

"What was I supposed to do? That was a weird situation," she said. This made him relax a little. He liked that she didn't want to hurt another person's feelings, but he would be checking up on this Adam guy to see if he was going to be any competition.

Chapter Five

When Bailey got to the coffee house, he was waiting at the door. He looked at her and smiled in a way that made her knees go weak. She had to grab hold of the door to catch herself from falling. "Bailey, what would you like to drink?" he asked.

"A caramel latte," she said. He just got a black coffee.

"How can you drink that without milk and sugar?" she asked. He shrugged.

"Just the way I've always had it," he said. In truth, vampires can eat and drink anything, but nothing has a taste. A vampire has no sense of taste, other than for blood and red meat, so he didn't need to add anything to his coffee, since he couldn't taste anything. It was just a warm liquid he drank to fit in with the human world.

"Okaaay," she said. "So, what did you want to do today?" she asked.

"How about you tell me about your family?" he asked. Bailey looked like a deer caught in headlights. He didn't know how to stop the look of panic in her eyes.

"If you want," he said.

"Not much to tell really. I have a sister named Amber. She is three years younger than me. My parents and I don't see eye-to-eye. They travel a lot, and I really don't know them at all. They really don't have a desire to truly know me or my sister," she said her voice cracking on the last statement. She was surprised she answered him so honestly. She usually hid the fact that her parents are absent from her life on all levels.

"I see," he said.

"How about your family?" she asked.

"My family passed away a long time ago. I've been on my own basically since I was 15," he said.

"I'm sorry, Ashton. That must have been hard."

"It was a long time ago." Bailey's eyes tightened on Ashton. There was something there underlying his face that let he know he was not telling her the full story. The mystery behind the mask intrigued her.

"How old are you?" she asked.

"Twenty, and you?"

"Eighteen," she said. He noticed that each time they were together, the light got brighter, and the tendrils of light that bound them grew in number as well as intensity.

"Are you in college?" she asked.

"No, I own a ranch in Texas. I took this season's herd in early to be sold and decided to see the world a little," he said.

"Oh, you're kind of young to own a ranch. I mean, that is something old guys do right?" she said.

He laughed, "Yeah, I inherited some money from my dad when he died, and I used that for the down payment." He didn't say he paid the ranch off over 48 years ago. She asked him if he had any other family around, and he said no. This made her feel sad for him. At least she had Amber, and Mary would always be family to her.

"How about we go for a walk? It's nice outside today," he said.

"Okay," she said. They headed toward the boardwalk on the beach. Bailey wasn't thinking that is where Annie, Kyle and Adam would be. She was focused on those beautiful green eyes that looked like they could see her very soul.

"Can I hold your hand?" he asked. She blushed and held her hand out toward him. She didn't understand herself. It wasn't like her to go goo-goo over a guy, yet her stomach was doing flip flops when he took her hand. When they rounded the corner of the walk, they ran right into Annie, Kyle and Adam.

"Hi—is this Ashton?" Annie asked in a seductive voice.

"Yes," Bailey said, rolling her eyes at Annie. Ashton read Annie's mind, and she was thinking *Poor, weird, or whatever, I'd be interested in him too, yum yum.* Ashton smiled at her. Bailey looked uncomfortable, but she didn't remove her hand from his, and he really loved that. Adam noticed they were holding hands, and jealousy flashed across his face.

Kyle, being the jerk he is, said, "You're kidding me. I thought something was wrong with Adam wanting to go out with you, and now you have this guy too."

Ashton shot him a look, and swayed his mind to say he was sorry. Kyle looked directly at Bailey and said, "Sorry, I'm a jerk." Kyle had this confused look on his face.

Did he just say he was sorry? Okay, this is strange, Bailey thought.

"Bailey, are you dating this guy?" Adam asked. He looked at Ashton for a reaction, but Ashton seemed to be focused on Bailey. Bailey didn't know what to say. She didn't have any experience with dating, and she didn't know if she was dating or not. She looked at Ashton, and he read her mind.

"Well, I hope we're dating," he said, a crooked smile crossing his angular face.

Adam looked at Ashton and said, "Are you up for a little healthy competition?"

Adam had this adorable mischievous smile on his face. Bailey noticed. Ashton and Adam glared at each other, and a flash of something not quite human shot across Ashton's face, causing Adam to pull back.

"We will let you guys get back to hanging out. Come on, guys. Bailey, call me later," Annie said. The three of them walked away. Kyle was saying, "Did I just tell loco back there I was sorry?"

"Shut up, Kyle," Annie and Adam said at the same time.

Bailey looked at Ashton and said, "I'm sorry about that. I wasn't thinking about them being here too."

"I'm not. Adam needs to know about me if he is going to pursue you as well."

She laughed. "Oh yeah, I have so many guys wanting my attention."

"It looks exactly like you do. However, I'm not worried." He smiled.

There was that self confidence, but this time she liked it. When she got home, her sister was there crying because her and Caroline got into a big fight over a boy. It was all a big misunderstanding. Unlike Bailey, Amber went to a co-ed academy. She had thrown a tantrum over being able to go to a school with boys. Her parents never had this problem with Bailey. When Amber made such a fuss over going to a school with boys, they decided it was not worth the fight, so they let her go.

"What happened, Amber?"

"Today is when we went on the field trip to the Tar Pits, and all the kids were being mean to this one kid. His name is Mathew. He has flunked a grade, and he doesn't have any friends. He's sort of an outcast. I hate seeing people be mean to anyone, so everyone was going on and on about him putting his window down because it was cold today. I didn't want to get involved, but I could see the pain each cruel word made on him, so I asked him nicely to put the window up."

He looked around and said, "For you, Amber, since you're the only one not being an ass about it." Then Caroline started making fun of me to the other kids, saying how sweet that Amber was taking up for her boyfriend and stuff like that. I don't think anyone would have made a big deal about it if Caroline had not sold me out. It hurt my feelings because she is supposed to be my best friend. I didn't want to say anything bad about Mathew to get her to shut up, so I didn't say anything.

Luckily, we were back at school about ten minutes after it happened, but I don't know if I want to hang out with Caroline anymore. She is shallow and selfish, and it just makes me so mad at her."

"Amber, I'm proud of you. It takes courage to stand up for people. It takes even more courage to stand up to your friends for people. I would talk to Caroline and let her know that if she is into bringing others down to build herself up, then you no longer wish to be friends with her."

"Do you think that is a good idea, Bailey? Caroline and I have been friends since we were in kindergarten."

"Amber, if she was truly your friend, she wouldn't do what she did to you today without being sorry."

"Okay, Bailey. I will talk to her about it."

"Just remember, Amber, it's the strong people who stand up for the ones who can't stand up for themselves. It's the weak people who push others down in order to build up their own self worth. I know that is not who you are." Amber thanked her, and they both went to bed. That night, Amber bunked with Bailey. Amber didn't want to be alone.

When Amber got to school the next day, she told Caroline they needed to talk.

"Okay, Amber. What's up?" Caroline was acting like nothing was wrong.

"Caroline, I didn't like how you made fun of me yesterday on the field trip. I get that you don't like Mathew, but it was not cool to make fun of me."

"Oh my God, Amber, don't make a big deal about it," Caroline said, rolling her eyes.

"It is a big deal. You are supposed to have my back…not stab me in the back," Amber said, anger visible all over her face. Caroline's eyes tightened on Amber. She was not happy with Amber standing up to her. "If you think it's okay to make fun of me just to get noticed then screw you. Being a bitch doesn't make you cool. If that is the person you choose to be, than I don't know you at all," Amber said, as she stormed off. Caroline wanted to scream at Amber, but deep down those words had cut her. She stormed off in the opposite direction. She didn't know why she opened her big mouth on the bus, but she had opened her mouth to get noticed by the popular kids. Now, she had lost her best friend over something that didn't seem to matter.

Amber and Caroline avoided one another throughout the day. They didn't sit together in any of their classes, nor did Amber go to the lounge for lunch. She couldn't stand to see Caroline's face. Amber walked into the school cafeteria, grabbed a turkey club and headed out toward the one picnic table on campus. No one was ever out there at lunch because kids were not allowed, but she was not in the mood to try and find a new place to fit in at lunch, so she dodged a teacher that was coming down the hall and slid out the side door. She walked over to the picnic table that was hidden behind the west building. Amber was feeling proud of herself for getting away with it. When she looked up, she noticed someone was already sitting there alone. She realized it was Mathew, but it was too late to try and find a new place to eat. He looked up at her flustered.

"Wow, they pulled you over to the dark side quicker than I thought possible," he said.

"What?" Amber asked.

"So, what do you have to do to get into Holly's club?" he hissed.

"I don't know what you're talking about," Amber said, with a puzzled look on her face.

"I thought you were different," he said, sighing a long sigh. "Don't try and bullshit me, Amber. Do you have to just sit with me during lunch and endure my company or do you have to do something more humiliating?" Mathew asked.

"I'm afraid you have me confused with someone who gives a shit about what Holly thinks. I am out here because of Caroline. If you must know we are not speaking," Amber said. Amber watched as the muscles on Mathew's face tried to relax, but stood guard as if any minute she would turn on him and strike him with a deadly blow.

"Do you sit out here at lunch every day alone?" Amber asked, as she began to unfold the turkey sandwich.

"Yes, I sit out here so I can stay away from freaking Holly and her droids of pretenders."

"I am not a Holly fan either. It's best to just ignore her little tantrums," Amber said.

"Holly doesn't do tantrums with me...she does other stuff," he said, clearly pissed off.

"Oh yeah, I've seen some of her stupid little stunts. I'm sorry...I bet it sucks."

Mathew wanted to smile at Amber, but this trick had already been played by Holly's group and he wasn't falling for it this time. The bell rang for next period, so Amber said bye and was walking away just as Holly and her club walked out of the lounge. Holly saw Amber and it was like a light bulb went on in her bubble blonde head. She realized Amber ate lunch with Mathew and her face shown an evil glare as she yelled in front of everyone. "Hey Amber, when did you and Mathew start dating?" Amber was mad, but after the conversation with Mathew it wouldn't be fair to try and smooth things over just to make her life easier. She was sick of being a second-rate citizen, so she just shrugged her shoulders and turned and smiled at Mathew.

"See ya tomorrow for lunch," she said, as she walked to her next class. Mathew's eyes widened. He knew they were not dating. Amber was not in his reach, but her kindness meant a great deal and the smile that lit up his face made Holly annoyed as she grunted and walked off to her next class.

Chapter Six

Perfidia felt something change with her link to Ashton, so she sought him out. She didn't want him to know she was searching for him. She could have summoned him to her, but he had been off her radar for so long now that she had basically lost interest. He was not the monster she had hoped he would be. For some reason, he was able to survive without killing humans, so she gave up on him ever being able to provide her with more power. When one of her vampires kills a human, she gains power from the torture and pain of the human before they die. She had become super powerful over the years, and even Kilguard didn't do anything to cross her. She was concerned that the link was fading between her and Ashton, so she wanted to find out why. She couldn't send anyone else to do the job for fear they would want to live like Ashton and possibly release all of her vampires. She would lose her vampire army, and maybe more, if Bailey was Ashton's soul mate. She used a glamour to make herself unrecognizable by Ashton, so she could walk right past him.

Normally, there would be strands of black tendrils coming from her body and connecting to his, forever linking them whenever she was near him. When she passed him, she noticed what once had bound him to her with more than a thousand strands of black light was now a mere few hundred strands of black light. *What had changed? How can this be? Is it because he will not kill humans?* she thought. She would have to do more research on this to find out. However, Ashton could not find out she was watching him.

Bailey was sitting in her room. It was a Wednesday, and she hadn't heard anything from Ashton since their last date. Was date the right word? Anyway, she guessed he had lost interest. Stop doing that. Stop worrying if he is interested or not, she was thinking. You do not live your life just to see if he will call. Why hasn't he called? Just then, the phone rang and Bailey jumped.

"Hey, Bailey?"

"Yeah, I'm here."

"I was hoping Annie gave me the right number. It's Adam."

"Oh, hi." She was thinking, *I'm going to kill Annie for really giving him my number.*

"Don't sound too excited," he laughed. "I have tickets to go see this new artist's work, and was wondering if you would like to come." She really didn't want to go out with Adam. He seemed nice, but her interest was truly with Ashton, but going to a true artist exhibit really excited her. She was experiencing some strong feelings for Ashton, and considering he hadn't called maybe this would help take her mind off him.

"When is it?" she asked hesitantly.

"It's Thursday night at eight," he said. She paused.

"Tomorrow night?" She was irritated he had waited until the last minute to ask her.

"I figured the less notice the less time you have to change your mind, and back out," he laughed, and even Bailey chuckled at that one.

"I can pick you up. Do you have a curfew on school nights?" She laughed.

"I haven't had a curfew ever. I guess that's the case if you don't do anything to get into trouble."

"I see, so not a party girl then?" He inquired.

"No, not the party girl type," she muttered.

"So, the art exhibit should be your scene then. Will you go with me?" he asked her again. Bailey thought about his invitation and decided what the heck, since Ashton hasn't called, and I would love to see a real artist exhibit, so she said, "Sure, but I'll meet you there."

"Bailey, it's downtown, close to Pershing Square, and I really don't want you to be driving around by yourself that time of night." She thought, *well I guess that is true.*

"Okay, you can pick me up then," she said. She gave him directions to her house and told him she needed to study for an Algebra test, so she would see him tomorrow night. They hung up.

Ashton hadn't called, or made any contact, because he sensed the presence of Perfidia. However, he so wanted to. He was so afraid she was there, and he wondered why after more than a hundred years of no contact she was searching for him. Maybe she was just in the area and not searching for him. Something about the loss of Elizabeth all those years ago, and then Perfidia showing up a mere week later, made him believe there was more to the story. He didn't want Perfidia anywhere near Bailey. He had felt her presence two days ago while walking down the street. He didn't respond, because he didn't want her to know that he knew she was there. He had to keep what control he could over the outcome this time. He had to see Bailey. He realized over the few days of no contact that maybe there was something more to her than just the fact she could free him from being a vampire. He was actually having true feelings toward her—feelings even stronger than the ones he felt for his Elizabeth. He wondered what was happening to him. He didn't think vampires could love. He was wrong, for he knew it as soon as it crossed his mind that he was in love with her—truly in love with her. He knew she liked him and that gave him hope that just maybe she could fall in love with him. He had to see her, so he went to her house invisible. He got there just in time to see her getting in the car with Adam. He never knew he could experience such pain or anger. He was livid. This was a supernatural jealousy. He was trying to hear her thoughts, the only thing that might ease some of his discomfort, when he heard Perfidia's voice behind him.

"So this is why," Perfidia hissed. He turned to see that Perfidia could see the strands of light that connected him to Bailey, but now he could also see the strands of black light that connected him to Perfidia. The connection with Bailey outnumbered his connection to Perfidia ten to one.

Perfidia's eyes were glowing yellow flames.

"I told you that you belong to me. What have you done?" she hissed.

Ashton stood petrified. He couldn't move or make a sound. Perfidia was standing there before him seeing the connection between him and Bailey.

"Well, at least she has her human male to keep her busy. From the looks of it, she is not interested in you."

Ashton snapped out of it and said, "You're right, I have read her thoughts, and she is deeply in love with the human male." Perfidia could not read thoughts. She could use mind control over some, but not all. Some had a screen that protected them from her control. Ashton had such a screen when he was a human, which made her want him more.

For the moment, Perfidia seemed satisfied.

"I warn you now to stay away from her." She turned and disappeared.

Bailey didn't understand why Adam would be interested in her. He was really smart, funny, very handsome and so the opposite of Kyle that she couldn't believe they were even related. He had beautiful gray-blue eyes and bleach blonde hair. He was toned, and very chiseled. He could truly have any female he wanted, and she was very curious as to why he was interested in her. They made small talk in the car. He was asking her about her love for art. He told her a little about his love for medicine. She told him she had a connection to art—a connection that she didn't think she would ever have with any other career. The thought of doing a job she loved for the rest of her life, even if she didn't make a lot of money from it, was worth it in the end.

"That makes sense. After all, your job will be what you spend most of your life doing, so you should love doing it," he said.

"Why do you want to be a doctor?" she asked.

"I have not always had a great family. I was adopted."

"Well, that explains a lot." He looked puzzled. She laughed.

"I mean, you seem like a nice guy, and Kyle not so much." They both laughed.

He continued, "After my mother died, my father abandoned me and my two brothers. We were sent to an orphanage. I was there a year before being placed in the first of three foster homes. I was adopted when I was nine by Kyle's uncle and aunt, so that is how we are cousins. I was the oldest, and I was responsible for making sure my brothers were okay. The medical conditions at the orphanage were not up to standard. When my youngest brother, Mark, got sick I didn't think anything about it. I thought he would be fine, but then Blake got sick too, and the doctors that came there didn't really want to be there. They became doctors to make money and not because they had a passion for it. I never knew what infection overtook their bodies. I was only six. My brothers were three and five. They never made it out of the orphanage, and I knew I would grow up and become a doctor, so I could save other kids. I have a true passion for saving lives. I owe that to my brothers." Bailey couldn't believe what she had just heard. She was crying. "I'm sorry; it's easy to talk to you. I didn't mean to upset you," Adam muttered.

"I'm sorry, Adam. I'm so sorry you had to go through that, and thank you for trusting me enough to tell me," Bailey said

They arrived at the art exhibit, and he opened her car door. She had to admit he was truly a gentleman—something that you just don't find in today's world. In the back of her mind, Ashton crossed her thoughts. She pushed him out and focused on Adam. They spent the rest of the evening discussing each other's views of the different pieces, and they found themselves laughing a lot too. When the evening was over, she told Adam she had a good time, and thanked him for inviting her. He asked if he could call her again, and she said yes before she even had time to think about it. She walked up the sidewalk toward her house not feeling the same tingle she felt after being with Ashton, but feeling happy. It was late and she had school tomorrow, so she tried not to make noise as she made her way to her room and fell into bed.

It had been a month since Amber and Caroline got into a fight. They both avoided one another like the plague. Caroline found another girl to hang with. Her name was Jessica. This left Amber fending for herself. Amber didn't like how this one fight had left her broken and alone. She hated Caroline for not apologizing. Caroline was able to move on and create a new best friend for herself. Amber didn't find this task easy, so she decided not to bother. Amber found herself spending more time with Mathew, not caring what others thought of them. She was able to grow as a person and this development opened her mind to a world of confidence she never knew existed.

Amber thought it funny that as soon as she stopped trying to fit in, she found a place to truly be herself, and she didn't need all the crap that came along with trying to rule the school. She was still a cheerleader, but just not the most popular. She still had guys left and right asking her out, but she didn't like any of them. She was surprised that she actually enjoyed Mathew's company, and he was honestly a true friend to her. They would eat lunch together every day at school, and Amber starting helping him with some of his school work. She realized he was smarter than everyone thought. She wondered why he played the role of someone dumb because he taught her a thing or two when it came to Algebra. She decided to ask him.

"Okay, I am confused," Amber said.

"About what? Is it Algebra again?" Mathew moaned. Amber smirked.

"Funny, but no."

"That's a relief. Cause if you don't have it by now...you're not going to get it."

"Why are all of your classes the easy courses for...slower kids?" she blurted. Mathew's eyes narrowed on Amber, his face clearly pained.

"You don't remember me from last year when I moved here do you?"

"No, why?" Amber asked.

"Because if you did you would remember my brother Jason. We were twins. He was slow and he needed my help, so I played the role to be with him." Amber's eyes shown confusion.

"Where is he now?" Amber asked. Mathew's face grew sad.

"He was born with a weak heart, and it finally gave out on him five months after we moved here. I couldn't move on after he died, so I stayed in the slow classes," Mathew said. Amber took Mathew's hand.

"I'm so sorry, Mathew. I didn't know."

"It's not your fault. I haven't been able to move forward, and none of the teachers have pushed me to do so."

"When you're ready I'll go with you," she said.

"Thanks," he said, giving her a smile of appreciation, but Amber could see the love he had for her, and she feared him taking action on it one day. She liked Mathew as a friend and couldn't see him as anything else. She could only hope that if he did like her as something more than friends it would not break his heart when she rejected him and they would still be able to remain friends.

Chapter Seven

Ashton's heart was relieved. Perfidia was gone, and Bailey was safe. The thought of never holding her hand again crossed his mind. How could he see her now with Perfidia's threat in the open air like he could reach out and touch it? He wondered why she was so afraid of this connection. Bailey is truly my soul mate, and I will not stand by and let her take her from me like she did Elizabeth, but I can't put Bailey in danger. He struggled with this. He was pretty sure that with his strength and supernatural powers, he would be able to protect Bailey from Perfidia, and history would not repeat itself. Deep down, he really thought Perfidia had killed Elizabeth, even though she had never come out and said it. He hoped one day she would admit it. With the fury that thought would bring, he could have defeated her with a mere finger.

Ashton waited until Bailey got out of school the next day before he called.

"Hey, Bailey. It's Ashton. I'm sorry I haven't called. I had some personal issues I've had to deal with the past four days. Can you forgive me?"

"Sure, it's cool. It's not like I was waiting by the phone. Things happen," she said. She sounded disconnected from him, and her voice was cold. He could tell she was pissed.

"So, what have you been up to the last few days and nights?" he asked.

She thought it was funny that he put in the "nights" part and wondered if he was asking if she had been out with anyone else. Bailey was truly one thing, honest, so she told him.

"School during the day, the usual soccer practice on Monday night, Tuesday evening was art class. Wednesday night Adam called and asked me out, and Thursday night we went to an art exhibit. It was really cool. I had never been to an exhibit where the artist is there in the room, and you can ask her questions about the different pieces. It was fun. How about you?" she asked. He loved her so much. He knew she was not trying to make him jealous. She just didn't believe in having secrets if she was interested in someone. She didn't try to hide anything. He didn't think he could love her more, but in that moment he did.

"Well, I mainly dealt with some things from my past," he said.

"What kind of things?" she asked. He hesitated.

"Things…I'm not able to tell you," he said.

"Why is that?"

"Because you wouldn't believe me if I did," he said.

"Try me," she said.

"I would love to tell you everything, Bailey. I love the fact you are so open with me, but there are some things from my past I don't think I'm quite ready to say to you. Can you trust me to tell you as soon as I can?" She thought about this for a moment. She didn't know why she trusted Ashton, but she did. She felt she could trust him with her very life.

"I trust you, Ashton. I'll wait until you're ready to tell me." She changed the subject. "What are you up to this weekend?" Bailey asked.

"If you don't have plans, I had hoped we could spend a lot of the weekend together," he said.

"Oh, how would you like to come to my house for dinner tonight? Mary and Amber will be out, so we can order pizza and watch a movie."

"Sounds great," he said. "What time should I be there? Oh yeah, and where do you live," he said quickly, so she wouldn't realize he had already been to her house on more than one occasion.

"How about seven?" She proceeded to give him the directions.

"I'll see you at seven. Should I bring something?" he asked.

"No, we'll order pizza, and we have on demand and about a billion DVDs. You can pick," she said.

"I'll see you soon, and thanks for being you, Bailey." He hung up the phone.

Ashton arrived right on time and rang the doorbell.

Bailey yelled, "It's unlocked," but she didn't hear Ashton come in. She was pulling up the pizza menu online because she wasn't sure what Ashton liked. Considering he drank his coffee black, maybe he didn't eat regular toppings on his pizza. She decided she better go check the door. She opened it, and he smiled.

"Hey, I'm sorry. I said it was unlocked, but you must have not heard me. Please come in," she said. As soon as she spoke the words, he felt the barrier that had prevented him from even touching the handle disappear. He followed her inside. He knew from now on he would be able to come and go as he pleased. If things didn't work out between them, at least he would be able to see her, even if she didn't know he was there. When you love someone it doesn't always matter if they love you back. Sometimes the fairy tale ending doesn't happen, and he was aware of this fact. Just to be in her presence was more comfort than he had been able to experience since becoming a vampire. Ashton hadn't had a connection, physical or mental, with another being since Elizabeth.

"What kind of pizza do you like?" Bailey asked.

"I'm not picky when it comes to pizza. Whatever you want I'm sure I'll like," he said..

"I love spinach pizza, but most guys don't like that." When she hung out with Annie, Kyle and some of his buddies, they were very vocal about the fact that real men eat as much meat on their pizza as possible. She wasn't sure if they didn't just say this to piss her off, considering she wanted spinach pizza. He laughed at her thoughts on this subject.

"What's so funny?" she asked.

"I didn't know they even had spinach pizza, but I would like to try it. I'm sure it's good." She frowned at him.

"We can order two, and get something with meat on it for you, so if you don't like it then you can have other options. It's always good to have a backup plan."

For some reason, the thought of Adam crossed her mind, and

Ashton heard it and sighed. He was going to have to deal with the jealousy thing. After all, in today's world women could date more than one man, and he hadn't asked her to go steady. He needed to catch up on the correct terms for today's dating world. He thought it funny she was concerned about him liking the pizza. If he told her he preferred a raw piece of red meat on his pizza she would throw up. Anyway, he told her that there was no need ordering two kinds. He liked adventure, and a spinach pizza sounded like it would be just that. She laughed and placed the order. He wanted to pay for it, but noticed she had already taken care of that part. He didn't want to offend her, and didn't know how to deal with this part.

"Can I pay for the pizza?" he asked.

"Already taken care of. Your treat next time." His heart jumped at the thought there would be a next time.

"Deal," he said. "Thank you for dinner."

"I picked the pizza. You can pick out the movie." She took him upstairs to the media room. On a side wall from floor to ceiling were DVDs. It reminded him of the libraries you see in old movies, and some he had encountered in real life. It even had the track with a ladder, so you could reach the upper shelves. She showed him to the DVDs, and then pulled up the on demand menu. He started reading the labels of the movies, and there were a great number of them.

"What type of movies do you prefer?" he asked.

"No way, Ashton. You pick means you pick." They both laughed. He noticed one from the old west and thought that one would be good, so he handed it to Bailey.

"I should have guessed, but this is actually a good movie," she said, as she loaded the DVD. "Can I get you something to drink?" she asked. For some reason a vampire couldn't really tolerate soda.

"Water or tea is good for me," he said.

She went over to a corner and pushed a button. The curtain pulled back from the right to reveal a complete mini kitchen. She made them both a glass of tea and placed a bag of popcorn in the microwave. The media room on the second floor of the mansion had about four rows of real movie seats, with the exception that these where actually lush, and comfortable. They were covered in a crimson fabric that matched the red velvet curtains on a very large wall in front of the chairs. Bailey pushed another button, and the curtains came back on both sides to reveal a full size movie screen right there in her home. No wonder she didn't have a TV in her room. Who would want to watch TV on anything other than this? The movie started and their hands touched inside the popcorn bowl. He only ate what he had to. Popcorn has a Werid consistency when you can't taste it. It was kind of like eating pieces of foam—the kind you package things up with.

The doorbell rang, so Bailey jumped up, looked at Ashton and said, "I'll be right back." She came back in a few minutes with the pizza and went to the mini kitchen. She opened a cabinet and pulled out plates. She turned and got some parmesan cheese from the refrigerator. The thought of how rich are these people passed through Ashton's mind. She handed him a plate with two slices, and she had a plate with two slices.

"I prefer mine with more cheese. Would you like some?" she asked.

"No thanks," he said.

He didn't like anything grainy, and that cheese looked grainy to him. He took a bite, and it actually had a hint of flavor. It wasn't strong. It was like eating after going to the dentist when the Novocain hadn't worn off completely. He was in shock. He could taste some of it. That is when he noticed that the strands of light coming from Bailey had magnified in intensity since the last time he noticed them. Her humanity was already coming through to him in those strands of light. He just didn't realize it yet. He ate both slices, and then ate two more. He was so overjoyed that he could taste something, even if it was so faint a human wouldn't have ever noticed.

"See, I told you it was good," she said. Bailey paused the movie, and they both took a bathroom break. When she came back into the room, Ashton was already there waiting for her, and the expression on his face was one Bailey didn't quite understand. *He is so beyond ordinary*, she thought. He smiled, thinking, *if you only knew*. She said down beside him. He could hear her heart pounding loudly inside her chest. His heart too was thudding like it was about to jump free from his chest. He leaned in close to her.

"Bailey?" He whispered in her ear, brushing his lips across her cheek.

"Yes?" She whispered back, her voice shaky.

"Would you mind if I kiss you?" he asked in a seductive voice.

She shook her head, and said, "No."

When their lips touched, the feeling of electric shock ran through them both, and they pulled into each other, both wanting more. Bailey was thrilled to her very core. The smell of him was intoxicating—a musky manly scent that wove around her and engulfed her like a security blanket. The taste of him was delicious, and she knew then and there it was also addictive. They didn't know how long they had been kissing each other. Ashton had never felt this kind of hunger. He wasn't hungry for her blood. He hungered to be as near to her as he possibly could. He ran his fingers through her hair, and she made a low moan. His lips ran along her neck and then back up her jaw line to her lips. The kissing was so intense that they both were lost in the moment, and they didn't hear Amber come running in the door with Caroline by her side.

Chapter Eight

Perfidia was certain that Ashton would not cross her. After all, no one had ever crossed her. If she said jump, even Kilguard, the High Wizard, and also her mate, said how high. She knew Ashton had always been different, and she couldn't completely let it go. If he was so connected to this girl, was she his soul mate? If she was his soul mate, what would that do if she gave herself to him freely? In all her years—close to a thousand years—she had never had a single vampire break the curse she cast upon him. Kilguard had never lost a vampire to finding his soul mate either. It's part of the reason they had gained so much power. For each vampire under their power, they grew in strength. Of course, not all survived the transformation. They had cursed some over the years whose bodies were just not strong enough to endure. One in five fledglings didn't make the change, and there were also the vampire killers out there. The Leader of Light, Faerie Bien Faire, tried to keep the balance of good and evil by killing vampires. Killing a vampire was almost impossible. No one knew how Bien Faire accomplished it, and those who learned were dead before they could speak of it.

All the folklore about vampires is just a bunch of foolishness. Humans didn't truly believe vampires existed, and those that knew it to be true never lived long enough to tell anyone. The common defenses for keeping vampires away were garlic, holy water or a cross—all useless and would do nothing to prevent a human's death. Beheading a vampire would slow them down, but not kill them. Vampires can reattach any body part, and the blood elixir that flows through their bodies would seal and heal the wounds. A stake through the heart is utterly inadequate. First of all, you would have to be fast enough to stake them. It would be like trying to catch a bullet shot from a gun—completely impossible. If a human was somehow able to stake a vampire, once the stake was removed, the elixir would heal the vampire, and the human would die a very slow, painful death for his defiance. Vampires are about control. They want a human to freely follow them and let them kill without a fight. When a human tries to resist the kill, they only create a game for the vampire—a game of cat and mouse. A vampire creator can kill her vampires with a wizard's blade. These are very rare—only five exist in the world. They were created by using the blood of innocence and the capture of a demon spirit that is trapped inside the blade. This blade could kill a vampire by piercing the heart. Perfidia thought about tracking Ashton down and using the wizard's blade to kill him now before he caused her anymore problems, but in the back of her mind he had somehow always remained her pet and she truly didn't want to destroy him…not yet.

"Oh my gosh! Are you having sex in the media room?" Amber asked.

Bailey wanted to kill her. *How could she say that in front of him?* she thought.

She knew Bailey was a virgin and even though Amber didn't have any reference of dating she had to know that was not cool. Ashton turned and said, "Hello ladies." They both looked like they were going to run and jump on him.

Bailey looked at Amber and said, through clenched teeth, "Can I talk to you for a minute?" She pulled her to the kitchen and said, "Get out of here! I thought Caroline asked you over to her house so you could discuss your *issues*."

"Her parents are out of town, and her nanny is going through some sort of mid-life crisis and needed to be off tonight. Caroline said she had been crying all day, and she didn't want to stay there with Weepy Willow."

"Amber, that is not nice. Does Caroline not love her as much as we love Mary?"

"I don't think Caroline thinks of her nanny like we think of Mary. Mary is family, but Caroline thinks her nanny is the hired help, and she is mad she is having a break down on company time. It would be really sad if it wasn't so funny coming from Caroline, the queen of breaking the rules."

"You need to leave now. Can't you see I'm busy?"

"We came in here to talk," Amber said, as her eyes flashed to Ashton. "This room is the only sound proof room. Is that why you're in here?" she asked, while a giggle escaped her lips. "Besides, you know there is going to be some screaming between me and Caroline over our *issues*," Amber said.

"Amber, as you can see I was here first. I need you to go somewhere else and go somewhere else now," Bailey said, her tone stressed.

"Bailey, you know Caroline and I have not been speaking for over a month. We need to fight this out in a room where no one can hear… and this is the room," Amber said.

"Go in the basement. It's soundproof. You're not staying in here," Bailey said, giving Amber an evil glare.

"Okay, chill. We're going. Who is this guy? He is hot, by the way."

"Noneya. Now go!" Bailey said.

"Okay, Caroline this room is taken. Let's go downstairs in the basement. I'm sure we can find somewhere to hash this crap out," Amber said, her voice a little icy.

Bailey turned to Ashton and said, "I'm sorry about that." He thought it was funny.

"No problem," he said, "So, do you want to finish the movie?" he asked.

She was thinking, *No, I don't want to finish the movie. I would like to get back to kissing you*, but she said, "Sure." He smiled. When she sat back down and hit play, he reached for her hand. Her whole body relaxed with him sitting there holding her hand. When the movie was over, it was past midnight, and he decided he needed to leave.

"Can I see you tomorrow?" he asked. She had a term paper due in English, but it was Saturday, and she could finish it Sunday, so she said, "Yes."

At the door, he said, "Goodnight," and kissed her hand before he walked to his car, got in and drove away. She wished he had kissed her goodnight, but she knew she would see him soon. He drove away the happiest he had ever been, even as a human. This made him wonder if he ever truly loved Elizabeth, or if he just thought at the time it was the path he should take. He loved her, but there was something more to the feelings he had for Bailey, and he didn't understand why.

Bailey woke up and looked at the clock. It was 11 AM. She never slept this late, but she was truly exhausted last night when she went to bed. She slept so soundly that she didn't even dream. Her sister and Caroline were up all night. She knew because she heard them a few times, but she was so lost in sleep she couldn't wake up to go yell at them. She got up and went to the bathroom. She brushed her teeth, showered, shaved and washed her hair—the works. She was putting on lotion when the phone rang. She assumed it was Ashton, so she said, "It's your art girl speaking."

"Okay, I like that you're my art girl," Adam said.

"Adam?" Bailey asked embarrassed.

"Yeah?" he said.

"Sorry, I thought you were someone else."

"Oh, so you're Ashton's art girl," he said in an irritated tone. She didn't know what to say. This was awkward. He changed the subject.

"I was wondering what you were doing today?" he asked. In truth, she didn't know, but she did know she had plans to do something with Ashton.

"I have plans today," she said.

"I see. Well, what about tomorrow then?" he asked.

"Adam, I don't think that will be a good idea."

"Bailey, give a guy a break. I'm really trying." She thought about how much fun they had at the art exhibit, and about how honest Adam had been with her, and how Ashton was not so forthcoming with the honesty thing.

"Well, what did you have in mind for tomorrow?" she said.

"I was wondering if you would like to go with me to this poetry reading here on campus," he said..

"Poetry?" She liked it very much that he knew what she liked. She didn't like that he had gotten the information second hand from Dill Weed Kyle. "Do you like poetry?" she asked in a sarcastic tone.

"As a matter of fact, I do, and I will be reading one of my poems tomorrow."

"Oh." This shocked her. She had to go now that she was curious, wondering if the poem would be something like "roses are red, violets are blue" and such as that.

"It starts at 3 PM. I can pick you up again, if that is cool?"

"Okay, but I have to tell you, Adam. I see us more as friends than anything else."

"It's a start." He hung up the phone.

She finished getting dressed and went downstairs to find Maria in the kitchen.

Maria is the house chef, but she usually doesn't work every day and not on Saturdays.

"Hi Maria, I didn't know you were working today," Bailey said.

"Yes, Miss Bailey. I was called in last minute, emergency order from your parents. They are going to be in tomorrow. The plan is a dinner party, and I had to come in today to prep the food. Can I get you anything for breakfast?" she asked.

"I would love one of your omelets, if it's not too much trouble," Bailey said.

"No problem, Miss Bailey. You sit down, and I'll have it ready for you in five minutes. The usual?" Maria asked.

"Yes, please. Thank you so much, Maria." Just then, the doorbell rang.

"Is Fernando here too, or should I get the door?" Bailey asked.

"Fernando is not here. He is coming with me tomorrow to help do butler duties then."

"Okay, then I'll get the door." She walked to the front door and opened it. Ashton was standing there holding a very large bunch of Gerber daisies. Bailey adored Gerber daisies, but she didn't remember telling Ashton this little detail.

"For my art girl," he said. She blushed.

"Come in. Thank you for the flowers, they're beautiful," she said.

"How did you know I love Gerber daisies?" she asked.

He thought quickly and said, "What girl wouldn't love them?" They both laughed.

"What do you want to do today?" she asked.

"How about going to the place where we met? Can I interest you in going to the museum?" She forgot all about the fact she was to be there today to work from 12 PM until 2 PM for her volunteer job. Looking at the clock, she realized it was 11:42 AM.

"I forgot I was supposed to be there to volunteer today. I'm supposed to be there in eighteen minutes."

"Get your stuff, and I'll get you there on time." She ran to grab her purse.

"Maria, I forgot I had to work at the museum today. I'm running late, but I do appreciate you making the omelet."

"Bring it, I'll drive you." he said. "You can eat in the car." Bailey shrugged and grabbed the omelet on her way out the door.

"Ashton, I'm really sorry. I forgot all about having to be there."

"I don't mind waiting until you finish working. I'll be back in two hours to pick you up."

Bailey smiled at him and said, "Thanks."

"Do you still want to spend some time here with me, or would you like to do something else?" he asked.

"I would love to spend some time here with you," she said.

"I'll see you in two hours, art girl." She got out of the car, and he drove away.

She got to her post just in time, with no one the wiser that she had completely forgotten. She was usually so focused on her responsibilities that she was surprised she had not remembered. She realized, for once she was lost in the moment, a typical teenager, and this excited her. In a way, Bailey had to always be a grown up. What other kid, at age seven, would be expected to see her parents leave for a two-month trip on her birthday, and still be able to hold herself together for her guests? Knowing Ashton had freed her for a while from being a grown up made her happy and carefree. Her two hours volunteering went by quickly. She guessed Ashton would come in whenever her got there and find her. She noticed a woman staring at her from across the room. She wondered what that was about. She looked away, but from the corner of her eye she could see the woman still staring. Ashton knew as soon as he got out of the car that Perfidia was there. He guessed she was with Bailey, and he was not having Perfidia anywhere near Bailey. He rushed inside to find her. Bailey was in the lobby waiting for him.

"Hey," and then she saw his face. "What's wrong?" she asked.

"Change of plans. If that's cool?"

"Okay." She followed him out to the car. He decided to tell her what he was. He knew it was breaking the rules, but he had to be honest with her. She had a choice here. She could truly love him or walk away. Perfidia had wanted him to love her, but he could never love her. He would give Bailey the choice he never had.

Perfidia saw Ashton come in and go to Bailey. She saw how protective he was of her. She didn't like it. She then saw that the light tendrils that connected her to Ashton were a mere ten strands of dull gray light where as Bailey had thousands of thick, golden strands that connected every part of her body to Ashton. Perfidia wanted to kill Bailey right there. All she needed was some of her essence, and she would cast the spell in ten days when there was a full moon. Perfidia didn't realize that Bailey's essence had changed. She was no longer just human, and nothing else. The ties that bind soul mates together truly change both of them. In a way, their bodies become linked, and she couldn't kill Bailey without killing Ashton. It's a supernatural covering of protection over her that even Ashton doesn't realize. She would get the girl's essence as soon as she could find her without Ashton.

Ashton asked Bailey if she knew of somewhere she felt comfortable with him telling her about his past. He wanted everything about this situation to be within her control. He didn't want her to fear him, but he was afraid she would, and the thought of that broke his heart.

"How about the beach?" she said. He grabbed a blanket from the trunk of his car, and they walked toward the beach holding hands. When they got there, he looked around for a private section. He found one near the gulf, where the rocks jut out. On the other side was a little sitting area where the water didn't quite reach. They walked over, and he spread the blanket out. He took her hand, and she sat down.

He looked into her eyes and said, "Bailey, I have to tell you something that is not going to seem real. I don't want you to be afraid, but if you are, please let me know, and I will stop and take you home. I would love to tell you everything before you decide to get to know me more, or not."

She looked at him, and said, "I will listen and try not to be afraid." He looked into her eyes for a moment and sighed.

"Sometimes what people perceive as legend or fantasies are real. I'm not like other guys, Bailey." She looked at him concerned, but said nothing.

"Ashton, whatever it is you can tell me," Bailey said.

He looked into her eyes and knew he had to tell her the truth, no matter what it cost him.

"Bailey, I'm a vampire." She glared at him.

"Be serious, please."

"Bailey, I am being serious." She knew he was, and he read her thoughts. She was afraid.

"Do you want me to take you home?"

She thought and said, "No, but I can't comprehend this being the truth. Vampires are not real, Ashton. Do you not want to see me anymore? You could have just said so." Her thoughts were hurt and betrayed, and this was tearing him apart.

"Baby, it's true. I can prove it to you."

"How?" she asked, eyeing him with a very suspicious concern.

"Just watch," and he disappeared right in front of her and then returned. She gasped.

"Vampires are *real*," she whispered in a cracking voice.

"I would never hurt you."

"Were you born this way? I mean, how did this happen?"

"I was born a human male back in 1880. I was twenty years old when I was cursed and turned into a vampire." She knew it was true. She could feel it. She could see it in his eyes. She felt so connected to him. She wasn't afraid of him, and she wondered for a second if he was using some sort of mind control over her. When in reality, she was screaming and wanting to run away.

He looked at her and said, "I can't use mind control over you Bailey. I can read your thoughts, most of the time." She flinched away from him, a little embarrassed at all the thoughts she had processed in his presence.

"Do you want me to take you home?" he asked in a shattered voice.

"No, just give me a minute," she said.

"I want to answer any questions you have. I assume you are wondering about the blood part. I do drink blood from humans. I don't kill anyone, but I sway their minds into letting me drink, and I heal the wounds and let them go."

"You drink human blood?" she asked, her voice so raspy now that she barely spoke above a whisper.

"Yes," he said defeated.

"I don't know what to do with that, Ashton."

"I know," he said.

"I saw you eat pizza and drink coffee."

"I can eat anything, but nothing has a taste to it except blood and raw, red meat." He didn't say that nothing had a taste until he met her. The look on her face was horrified.

"Do you want me to take you home?" He murmured.

"No, I'm listening, Ashton. I'm trying to listen to everything you want to tell me. I told you I would," she said while her voice quivered slightly.

He sighed and said, "I have other abilities. I can float in the air and move at super fast speeds. I am very strong and when I am angry my eyes change color. They go from green to metallic silver. I realize it's hard to understand the longing for blood. When I was first transformed I didn't realize I was going to have to drink blood. I grew very weak and couldn't stand to be around people. I am not like other vampires. Other vampires are out to kill and drain all the blood from a human's body. I take about what you would give if you donate to the Red Cross. I have to drink human blood. It's a desire so strong I would go insane if I didn't drink blood at least every few days. The blood is what maintains my body. It keeps me young and my organs vital. I'm telling you this because I have fallen for you. I think—no, I know—I am in love with you. I would love to continue to get to know you and spend more time with you if you will let me."

"How can we? Her voice was cold now, and broken. You're over a hundred years old. I usually don't freak out about the issue of age, but that's a lot of numbers. Then there is the issue of you never getting any older, while I will. You will never die, and I will." She spit the words out at him, like a snake striking at a mouse.

"I can die, Bailey. My body will start to age once I have lived a thousand human years."

"Well, considering I will be lucky to make it to a hundred years that seems irrelevant. I mean, we don't have anything in common."

"You're wrong. We are connected even if you don't see it. You're afraid to admit it, but you feel it too. I am in love with you, but it's got to be your choice to want to be with me. Even if I could force you, I would not. I love you enough to let you go." His voice broke, and he had to fight back the emotion that wanted to overtake his body.

Bailey looked at him, anger in her eyes, and said, "I would appreciate it if you took me home now." He nodded, and walked to his car. On the way back to her house, her mind was spinning.

"You don't burn up in the sun," she said this like fact because she had seen him outside while the sun shined brightly above them.

"No, the sun just weakens my supernatural abilities."

"Do you sleep in a coffin?" He laughed, "No, I sleep in a very nice bed. I don't require as much sleep as I did when I was human, but I sleep."

"How much sleep do you require?" she asked.

"I sleep about four hours within a twenty-four-hour period."

"Oh," she said. Bailey spoke these words with fear in her voice. "If I never want to see you again, are you going to hurt me?"

He moaned a sorrow filled sound and said, "Bailey, I would never hurt you. I could have continued to hide the truth from you, but I wanted you to know who I really am. It will break my heart to never see you again, but as I said, it's your choice." He pulled up in her driveway, and she got out of the car.

"Please don't call me. I need a few days. I will call you when I'm ready to talk about what happens from here."

"Okay," he said. His car pulled away from the curb, and she didn't look back as she walked into the house. As she made her way inside, the tears began to flow.

Chapter Nine

When Bailey walked inside the house, her father was there, but he didn't even say hello. Her mom was talking to Maria about the dinner for the guest tomorrow evening. Mary saw Bailey come in and said hello. She could see Bailey had been crying.

"Are you okay?" she asked.

"Yes," Bailey said. Just then, Joanne walked around the corner.

"Bailey, you're home. Your father and I are having dinner guests tomorrow evening, so you should make plans to be out all day, or go through the servants' entrance to get to your room if you have to be here before ten tomorrow evening. People should start arriving at six, so you're free to be here until two, when all of the catering and set up will happen. Do you understand?" Joanne asked.

She looked at her mother, the woman she hadn't seen in over three months, the woman who didn't show any kind of emotion of missing or loving her. She replied in a cold voice, "Yes, I do. I already have plans."

"Good then." Joanne walked out of the room. This was just another blow to her already weak psyche. She went upstairs and wanted to scream out with the pain of it all. She knew her mother's behavior had not tormented her very soul. It was Ashton that she was heartbroken over. How could she love him when he was not human? How could she want him when he was not from her world? How could she trust that what they have is real? All questions she had no answers for. Just then, her cell phone rang.

"Hey, Bailey?"

"Hey," her voice cracked out.

"Did I catch you at a bad time?" Adam asked.

"Well, it's cool, but yeah I'm upset."

"Can I help?"

"I don't think so, but thanks for offering." He paused, but decided not to push the subject. "I was calling to confirm our date for tomorrow and to see if I could pick you up early for a lunch date. We could go out, or I would be happy to pack a picnic for us to have on campus." This very gesture made her laugh.

"You can make a picnic lunch?"

"I can and will create a culinary masterpiece for you." She laughed again.

"I would love to see this culinary masterpiece, so I say picnic on campus."

"Okay," he said. "I'll pick you up at noon."

"Actually, my parents are having this big party thing here, so can I meet you somewhere?"

"How about meeting me at the shopping center parking lot on third? I'll take you from there."

"Sounds good, I'll see you at noon," Adam said.

"Adam thanks for making me laugh."

"You're welcome, Bailey." Goodnight they both said. Bailey didn't sleep well that night. She didn't really sleep at all. Her mind was racing with "what if" questions. She was just so torn between loving him anyway and telling him to never come near her or her family again. Sometimes ones destiny is not always the road one wants to take.

Ashton was in utter misery. He didn't know what he was going to do when Bailey told him to never contact her again. He felt lost again. He was so lost now that nothing for him would ever be the same. He wondered if it would have been better to have never found her. At least he was able to exist in the world and survive. How could he survive now without having her to hold? He yearned to be near her. He didn't want to disrespect her space, and now the very idea of being near her without her knowledge was beyond insolent. He would not tarnish her soul any more than he already had. He would be strong and accept the fact that he would have to let her go. The only factor now was Perfidia. Why had he not just walked away when Perfidia had warned him? He knew he would have to protect her, and that might mean watching her without her knowledge. He would accept this and protect her no matter the cost.

Bailey got up early to meet Adam in the shopping center parking lot at noon. She wanted to get out of the house before seeing her parents again. The sooner they left the better. In reality, she was used to their absence. Their behavior when they were around was so bad, she preferred that they stayed away—away from her and her sister. A woman approached her car while she was waiting. Bailey rolled down her window a crack and asked what she needed. The lady said her car had a flat tire, and she wanted to borrow a jack. Bailey didn't trust this woman for some reason. She lied and said, "I'm sorry. I don't have a jack." She then rolled her window back up. The doors in the car were locked, so Perfidia wouldn't be able to jerk the door open to get her essence. She walked away and then disappeared. This scared Bailey. Bailey saw her disappear. The first thing she thought of was Ashton. She dialed his number. He answered on the first ring.

"Bailey?" Ashton asked.

"Yeah."

"I didn't expect you to call so quickly." Her voice sounded afraid and like she had been crying.

"Something happened. I'm afraid."

"Where are you?"

"I'm in the shopping center parking lot on Third."

"I'll be there in three minutes." He was there in two minutes. When he said he was fast, he didn't lie. She opened the door when she saw him and ran into his arms.

"What's wrong, baby?"

"A woman approached my car. She wanted to borrow a jack, but I didn't feel right about her. When she walked away, she got a few feet from me and vanished into thin air. Was she a vampire? Was she after me?" Just then, Adam pulled up.

She saw the look on Adam's face and felt really bad. Here she was in the arms of another man—well, to Adam he was another man—and they were supposed to be going on some sort of date. She looked at Ashton and saw the hurt on his face as well. She thought his eyes flashed sky blue, but she couldn't be sure. She watched as his expression hardened into something she couldn't read, but she had seen the hurt there.

"I understand, Bailey. Please don't feel bad. I'm glad you called me about the woman. I will check it out and get back to you. Can you please text me and let me know where you're going? I'll need to keep track of you to make sure she doesn't get anywhere near you. I'm not mad. I know what we discussed yesterday was a lot for anyone to take in. I get it." He could read the worry and concern for him in her thoughts, and this gave him comfort.

"Go. Call me when you're ready to talk, or if she approaches you again. Do not let her get near you, Bailey, please." His voice was pained.

"I won't let her near me," she said.

"Do you want me to explain to Adam?"

"No, he'll just wonder why I didn't call him. And it's not like we can tell him she disappeared."

"Okay." He walked away.

Adam made no attempt to get out of his car once he saw Ashton. There was something about that guy that gave him the creeps, but Bailey would have to see that for herself. He would be there to pick up the pieces in the end. He already felt she was a keeper. He had fallen for her, in a way. He wasn't for sure it was love, but he liked her a lot. Sometimes he wondered if he was a little obsessed with her. Once Ashton started walking away, he got out of the car and walked toward Bailey.

"I'm sorry about that," she said. "Something came up, and he had to talk to me briefly." Adam looked at her and saw she felt bad, so he told her it's no big deal.

"Are you ready to go?" he asked.

"Yes," she said.

Once in the car, she relaxed, and they started talking about their favorite poets. She preferred "The Journey" by Mary Oliver, while he preferred "The Road Not Taken" by Robert Frost. When they got to his campus, he took her to a beautiful section of fluffy, green grass close to a little creek. He spread out the blanket and started placing food from the basket onto plates. She was actually impressed. There was an assortment of cheeses, fruit, crackers, turkey, and then he pulled out two chilled bottles of Dr. Pepper. He remembered her remarks about Dr. Pepper being her one weakness. She couldn't drink the diet stuff. She had to have the real deal. They sat, ate, and talked. It was easy to be with Adam. He was so sweet, smart, and as far as she knew, he was human. It's funny how she didn't see herself with anyone who would want to be a doctor, but she could see herself with Adam. These thoughts were beyond the boundaries of friendship. She wondered if she would be having these thoughts if Ashton hadn't dropped the bomb of being a vampire on her yesterday. *Did she just think that? Wow, he's a vampire. How can anyone deal with that thought?* Adam looked at Bailey.

"What are you thinking about right now?" he asked.

"You wouldn't believe me if I told you." She laughed.

"I see. So you're thinking about how much you like me then." They both laughed.

They finished up their lunch, and Adam packed everything back into his car. He took her hand and asked if she was ready to go to the poetry reading. They had spent several hours there by the water eating, talking, and getting to know one another. Bailey felt Adam was real, and he was growing on her. She was so confused. When they got to the poetry reading, someone was already reading. They both sat down and watched. It was about an hour later when Adam's name was called to come and read. He looked directly at Bailey when he said the poem by heart. "She walks in the room, and it lights up brighter than the sun. She's smart, creative, and different, could she be the one? She laughs, and my heart sings. She cries, and my heart stings. Is this love I feel? Can this be real? Only Time will tell." It was a beautiful poem, but it made her uncomfortable. She didn't know why, but something about Adam was not the same as their first date. He took her hand when he sat back down beside her and the crowd awed. She blushed scarlet. He smiled. When the readings were over, and they were walking back to the car he stopped beneath a willow tree. He looked longingly into her eyes.

"Bailey, I have wanted to kiss you from the moment you told me to hold on while you took a call from another guy. I don't care. I would like it very much if you would let me kiss you." She didn't know how to say no. She nodded, and he leaned in and kissed her. It was nothing like the kiss with Ashton—no electric shock that ran from the tips of her toes to the top of her head—but there was heat there. There was tenderness and a feeling of something beyond friendship. Adam was in shock that she was kissing him back with a passion that was more than he expected. This gave him hope that maybe he wouldn't have to pick up the pieces. Maybe she would choose him over Ashton, and he would not ever break her heart. He would cradle her heart like a delicate flower, protect it, and keep it safe from anything or anyone who wanted to cause harm.

Perfidia was beyond mad. She was so tempted to summon vampires to kill the girl. It would be easy for them, but her pride kept her from doing so. She knew she would be able to feel the pain this would cause Ashton, and she yearned to make him suffer. He had been the only male to ever refuse her. The rest refused her over time, but she was able to lure them away and torture them before she had to turn them into Vampires. With Ashton it was different. She felt that even though she changed him into a vampire, he had somehow maintained control over his life, and this thought made her so mad that she killed two people on the way home out of pure hatred. Of course, the news would say they died in a car crash, but the truth was that she appeared in their car and scared them so badly they drove off the bridge and dropped two hundred feet to their death.

Bailey was so very confused. She had feelings for Adam and, even though she knew Ashton was a vampire, she still had feelings for him also. She didn't know which feelings were stronger. They both had been able to offer her a feeling of comfort and self acceptance. She felt she could be herself with either, and she just didn't know how she would ever decide who she wanted to love. She had feelings for both of them, but they were different. She would have to sort through the emotional part of this situation, and that was something she was not looking forward to. She tended to vent her emotions through her artwork. This would actually take consideration and coming to terms with who she was and the person she wanted to be.

On the one hand, Adam was great. He seemed like a nice guy, but there was something that didn't sit right with her about him. She thought maybe she was being overly sensitive now that she knew the truth about Ashton. Adam was a guy she could fall for, a guy that would love her and treat her well. The heat between them was there too. On the other hand, Ashton had offered her this sense of adventure beyond the natural world. He had declared his love for her freely and honestly. He had told her all his dark secrets about who he truly was and was willing to walk away from her if she chose another path. Ashton also offered something beyond heat. It was an undercurrent of belonging to someone. It was a connection beyond the bounds of this world. It was something she longed to have again. She actually missed him. She picked up the phone and dialed his cell.

"Ashton?"

"Yes?"

"It's Bailey."

"Hey baby, are you okay? Did you see her again?" She noticed the panic in his voice.

"I'm okay, and no I didn't see her again."

"Is everything alright?"

"Yes."

"Do you want to talk about it, or are you ready to tell me something?"

"I was actually wondering if you could come over. My parents flew out two hours ago. You can come in through my patio."

"Are you sure you want me to come over this late?"

"Yes, I'm sure."

"Okay, I'll be there in three minutes." He was there in two. She watched as he floated onto the balcony and waited for her to open the door. It was unlocked, but he waited for her to let him in. Once inside, she put her arms around him, and he pulled her closer to him. They sat on one of her huge bean bags, and she just let him hold her. He was so happy, but concerned. Her thoughts were too erratic to read, so he held her and waited. Finally, he said, "Bailey, baby, do you need to tell me something? Do you want to talk about it?"

"I don't want you to ever let me go." He sighed a long sigh. "I'm trying to let my human brain accept the fact that there is a great possibility I am in love with a vampire." He froze. What? Did I hear her correctly? Did she just say she thinks she loves me? She thinks she loves me, and she knows what I truly am. He watched as the strands of light grew, and he felt the connection to Perfidia completely disappear.

Within minutes, Perfidia was at the balcony doors. Ashton was so preoccupied with the feelings and emotions that he didn't feel Peridia's presence. The one place Perfidia could not appear and disappear was a person's home. Her blonde hair had turned into flames of fire. Her eyes were glowing, orange flames. She even appeared to have waves of flames flowing over her skin. She had never known this kind of pain. For once, instead of giving pain, the links that bound her to Ashton that Bailey had severed were causing her physical pain—her hair, her eyes, even her very skin felt like it was on fire. She cried out in pain, and Ashton turned just in time to see her disappear.

Ashton jumped up and ran to the doors. He pulled them open, knowing she couldn't enter, but he didn't feel her presence. He realized he wasn't connected to her anymore, so he could no longer feel if she was near or not, but with the loss of that ability came another sense. He could smell her very aura. He knew she was still alive. He knew she was in great pain, and this brought to him happiness for a second—then he realized that if and when she recovered, she would not let this go unpunished.

"Is everything okay?" Bailey asked. Bailey hadn't seen Perfidia. She didn't know of any of this, and Ashton was bound to keep the secret. The curse prevented him from telling her about the witch who cast the spell. It also prevented him from telling her it could be broken. She had to choose to love him beyond the natural world for that is where the spell came from, and this would set him free.

"Yes, baby. It's okay. I just thought I saw something. Are you ready for me to leave now?"

"Can you stay?" she asked in a shy voice. He thought about this for a minute.

"I can," he said. She smiled. Bailey was having even greater feelings for him than she did when he walked through her balcony doors. She didn't understand it, but she could feel the undercurrent pulse through her skin, linking her to him, and she was not afraid. She was excited. She kissed him, and the passion consumed them both. The thought ran across her mind that after tonight she might not be a virgin anymore, and Ashton stiffened. He pulled away from her and looked into her eyes. He could see she was truly happy. From the thoughts of love and longing running through her mind, he didn't know if he would be able to resist. When Bailey woke up, Ashton was exploring her studio. He was looking at all of her artwork. He noticed how they all seemed so sad, isolated and pained. He wondered if Bailey would ever not feel this way. She got up, slipped into the bathroom, did her business, brushed her teeth, fixed her tangled hair, and then strolled over to him and put her arms around him.

"I see you're awake," he said.

"Yes, thank you for staying last night."

"No, thank you for letting me stay." They both laughed.

Bailey was still a virgin. She was trying to figure out why. She didn't know why she told him to stop, but she did. A part of her was just not ready to let go completely. She knew she had feelings for him, but she wouldn't give herself until she loved someone completely, and was able to say it aloud. They spent the day together hiking to the Hollywood sign. It was a beautiful day and the trail leading up to the sign was almost deserted. They only passed one woman who appeared to be doing this for exercise and not entertainment. She looked like she walked to the beat of her own drum. When they got to the top, they sat down for a while, holding one another while they looked at the city views. It was a clear day, so they could see downtown Los Angeles as well as the ocean. They enjoyed the simple things in life...just being together.

Chapter Ten

Perfidia was down for the count. She was crying out in pain. Kilguard tried to cast spells to release the pain, but he couldn't. However, he could feel himself growing stronger with every lick of flame that coursed through her body. She wanted to kill someone. She wanted to get away, But the burning continued. The tendrils of light that once connected her to Ashton where truly burning themselves free from Perfidia's very skin. She was not able to feel any pain until every last light that had once been connected to her was completely severed. Then, the torture began. Kilguard didn't know what to do. They had never gone through anything like this. Kilguard was tired of following orders from Perfidia. It was time she showed him some respect. Besides, he could feel her powers transferring to him daily. For every flame that burned her, a hint of her powers were given to Kilguard, and he liked it.

Adam is one of Perfidia's human minions. She went and took him the very night he got back from taking Bailey to the art exhibit. He now followed her orders. Some of her human playthings were kept in a dungeon. This made it convenient for her to cause them pain and drink it in like it was water. Others, like Adam, were now pawns in her plan to keep Bailey away from Ashton. She took him that night as a backup plan. After all, he was very beautiful. She loved pretty toys. She thought it would be easy planting the words he would say to Bailey in his mind, controlling his every thought. She also liked to have minions high up on the social ladder in today's society, and one day Adam could be just that. Somehow, Ashton was still holding his own with Bailey. This infuriated Perfidia. How can this human girl want to be with a vampire?

Kilguard had human playthings too. Not even Perfidia knew he was a father to a human girl. If she did, she would have killed him and the girl. Kilguard and Perfidia would torture their humans and receive power. However, Joey was different. He found her almost nineteen years ago. She was engaged at the time, but not yet married. She was different. She was not the typical girl. She had been into music and loved all types. She would spend hours rehearsing and trying to write her songs. Kilguard was bewitched by her after seeing her one day walking down the street. He started to pursue her. She was more than just another plaything. He could feel it in every part of who and what he was. She could be someone he loved.

Granted, he was cold hearted, but every being of this world longs for true love. He had been with Perfidia for almost 800 years. Perfidia had found him and turned him into a High Wizard. That is how she still had some control over him. He had once thought he loved her, but now he realized he never had a choice. Now, he loved Joanne. He played the role well with Joanne. He seduced her, and she became pregnant. He knew that if Perfidia found out, Joanne and their child would be destroyed, so he sent her away. He told her he didn't love her and that he had just wanted to take her virginity. This broke Joanne's heart and turned her into the woman she is today—a cold-hearted person who truly lost the ability to love.

She married Bill, the man that she had been engaged to when she fell for Kilguard. He called himself Kingston to her then. Bill loved her and forgave her. He claimed the child as his own. She had the baby and named her Bailey, but she was never able to love her. She had another child a few years later—Bill's true child—and named her Amber. Joanne's betrayal had pained Bill so that he could offer no love for either Bailey or his natural daughter, Amber. Kilguard didn't know that the person causing Perfidia pain now was his own daughter. Time will tell where Kilguard's loyalty lies.

Graduation was one week away for Bailey. Her life as a senior just flew by. She was already accepted into UCLA, and Ashton had plans to follow her there. He too had enrolled and decided to pursue a different career path. He had once thought he would always live on a ranch, but with Bailey in his life now, he honestly didn't know where he would end up and wanted to have a backup plan in order to provide for them both. Besides, he no longer wanted to live a lonely life anymore. He couldn't. She had changed him so much. He actually felt more human than he thought possible. He was actually feeling all types of emotions. He hadn't been able to cry in over a hundred years, but they were watching The Notebook one night, and the tears flowed freely. He couldn't believe he was crying. *How could this be? Vampires don't cry,* he thought.

Bailey just looked at him with tear-filled eyes, as she handed him a tissue. They both laughed. Bailey had to admit that she loved him. She just couldn't get her brain completely around it yet. Right now, for once in her life, she was just living in the moment. Ashton had to leave her every now and then to hunt. They never discussed this. That was one thing she could not fully accept, so she preferred not to talk about it. She didn't think this made her like him less. It was just so beyond the normal that she was not able to talk about it.

The last official week of Bailey's high school career went by so fast that she couldn't really remember what all had happened during the week. Graduation night was more or less any other night for Bailey. Mary and Amber stood rooting for her when she walked across the stage to accept her diploma. Bailey's parents were not there. Even though Bailey was used to them being absent from her life, for some reason it bothered her that they didn't have the desire to see their oldest child graduate from high school. She felt better when she made eye contact with Ashton. Ashton gave her a smile that made her feel warm all over. Once everyone threw their caps into the air, Bailey walked away from the cheers and right into Ashton's waiting arms. "It seems my art girl is now a woman." They both smiled. Mary walked over and hugged Bailey.

"Bailey, I'm so proud of you. Your parents couldn't make it. They had some big corporate event, but they truly wanted to be here." Ashton read Mary's thoughs. *I can't believe they didn't show up. I hope they lose millions. Two daughters and they don't even know them. Money doesn't buy happiness. I could strangle them both for this.* He knew she was saying this to prevent Bailey from more pain, and he respected her for it.

"Bailey, I can't believe we're no longer going to be living in the same house," Amber said. "I'm going to miss you so much. I hope you will call and text me as much as possible once you go away to college. I'm going to miss you like crazy."

"Amber, you will always be a big part of my life. I love you, little sister. Besides, I know you're hoping Mary will let you take over my room, and the answer to that is yes."

Amber squealed and hugged her sister. Bailey knew deep down that once she walked away from her parents' home, she would never live there again.

Bailey stopped by the museum to turn in her volunteer stuff. She had enjoyed her time there, but truth be told, she was happy that she had a summer completely free from responsibilities. She was able to talk Ashton into going with her to her parents' beach house. They had planned to spend most of the summer there. Amber would be going away to her usual cheerleading camps. She went to four all together, and that would keep her busy for most of the summer. She had plans to spend the last week before she went away to college with Amber at the beach house, and Ashton said he would give them some sister bonding time. Bailey spent most of the morning packing up her room. She was getting things ready to send to her new loft apartment close to campus. She would go there some during the summer to make sure everything was being placed and decorated to her standards. The one thing about having money is that you always have someone who will do what you want. Bailey usually did things for herself, but moving her stuff was something she felt she could afford to hire someone else to do.

She had just walked out of the museum when she saw Adam coming toward her. He had this look of determination on his face. For an instant, the intensity scared her.

"Hey, Bailey. I've been texting and calling you for weeks." Adam was scowling at her. "Why haven't you returned my calls?"

"Hi, Adam. I'm sorry. I've been busy." She tried to play it cool. "What's up?"

"Bailey, I haven't seen you for a month. I don't get it. I mean, I thought we had a connection, and then you just shut me out. Is there something you want to tell me? Why are you doing this to me?" Adam couldn't tell her that Perfidia tortured him for every text left unreturned. For every unanswered phone call, he suffered. She noticed that he looked exhausted. He didn't look like the Adam she knew. Even though she didn't love him, she felt enough for him to ask.

"Are you okay, Adam?"

"I'm fine. I just…" he paused. "I'm lost without you, Bailey." Bailey was scared now. Oh my gosh, she had somehow gone from not having a boyfriend to now having a vampire boyfriend and a possible stalker. She made eye contact with Adam.

"Adam, what does that even mean? We have only been on two dates," she said.

"Bailey, connecting to people is hard for me. I thought it was hard for you too." He sighed. "I guess I just gave away my heart too quickly, and now I'm suffering for it." He walked away, leaving Bailey standing there confused.

Bailey didn't know how she was going to deal with Adam. She feared that if Ashton found out, he would be jealous. She felt the need to try and focus on not thinking about Adam around Ashton. When she got back home, Mary was waiting.

"Bailey, I have something to tell you, and I don't think you're going to like it. Jack asked me to marry him. I am in love with him. I don't know what to do."

Bailey had truly hoped this day would come after Amber had graduated high school. Now the burden of being responsible for Amber was still on Bailey's shoulders and she wanted to be free from it all, but she couldn't let Mary down…Mary, who always put herself last.

"Congratulations, Mary. I'm truly happy for you," Bailey said in a haze.

"You and Amber are like my own daughters, but I fear your mother will not let me continue working here if I marry Jack. Jack and I have discussed it, and we have worked it out to where I will stay here like normal, with the exception that I spend as much time as possible with him during the day. When Amber goes to sleepovers, I will go to Jack's house…well, my house once we are married." Bailey looked at Mary and felt so much love for her that she was overwhelmed. Mary was still worrying about them. She was so unselfish.

"Mary, I am so happy for you. Joanne and Bill are never here. They don't have to even know. Amber and I will keep in quiet. Joanne and Bill usually give advance notice about coming home, so Jack is welcome to stay here with you."

"I don't know if that is a good idea, Bailey."

"Just make sure there is no trace of him when they visit. I will speak to Maria and Fernando and let them know it's okay. You can trust Amber and me not to let the secret out."

"I don't know what to say, Bailey," Mary said.

"You can have the wedding at the beach house. I will speak to Maria about the catering. I will take care of the cost. Consider it my wedding gift to you," Bailey said.

"Bailey, I can't let you do that. I appreciate it, but I can't let you do it," Mary said.

"I love you so much, Mary. Thank you for being a mother to me, and thank you for always putting me and Amber first. It is the least I can do for you and I want to do it."

"Thank you, Bailey," Mary said.

"Do you have any idea what kind of timeline we are working on? I was thinking, if you have it soon, then you could go on a long honeymoon while Amber is away at one of her many cheer camps this summer," Bailey said.

"Oh Bailey, thank you so much. I didn't think we would be able to have a honeymoon, but that makes great sense. We can spend the summer together before things get back to normal. Well, normal for here that is." They both laughed.

Bailey threw herself into wedding plans. She had Vera Wang designing a dress based on Mary's likes and dislikes. Mary deserved more than the very best, and Bailey would make it happen. Bailey had her own bank account that her parents added an allowance to at the end of each month. Bailey had never spent more than a hundred dollars from that account. She thought it fitting to spend every last penny of it to ensure Mary's wedding was a fairytale. Bailey went to the bank to see how much she had. She couldn't remember the last time she looked at the balance, or even if she ever had. The teller printed out the statement and handed it to Bailey. Bailey's eyes popped out of her head. Her parents had added $3000 to her account every month for the last

18 years. She had over $700,000 in her bank account. For once, the thought of this money—her parents' money—made her happy. Mary would not accept such a gift if she knew how much Bailey was going to spend, but she didn't really want her parents' money. Money does not equal love, and money was all they had ever offered her.

The wedding planning was a huge success. Mary looked great in her dress. The wedding was on the beach. There were around fifty people there. A boardwalk had been built to hold the wedding party, and chairs were placed in small sections for the guests. Mary never looked so beautiful when she walked down the aisle. She was so happy. Bailey and Amber were her bridesmaids. They both wore cream sleeveless dresses that grew tight around the bodice. They both had on thin-strapped high heels that were a natural color. Bailey had her hair swept back in and up-do away from her face. Amber's hair was hanging down, too short for an up-do. Amber had always envied Bailey's hair. It was the sandy brown-blonde color that most girls dream of. She had her father's hair. It was more of a reddish brown than anything else. She had been tempted once or twice to dye her hair, but she always chickened out. She thought there was nothing worse than someone with dyed hair looking like they had dyed hair. Still, both girls looked great. Ashton wore a nice, crisp black suit. He had a beautiful, ocean-blue tie on. After all, Bailey loved blue, and he lived for the small pleasures in life. Amber thought he looked like a secret agent—a gorgeous secret agent, but a secret agent indeed. Bailey thought he looked like someone she loved.

He smiled and mouthed the words, "Wow, you look nice."

She smiled back and mouthed, "You, too. Love the tie." Amber noticed them cooing over each other and rolled her eyes. She wasn't so sure she liked her sister liking boys now. All of this love stuff was kind of making her want to barf. Maybe she wouldn't feel that way if she was in a relationship, but right now that didn't look like a possibility. The boy she was in love with didn't seem to know she existed, and the one that did notice her she wished did not.

The reception was lovely. The food, wine and dancing turned out to be perfect. They had the reception on the beach. Mary thanked Bailey for giving her something so perfect that she never thought it possible.

"Thank you for giving me and Amber your unconditional love," Bailey said as she handed her the tickets for her honeymoon surprise—

tickets to Paris with a full itinerary of adventure waiting for her and Jack.

"Bailey, how can I ever thank you enough?"

"Mary, how can I ever thank you enough? This is but a glimpse of what you have given me. Have fun and call me when you get back. I'll pick Amber up from her last camp and bring her back here to the beach. Your honeymoon plans entail an entire summer, so I guess I'll see you in August." It was June 5th. Mary was crying when she got in the car with Jack, and they drove away. Bailey and Amber were crying too. As the caterers and other hired people were cleaning up, Ashton pulled Bailey to the side and said, "I didn't think I could love you more, but you're such a giving person. I love you more every day." She sighed, and Amber walked up.

"Okay, Amber, are you all packed? The driver will be here to take you to the airport in fifteen minutes."

"Yes, all packed. Wow, this wedding was awesome!"

"Remember, not a word to anyone. Bill and Jo—I mean, mom and dad—cannot find out. Got it?"

"Got it," Amber said. "I'll see you in two months, Big Sister." She whispered in Bailey's ear, "He gets yummier every day." They both laughed.

"Go." Amber got in the car and it pulled away. "Don't forget to call or text."

"Okay, I will. Bye." When she pulled away, Bailey fell into Ashton's arms.

Perfidia had been burning now for days. She didn't realize that she would continue to burn for another two months, the time it would take to release the links of Ashton's essence from her skin. She cried out day and night in pain. For brief periods of time, she was free from it and had time to torture one of her human playthings, helping to recharge her body with power. If she burned like this for long without being able to gain power from others, she wondered if it would kill her. So did Kilguard. A part of him hoped it would destroy her and completely vanquish her existence. The other part feared what his life would be like if he didn't have to worry about pleasing her, but he had decided either way it was time for him to move on.

Kilguard stayed close to her, drinking in as much of her power as he could without her knowing he was doing it. He was growing very strong. He felt once it was over, if she didn't die, he would be able to have control and tell her he wanted to go his own way now. He would wait until she could fight back before telling her this. He knew that if he didn't, she would seek revenge, and he would rather face her wrath than run from it.

Bailey and Ashton enjoyed their first carefree summer day, with Amber gone to camp and Mary off on her honeymoon. It was the first time in Bailey's life she felt free of responsibility. She was so happy to be spending her days lounging on the beach or frolicking in the water with Ashton by her side. She relished in each adventure her nights held for her. So far, Ashton had been a complete gentleman with her. They would make out and such, but it never went beyond that. She loved waking up each morning wrapped in his embrace. He was experiencing a different life than he thought possible. He was so in love with her now that he was afraid he could not walk away from her if she decided she didn't love him. He thought humans were different. They can love you one minute and hate you the next. Once a vampire loved you, it was for an eternity.

Chapter Eleven

Ashton had to go away to hunt, and Bailey would be alone for the day. She was out on the beach when she saw Adam. He was surfing. He looked better, and she was grateful for that. She hated the fact that she hadn't thought about him since the last time she had seen him. She didn't know Annie was going to be at her parents' beach house, nor did she expect she would be there with Adam. She thought it against the code to date your cousin's ex-girl, but it was none of her business. Annie hadn't called her since graduation. She assumed she was already off on her two-year trip around the world. Maybe she hadn't called because she was dating Adam and thought Bailey wouldn't like it. Just then, she saw Kyle and Annie walking down the beach holding hands. I should have known better, she thought. Annie may be lots of things, but she would never date her ex-boyfriend's cousin, nor someone I had gone out with. It broke the unspoken girl-and-boy code. Annie saw her then and let go of Kyle's hand to come running toward her.

"Bailey, I didn't know you were here! I thought you would be gone on some summer adventure before school started in the fall."

"I thought about it." They both laughed.

"I'm sorry I haven't had a chance to call you. Kyle and I have been together non-stop, and you know how that goes."

"I do. Ashton and I have been together non-stop as well."

"Really? Do tell." They both laughed again.

"Well, has the eagle landed then?" That's when she remembered the code name she and Annie came up with years ago for losing their virginity. Bailey laughed so loud she spit Dr. Pepper everywhere.

"No, it has not. Don't say things like that when I've just taken a big chug of Dr. Pepper!"

"You mean you haven't done it yet?" she said with a look of disbelief.

"No. Let's not talk about this."

"And he has been here with you since graduation?"

"Yes."

"Has he tried?" Bailey sighed, exasperated.

"Our relationship is not based on that alone."

"I'm sorry, Bailey, but boys will be boys."

"Well, that's where you're wrong. Ashton is not a boy. He's a man. He respects me, and is willing to wait until I'm ready."

"Wow, I'm impressed. He sounds like a keeper." They both laughed. Kyle walked up.

"Hey, Loco," Kyle said, giving Bailey his usual scowling grimace.

"Hey, Dill Weed," Bailey responded.

"Guys, can't you get along?" They both glared at each other.

"I doubt it," Bailey said. "I have no patience for the mere stupid."

"Yeah, well I have no patience for the queen of crazy," Kyle spat back.

"Shut up, Kyle," Annie said. Adam walked up then. He didn't realize it was Bailey, and when he did his face looked like it was pained.

"Hey," Bailey said.

"Hey," Adam responded in a flat tone.

"I didn't know you could surf," Bailey said.

"Yeah, I try," he said.

"It doesn't look like trying. It looks like knowing what you're doing," she said. He smiled.

"Annie, are you guys staying all summer or what?" Bailey asked.

"No, we're just here for the next week, and then Kyle and I start our travels around the world together."

"Oh, I see. Where are you going?"

"Where are we not going?" They all shared a laughed. "Starting off in Europe and then we will see where the wind takes us. You know, you should make plans to meet up with us at some point," Annie said. Kyle glared at Annie. Bailey laughed.

"I think for the sake of your relationship that is not a good idea." They all laughed.

Annie wasn't thinking when she asked, "Where is Ashton?" Adam's face fell. Bailey noticed.

"He had a few errands to run. He'll be back here later this evening."

"So, you're free to hang out with us today then?" Bailey felt awkward. She would love to hang with Annie. She could do without Kyle, and she didn't want to hang with Adam, considering he really seemed to like her, and she had already somehow hurt him.

"Annie, can I talk to you for a minute?"

"Sure, hold on, guys, we'll be back. Girl chat," she laughed.

"Annie, it's not a good idea for us to be hanging out. Adam gave me the creeps the last time I saw him. He seems to really like me. I thought I liked him, but my feelings for Ashton are greater, so I don't think we should hang out together. It might send the wrong signal to Adam that I like him, and I can't deal with that. I don't think Ashton would like it either."

"Bailey, it's not like you're going to be making out with him. We'll all play a game of beach volleyball, and swim and just be teenagers. It's not like you're going to be alone with Adam. You have always been so uptight." Bailey frowned.

"Okay, I guess. I would like to spend time with you before I don't see you for two years."

"Come on, we'll see each other."

"I doubt it. My school schedule is going to keep me busy, and I can't jet off to meet you in Europe at any given time."

"I know, but we will keep in touch. I promise." They walked back toward the guys and Annie said, "Beach volleyball anyone?" They played and had fun for a while.

Kyle didn't want to play anymore because Adam and Bailey kept beating him and Annie, so he said, "Let's all go for a swim." They all ran and jumped into the water. Bailey was swimming around when she felt something glide just under her. She screamed. It was Kyle being a jerk.

"Go away, Kyle!" she yelled. He laughed. He took off toward Annie, pretending to be a shark, and she was swimming as fast as she could to get away from him. He got her in the end, and pulled her under the water. When they came back up for air, they were making out. Bailey rolled her eyes. Bailey glanced over to see Adam. He was watching her, but keeping a distance. This made her feel bad. What had she done that made him like her so much in such a short period of time? How could she fix this? She would really like to be Adam's friend. She floated over to him. "Adam, how's school going?"

"Good, I guess. I took the summer off. I was just overloaded, trying to get too much done too fast, and it almost burned me out. I decided I needed a break." They were out in pretty deep water, and Bailey got a leg cramp. She started to go under. She was scared. She couldn't keep herself afloat. At first, he thought she was kidding. He didn't picture her the drama-girl type, and didn't get her pretending to drown. When she came back up the last time and he saw her face, he knew she wasn't kidding. He went for her as fast as he could and pulled her to shore. Bailey wasn't breathing, he was frantic. He started CPR and had her breathing again within minutes. She started coughing up water. He was out of breath.

"Are you okay, Bailey?"

"Yeah, I think so." It hurts to talk. Her throat was all scratchy. He picked her up and took her into the house. "Thank you for saving me," she whispered. "I didn't think I was going to make it."

"I didn't know you were in danger. I thought you were playing. I'm sorry it took me so long to see you were in trouble."

"It's okay. You did see…you saved me. Thank you." He leaned in and kissed her forehead. She was too weak to say anything, but Ashton arrived just in time to see it, and he was not happy.

Bailey looked up in time to see Ashton coming through the door. She also saw the look on his face and the color of his eyes. They were metallic silver. She remembered him telling her when he was super angry that his eyes changed color. She wasn't afraid for herself, but she was afraid for Adam. "Adam, can you put me down?" she croaked. He did as she said, and he looked up in time to see Ashton walking toward him at a super fast pace. Bailey called Ashton's name. He didn't stop moving toward Adam. It was something she had never seen before. It was the look of predator hunting prey. She had to stop him. She was afraid he was going to kill Adam, and she knew her Ashton, if under control, would never do that. "Ashton!" she yelled again. He didn't listen. Adam was under some kind of mind control. The look of horror on his face was so frightening that Bailey wanted to run from the room. She would not let this happen. Just then, Ashton pounced on Adam, and things for Adam went black. Bailey threw herself over Adam. She looked at Ashton. He was not Ashton anymore. There was an animal look on his face. For a second, she was scared for herself. "Baby, please come back to me! Adam just saved me from drowning!" It was hard for her to talk. Her throat felt on fire, but she pleaded with him. "Please, I need you to come back to me." He snarled at her. "I know you're upset, but you can control this. This is not who you are, baby. I love you. Please don't do this." He snapped out of it as soon as he heard the words. He fell to the floor, placing his face in his hands.

"Bailey, I'm sorry. I don't know what happened. I've never done that before."

"Baby, you were jealous, and jealousy is a strange beast. Now, how can we fix this? Adam can't remember what went down here."

"I'll sway his mind. Give me a minute." He pulled himself away from her, and she went to him. "Aren't you afraid of me, Bailey?" She could hear the pain in his voice, and this broke her heart.

"I have to admit, you did scare me, but I know you. Now don't beat yourself up about this. We are both experiencing feelings we didn't think possible, so we have to learn how to control them. Now, don't pull away from me."

He held her close and said, "I love you."

"I love you," she exclaimed like a declaration. That's when he remembered what she said. "Did you just say you loved me?" Bailey was a little shocked. She did say out loud that she loved him. She smiled up at him.

"Yes, baby. I did."

Adam had a cut on his forehead. Bailey bandaged him up, and Ashton swayed his memory. He would only remember pulling Bailey from the water. The rest they would make up. When they took Adam back down the beach to Annie's house, Annie and Kyle were waiting. "Oh my gosh! What happened?" Annie asked. Annie gave Ashton a dirty look. He didn't smile at her this time, for she was thinking Ashton went crazy and beat up Adam. Ashton knew she was right.

"Adam saved me from drowning, but he hit his head on a rock. After he did CPR on me, he passed out. He should be coming to any minute," Bailey said.

Adam woke up and said, "What happened? Where's Bailey?"

"I'm here. Thank you for saving me. Adam, you should rest now. You hit your head while pulling me from the water. If you need anything, let me know."

"Should we call the ambulance?" Annie asked.

"No, I'm fine. I'm glad Bailey is okay," Adam said.

"Me too," Annie said.

"We will see you guys later," Bailey said. She took Ashton's hand, and they walked back down the beach toward the house.

When they got back to the house, she was trying to figure out how she was going to comfort him. Ashton looked so broken that she was truly afraid. "Ashton, talk to me!" she exclaimed.

"Bailey, I almost killed you, and Adam. I may not like the guy, but I have fought every ounce of vampire instinct in me to not kill any humans."

"Baby, you didn't kill, nor will you kill, any humans. Look at me, please!"

"I can't. How can you look at me the same way again? I am not human, and I don't think I am safe for you to be around anymore. If I can lose control over seeing him kiss your forehead, what would have happened if he had kissed you on the lips?" He shuddered. "I would have ripped his head off, and I don't think you would have been able to stop me." Bailey flinched.

"Yes, I would have. You're overreacting. It's your instinct to protect what's yours and Ashton I'm yours—I'm all yours. I'm not holding back from loving you anymore. Part of loving someone is loving the good, the bad, and the ugly. Now, let me tell you about the day, so we can move on. I love you and there is nothing you can do to change that!" This made him smile, even though he didn't feel like it. Warmth spread throughout his entire body—a warmth he had never felt before. It was the feeling of unconditional love. She told him about the volleyball and Kyle being pissed off because he kept losing. She told him about swimming and almost drowning, and Ashton shuddered again.

"I can't lose you, Bailey," he muttered.

"You didn't." She pulled him close, and they held each other. "Wow, who would have thought I would have been able to calm you down when your very presence soothes me," she said. He smiled. "We'll have to be more careful. I won't see Adam again. I knew it was a bad idea, but I felt bad for him. It's not normal how he has attached himself to me. I mean, on our first date we connected, but it was not love. I think we liked each other, but for me it was a kinship. We both have our issues, and we connected from that, but on the second date things went to unnatural levels. I mean, who writes a poem about a girl you have only been on one date with?"

"He wrote you a poem?" She saw his eyes flash silver.

She smiled, "Calm, remember? Is Adam holding me? No, you are. Now, maybe I'm a skeptic, but I do not believe in love at first sight, not as a human anyway. That's not all though, his personality changed. He went from carefree to somewhat controlling and then domineering. It really scared me."

"What did you say?" Ashton asked.

"He kind of changed. I thought maybe he wasn't the person he pretended to be that first date. He was just too pushy and lovey dovey on the second date. By the time I saw him the third time, he seemed to be more like he was a stalker than anything else."

Ashton stiffened. He knew only one being that could change your personality, and he knew Perfidia had turned Adam into one of her minions.

Ashton wanted to seek Perfidia out, but he feared leaving Bailey alone for one minute with Adam now under Perfidia's control. He wanted to tell Bailey to stay away from Adam now because he was no longer under his own control, but he feared she would think he had mind control over him, so he decided the best defense is a good offense. He would take precautions. If Adam was a minion, he could still use mind control over him to sway him, and he would have to try and be around Adam more to read his thoughts and get as much information from him as possible. He decided he would go see Adam.

Bailey had called Annie and told her that she just didn't feel comfortable hanging out with Adam, considering their past and that she didn't want Ashton to feel uncomfortable. She told her to pass along her gratitude to Adam for saving her from drowning and to let her know if he needed anything.

"He's already back to normal. He went out surfing this morning," Annie said. Bailey was relieved.

"I get it, Bailey. It's kind of a weird situation, even Kyle gets it. We decided to head out early for our trip anyway, so I'll call you in a few weeks from wherever we are."

"Okay, be safe and have fun."

"We will, and you have a fun summer too. After seeing Ashton again I'm sure the eagle will land soon." Annie laughed.

"Annie, that's not funny!" They both said goodbye. When she hung up the phone, she was glad they were leaving early. That meant Adam would too. Annie forgot to mention that Adam had the beach house for the rest of the summer.

When Ashton got to the beach house, Annie and Kyle were already gone. He saw Adam on the beach. He walked over to him. "Hey, I wanted to come and tell you thank you for saving Bailey yesterday."

Adam looked at him with a scowl on his face and said, "Don't pretend you like me, and I won't pretend I like you. There is something not normal about you. I can't put my finger on it, but I know it's there." He heard Adam trying to recall the events of what happened after he pulled Bailey from the water, but he couldn't reach them. Ashton's voice grew cold as ice.

"You're right. Let's not pretend. Let's also not pretend that you don't have something you're hiding as well." Adam's eyes flashed, and he knew Ashton knew he was under Perfidia's control.

"Look, I don't know what you're talking about." Ashton heard his thoughts, *how does he know about her? Perfidia.* He shuddered. A flash of torture beyond understanding went through his mind, and even Ashton felt the pain from it. *Why can't she leave me alone? I haven't heard from her in a month. Maybe she forgot about me. I'm finally myself again…no one controlling my thoughts. How does he know about her? Does he know, or am I overreacting?* "What are you talking about, Ashton?"

"I'm just saying, we all have things we hide. Some of us can just hide things better than others. I thanked you for saving Bailey, but I'm telling you now for your own safety to stay away from her." His eyes went silver, and Adam knew, no matter what torture Perfidia put him through, he would not go near Bailey again.

"You have my word I will not go near Bailey again," Adam said as he walked away.

Chapter Twelve

When Ashton got back to the beach house, Bailey was lounging by the pool asleep. He bent down and kissed her. She opened her eyes. "I was wondering when you would be back. Come here." He went and lay down on the lounger beside her, and they started kissing. He pulled off his shirt, and threw it on the ground. He already had on swim trunks. She was in a sporty one-piece swimsuit. Bailey was not into showing her body off to others. She was modest, and when the time came, there would only be one person who would know what her belly button looked like. They kissed for a long while, and then he picked her up and threw her into the pool. She started laughing. He jumped in after her. They played in the water all afternoon—sometimes making out, sometimes just goofing off.

It was around 6 PM when Bailey said, "I'm starving." She hopped out of the pool and went inside to find herself something to eat. Ashton followed her. They both went upstairs and changed clothes. He had his own room, and she had hers. Although he slept in her room every night, he respected her enough to let her get dressed without him watching. When and if she was ready for something more, he would be ready too. When he came back downstairs, she was already setting the table. He ate with her, partly because his experience tasting food had become stronger. He also enjoyed being able to feel somewhat human when it came to eating food. Bailey knew he needed nourishment, so he would not grow weak. She loved him, and she would deal with what he needed to eat to survive. She came out with tea for both of them.

"Can I help?" he asked.

"No, babe. I got it." She came back out with two dinner plates. She placed hers down first—a nice salad with grilled chicken. The one thing about cowboys—they really don't like salad. He would eat it anyway. When the plate was sat in front of him, he smiled. It was a very large, bigger than the plate, cut of raw, bloody, red meat. She also gave him a steak knife and fork. She bent down and kissed him.

"I know you are not affected by E coli, but I could be, so after you eat please brush your teeth before we make out again." He laughed, a little surprised.

"Thanks for thinking of me." It kind of shocked him that she was going to be able to sit with him and eat her dinner while he ate raw meat, but she did. She didn't even act like it made her sick. He wanted to laugh a few times when she kept saying to herself, *mind over matter, mind over matter. Pretend it's cooked, pretend it's cooked,* Finally, she thought, *it's just cooked with red sauce*, and she didn't think about it anymore after that. However the thought of *I really love him,* ran through her mind. Ashton smiled at Bailey.

"I really love you," he said. Sometimes she forgot he could read her thoughts. She smiled, face flushing a bright crimson.

"Stop doing that, please. Can't a girl think without you listening in?"

"I try not to, but sometimes it's hard not to hear you."

"Okay, I forgive you. What do you want to do after dinner? Stroll on the beach?" she asked.

"Sounds good to me," he said.

She cooked. He cleaned. He was fast. He had the dishes cleaned up and everything put away, as well as his teeth brushed, before she came back downstairs from freshening up. He took her hand, and they headed out toward the roaring waves. The sun was about to set as they walked, talked, and held each other. Adam watched from a distance. He was under orders. He wouldn't go near Bailey if he could avoid it, but he would report back anything, and everything he could to Perfidia.

Maybe if he had enough information, she wouldn't torture him so, but he doubted it. She was truly wicked.

Kilguard didn't know why he was seeking Joanne out. He hadn't seen her in years. In the beginning, when he first told her he didn't love her, she was on his mind so often then he thought he was going to have to do something to provoke Perfidia to kill him to make the pain of it go away. He followed her in the beginning, after telling her he didn't love her. She just didn't know it. He thought maybe he could figure out a way to keep her. He saw the light that once shined through her slowly wither and fade to nothing. He knew he was the one who took her light. If he could die to give it back to her, he would have, but mistakes made are not always fixable. He watched everything she had once lived for—music, the laughter of children, and the love for life itself—just slip away. It was like dreaming, when you're so lost in the dream you don't ever want to wake up, but for some reason your subconscious pulls you to wake. Joanne could no longer hold onto anything she had once loved, because she couldn't hold onto the one person she truly loved, Kingston.

Joanne turned into a person who played her part in life. She became who Bill needed her to be—a trophy wife. She had to be who Bill wanted her to be in order to keep him. She had lost everything that made her who she was. Before Kingston, she use to be independent, strong, someone who could take care of herself. When he walked away from her and their child, she feared being alone. She feared not being able to care for the baby. Mainly, she feared not being able to love the child—the child that caused him to leave. She didn't know who she was anymore, and this is when her light for life faded to nothing. She never connected to either of her children. She treated them like they were disconnected from her, and she felt she didn't need to be near them, nor want to be, most of the time. There were times when she longed to be the person she was before Kingston—the person who would have loved to have two beautiful, smart, independent daughters. Bailey reminded her so much of herself before Kingston that it was torture to be around her for even a second. She pushed herself to stay away. It didn't help that Bailey looked so much like Kingston. Every time she looked in Bailey's eyes, she wanted to scream, so she made little to no contact. Bill's business kept them away so much that, to her, it was a blessing. When she did have to see the girls, she saw the pain she had caused every time she looked at them. Both girls felt she had abandoned them, and she knew they were right, but she didn't know how, or if, she would ever be able to fix it. Joanne didn't feel like she had anything left inside her to give to her girls. She truly wished she did, but Kingston had taken every ounce of her love with him when he walked out the door.

Bill had made life miserable for Joanne. When she told him what had happened, he too changed. Bill was an all-American boy. He was the good guy—the guy you want to bring home to Mom and Dad, the guy you want to marry. He showed her how much he loved her daily. He would have given her the world, and that was his goal in life, but things changed within their relationship after that. Bill was no longer the loving man he had been. He was cruel to her. He wanted her to suffer as much as she had made him suffer for choosing someone else. It was not so much that she fell in love with someone else; it was the fact she carried on a relationship with this person for four months while still planning to marry him. When she told him of the betrayal that was bad enough, he was beyond crazy and wouldn't speak to her for weeks, but when he found out she was pregnant too, Bill's light faded to nothing.

Bill told her he would still marry her and take the baby as his own, but he would never trust her again. She would have to live with that fact, along with the consequences. Bill's consequences consisted of Joanne never being able to be alone. She had to be with Bill or her personal assistant, Lily, at all times. If for one minute she was alone, she would get the third degree. She didn't argue with him because she felt she deserved his distrust, so she lived a life of having to have a babysitter—a babysitter Bill paid to watch her, to keep her in line, to make sure she never betrayed him again.

Kilguard had not seen Joanne in over eighteen years. It took him a while to find her. She was on some tropical island with Bill. Sometimes he truly wanted to kill Bill. He knew Bill had given her a good life—well, at least a good life by human standards—but he could tell she had never truly been happy. He understood this more than she would ever know. She had affected him in a way that made him change too. His heart was not quite as cold as it was before her. If he could have ran away without Perfidia finding them, he would have all those years ago. But Perfidia was much too powerful then, and he knew betrayal would have meant more than death for both of them, but also for his child. He loved his daughter, even if he would never know her.

When he found Joanne, she was sitting alone. She had aged well for a human. She didn't look her age to him. He would always see her as the girl he loved. She was crying, and she was looking at two pictures. One was a picture of two girls. These must be her daughters, one of which was his daughter—the older one, the one with the beautiful blue eyes. His eyes…Wow, she has my eyes. She also has shoulder length brown-blonde hair—that too she took from him. He couldn't believe how much Bailey looked like him. He could tell she was not the conventional girl. He could see a glimpse of the girl Joanne had been on the day they met when looking at Bailey, with the exception of her eyes. Joanne had brown eyes. He noticed neither girl smiled in the picture. They both looked like they would rather be somewhere else. It wasn't a bad picture, but it was a candid shot done by a personal camera. In Joanne's other hand was a picture turned over on the backside. It looked very old. The edges were tattered. It looked like it had been carried around in Joanne's purse for many years. Written across the back in black letters—Kingston. When she turned it over, it was him. He was in shock. *After all these years, she still loves me*, he thought. *How can she still love me? I broke her heart.* He had to get away before she heard him moan out in agony.

Chapter Thirteen

Perfidia ordered Adam to get some pictures of Bailey. She had her pride, but she was in a lot of pain and she didn't know if, or when, it would stop. She thought, if the girl is dead it will stop, so the plan now was to kill the girl. She would kill her as quickly as possible. Also, she told Adam to get some of her hair. It would not be as good as getting her essence, but it would do the trick. She would be able to cast the spell that would kill her on the next full moon.

Adam was able to sneak into the house when they were out one day on the beach. Something told him to wait until he was sure Bailey had Ashton completely preoccupied before he went into the house. He got some hair from her brush in the upstairs bathroom. He noticed, while walking through her bedroom, that Ashton's clothes were not in there. He glanced in the room next door to see Ashton's things, and he wondered what that was about. He would keep that information and use it on a day Perfidia was torturing him. Maybe this would make her stop. He waited until two days later, when Ashton had left for the day, to use his zoom lens to take pictures of Bailey while she lounged by the pool.

He took everything back to Perfidia and, for once, she didn't hurt him. She told him he could go until she needed him again. He thanked her and left. Part of him was very angry. Why had he let her do this to him? He was a coward. Here he was putting Bailey in who knows what kind of danger just to prevent himself from the feeling of being skinned alive. That is what her torture felt like. It felt like she was taking a razor and removing every inch of skin from his body.

As he was walking up from the dungeon to get back to the main level, he noticed it in the hallway—the picture that had been on the orphanage wall back all those years ago. He looked at it. Why would Perfidia have a picture of a group of children playing on a playground—faces filled with laughter and joy? He looked closely. He could have sworn he recognized two of the faces. When he looked back, the faces had changed. He was sure it was the exact picture from the orphanage. He couldn't comprehend why, or how, she had this picture. He wanted to know this, and he wanted to know now. He would go back and ask her. He didn't care the pain he would endure. He had to know why she had this picture. He knocked on her door. She was crying out in pain.

"Perfidia," Adam said so low it was hard to understand him his voice was shaky and hoarse.

"What do you want? I told you to leave," she snarled.

"I want to ask you something. I have information that I will exchange for the answer to my question." This interested her. What did he think he could give her, and what did he want from her? His freedom she guessed, but she was curious as to what he wanted to offer her.

"I have information that might help you somehow with Bailey. I need to know where, and why, you got the picture of the children upstairs in the hallway."

"I see. What information is it you have not told me about boy?" she hissed.

"I've told you everything but this, and I just noticed it today." Adam's voice grew strong and defiant. "I need to know about the picture." Perfidia laughed a very hard laugh.

"Do you think mere death is all you have to worry about? My young, dumb blond, death would bring peace compared to the pain I can conjure. However, I do think telling you will bring more pain than not." Perfidia couldn't read human thoughts, but once she turned someone into her minion—for about the first thirty minutes, the human mind fights for control—she could see your life flash from birth to present.

Every birthday, every tear, every secret, every pain, she knew about. She knew you, as if you were an open book. She didn't want to torture Adam today. After all, he had followed orders well, but she was growing weaker by the day, and the pain this was going to bring him would feed and keep her strong for days.

"Adam, you can keep your secret about Bailey for another time. I am going to tell you, but remember you asked for it. That picture has always, and will always, be my picture. I hung it in the orphanage where I worked. You see, the mere memories bring me hints of power. I keep it to remember all the children lost under my hand, and the pain that inflicted on each older brother and sister. I worked in the orphanage for years. I love working with children." A smile so evil fell upon her face that Adam wanted to run away and never see her again. He knew she was pure evil.

"You see, I only took those who had strong siblings. You were strong. Blake and Mark were weak. Your pain and suffering kept me strong for an entire year. A child's torture gives me maximum power. So, if you're wondering what that means, your strength brought about Blake and Mark's deaths." She said this with such happiness that it took Adam a minute to focus. He wanted to throw up, but instead he hurled himself at her. "Silly boy, I really didn't want to mess up your pretty face." She tortured him for hours, until he passed out. She had another minion take him home.

When Adam woke up back at the beach house, he could barely move. He was bruised from head to toe. He was in so much misery that he didn't know if he even wanted to survive. He couldn't believe this, after years of thinking he had killed them. In reality, he had. He was strong, and they were weak. Perfidia had said so herself. They died because of his ability to endure. He cried out in anguish. It was so loud that the sound touched Bailey, who was walking on the beach. Ashton was gone and wouldn't be back for a while, but that sounded like Adam. Was he in pain? He had saved her life. What if he was hurt? She had to go find out. When she approached the house, the sliding doors were open. When she first went inside, she didn't see him. "Adam, are you okay?" Bailey asked.

"Go away, Bailey. Please, just go away," he said in a broken voice. It sounded as if every ounce of life had been drained from his body. That's when she saw him curled up in a ball on the floor by the sofa. He was black and blue from head to toe. She gasped.

"What happened to you? Are you okay?" A flash of, did Ashton do this, ran across her mind, and she was glad he wasn't there to read her thoughts. Of course, he would never do this. What was wrong with her? How could she even think that?

"Bailey, I'm fine. Just go away," he moaned.

"Adam, I'm not going to leave you until you tell me what has happened," she said, her voice strong and motherly. Most of Perfidia's minions couldn't even speak her name. She had made sure of this by casting a tongue-tie spell on them that prevented them from telling others about her. She had been so angry over losing Ashton that she didn't cast the spell over Adam. The next time she thought to do it, she decided he was too afraid to say anything and she was too weak to conjure it up, so she would let it slide. No one would believe him anyway. He would get locked up if he said anything. If he did get locked up for talking, she would appear in his room and kill him. Even though she could not enter into someone's home, she could enter public places such as hospitals. She would make it look like suicide.

"Bailey, I don't know if I can tell you. He sounded so guarded. This truly scared Bailey. "To be honest, I don't know who I am anymore. I don't know what has happened, or why this happened to me."

"You can tell me, Adam," she pleaded. "I will believe you. I promise."

"You may say you will believe me, but you will think I'm crazy."

"I give you my word, I will not think that."

Adam sighed, and said, "I have been cursed." Bailey froze. She thought, *is Adam a vampire too? How does one get cursed?*

She was scared, but she said, "Okay." Adam took her sudden stillness as though she thought he was insane.

"I told you, just forget it," he said.

"Cursed how?" she asked.

"I know you're going to freak, but a High Priestess Witch has turned me into some human servant, and I serve only her. I sometimes don't have control over my actions, or thoughts. Like on our second date, and then again when I approached you about not calling me back or answering my text. For some reason, this witch is after you." Bailey shuddered, and the fear of what Adam was saying shot down her from the top of her head to the tips of her toes. Bailey took a deep breath to calm herself down.

"I believe you. We have to tell Ashton," Bailey said.

"NO!" Adam shouted.

"I have to tell him. I bet she was the woman who approached me at the shopping center before you arrived. When I wouldn't help her, she turned and disappeared. "Did you tell her where we were meeting that day?"

"Sometimes I don't remember what I tell her, but I'm sure there is a chance I did tell her." This upset Adam. "She had come after you on her own," he whispered. "Bailey, this witch, Perfidia, is evil beyond understanding." Bailey looked at Adam like she was thinking about something.

"I knew you were different on our first date compared to our next, and then the way you appeared to be stalking me," Bailey said. Adam just looked stunned. He didn't realize he had stalked her.

"Did I stalk you, Bailey? I'm so sorry. She can make me do these things when I'm under her control. I don't remember much that happens. She usually just gives me tasks to get completed, or so I thought. I don't really remember much about our second date. I assumed I was in some sort of love struck haze." He laughed. "Don't get me wrong, Bailey. I do like you, but love is not something I take lightly," he said.

"I knew it. I knew something had changed about you. You were such a genuine person on our first date, and then you went all smothering. It really pushed me away. I assume that is her only experience with love, having to force someone into it," Bailey said.

"I didn't think about it that way," Adam said. "Wow, no wonder she acts miserable and crazy."

"Ashton can help us with this. I know you don't like him, and he doesn't care that much for you, but you need help, and apparently you need help because someone is after me, so we are all in this together."

He sighed and said, "Okay, I don't know if you need protection from me, Bailey. I want you to know that."

"Thanks for telling me, Adam. We will figure this out. Now, I need to find a first aid kit. I know Annie has one around here somewhere. She is always falling down and stuff." They both laughed.

"You're right. She is always falling down or running into something."

"Yeah, I honestly don't understand how she is alive. When we were kids out having adventures, it seems each adventure ended with me having to carry her back to the house, so her nanny could clean some sort of mortal wound." She went about trying to find something to help soothe the pain. She found some aloe and this seemed to calm down the burning, and he started to feel better.

When Ashton got back to the house, he assumed Bailey was on the beach. He scanned the beach and didn't see her. A vampire has supernatural eyesight. He looked up and down the beach in both directions, and he could see the distance of the beach on both sides. It was like looking through binoculars. He then started to scan the houses. He saw a woman bathing a child in the house next door. The next house up had a couple making out upstairs, while a possible husband was coming up the stairs to catch them in the act. Then he looked at Annie's house where Adam was. He knew Bailey would never go there, but he looked anyway. He saw her sitting beside Adam. Adam had his head in her lap, and she was caressing his hair. He felt the control slipping. *Don't overreact. Don't overreact. Bailey loves you. Bailey loves you.* He repeated over and over in his head. He was able to hold onto this thought until he reached the sliding door, and he heard them laughing. He saw Adam touch her leg, and he lost it. Bailey saw him in the nick of time. His eyes were metallic silver.

"Ashton, it's not what you think." Bailey was starting to panic. "Look at me, Ashton." He moved forward, ignoring her completely.

"Babe, some witch named Perfidia did this." He stopped in his tracks.

"She's after me." His eyes narrowed, and he looked at Bailey and then to Adam.

"How can you know that?" Ashton asked. "Did he tell you?" She looked at Ashton confused.

"Do you know Perfidia?" she asked. He nodded. "Is she the one who cursed you?" He nodded again. "You couldn't tell me could you?"

"No," he said. Her eyes were overflowing now with tears. She ran to him and threw her arms around him. "It's my fault, Bailey. I'm so sorry. I should have walked away, but I needed you." His voice was breaking now with each word he spoke. "Once you touched my heart, I couldn't survive without you."

"I couldn't survive without you either. We will figure this out. It's not your fault, Ashton."

"It is! You know it, I know it, and even Adam here knows it." His voice was harsh and angry. "I will protect you with my last breath," Ashton hissed. Adam glared at Ashton.

"You don't mess around with this witch. You don't know what she can do," Adam said.

"I do, Adam. I know more about her than you do. I have known her many more years. It's okay if we don't like one another. Right now, we have to figure out how we can survive her. How are you able to speak of her? I can't say her name. Did she not cast a tongue-tie spell on you?"

"No, she didn't," Adam said.

"You look like you have been tortured," Ashton said.

"She tortured me yesterday for over five hours. I finally passed out. When I woke up, I was here. She has been using me to get to Bailey. I didn't want to do it, but I didn't have any control over my own actions."

"I know," Ashton said. "It's not your fault, Adam. Just know anything she does is not your fault." Adam's face was pained, and he spoke barely above a whisper.

"She killed my brothers because of me. That's my fault," Adam said. Bailey looked at Adam horrified.

"What?" she gasped.

"It's true, that is why I look like this. I had to take your picture and some of your hair to her yesterday. I'm so sorry, Bailey."

"It's okay. Now, what about your brothers?"

"Well, you know I told you they died in the orphanage. I was six and assumed it was the medical conditions. That is what I heard the nurse say." In his mind, he saw her face. He screamed out, "NO, IT CAN'T BE!" His face grew distant, and then a flash of pain beyond comprehension was engraved in the depths of his eyes. "It was Perfidia. She was the director at the orphanage," he choked.

"Oh no," Bailey said.

"She told me she gained power from the misery of people, and children's misery gave her the most power. She said the deaths of my brothers were due to my strength, and their weakness. She was able to survive off my pain for an entire year," he said.

"Oh, Adam." She went to him and took him in her arms. Ashton didn't move. He was figuring out for himself what had truly happened to Elizabeth, and his heart was truly breaking all over again. He would tell Bailey later when they were alone. Adam needed her now, so he walked into the kitchen and got everyone a glass of tea. Adam sat in silence for over an hour while Bailey held him.

They decided they needed to work together on this, so they were going to have to do some research to see if the mind control Perfidia had over Adam could be broken. They discussed all options of what they could do to fight against her. "Can she enter the house?" Adam asked.

"No," Ashton said. "She must lure you out of your home."

Bailey looked at Ashton. "But Adam can enter the house," Bailey said.

"True, but I will keep Adam away from you if she sends him." Ashton looked at Adam with a look of sincerity. "Adam, I will try not to kill you if you come for her. I'm not making any promises. I know she could transfer some of her power to you, giving you strength to fight me, but I don't think it would be good enough. I'm beyond strong, so I'll try and control my anger if that happens. I will try just to incapacitate you." Adam looked at Ashton horrified, and nodded.

"She is doing some sort of spell the next full moon," Adam said. "That is why she needed the hair and stuff. I heard her saying the girl will be dead within 24 hours after the spell is cast." Ashton stiffened. He knew it then and there. Perfidia had cast this spell against Elizabeth on the night of the full moon, and she had died within 24 hours. She had killed Elizabeth to get to him, and the fury rolled through him like a thousand roaring lions. Adam and Bailey both jumped.

"That is how she killed Elizabeth," he said, his voice filled with anger. Bailey and Adam looked at each other and shrugged.

"Babe, who is Elizabeth?" Bailey asked.

"She was the woman I had asked to marry me before I was cursed. I was in love with her. She died on the night of a full moon. They claimed scarlet fever, but the doctor kept saying it's not possible. It came on too fast, and took her too quickly. The coroner settled on saying it was scarlet fever, even though they argued about it for over an hour." Bailey ran to him and pulled his face down to meet hers.

"I'm so sorry. I didn't know you had been in love with someone who had died. How can I ever say how sorry I am for you?"

"You're here. Thank you for being here. I'm afraid. What if she cast this spell against you, Bailey? I can't live without you," Ashton exclaimed. Bailey had this aura about her. It had developed within the time it took her to say the words.

"The spell will not work on me," Bailey said with a mindset of perceptiveness.

Ashton looked at her incredulously. "What are you talking about?"

"Ashton, you have changed me, just as I have changed you. I know you feel it too. There is a…I don't know how to say it—a covering over me, like a blanket of protection. I don't think she can do any kind of dark magic that would be able to penetrate through that layer of protection." He felt the truth in her words and knew Perfidia would not be able to take her away the way she had Elizabeth. The relief washed over him, and he was ready to figure out how they could fight her when they needed to.

Chapter Fourteen

On their way to the library, Bailey's phone rang. "Hey, Amber."

"Hey, so anything interesting happening around there?" Bailey laughed an odd laugh and Amber noticed.

"Oh my God, you're acting weird. You did it, didn't you? I can't believe you did it. What will mom and dad say?" She laughed.

"Amber, you're silly. No, I have not done that yet."

"Yet? So, you plan on getting it on with Mr. Secret Agent Man?"

"Amber, I'm hanging up now."

"Okay, I'll be good. Cheer camp is awesome! Can you believe this cheer camp is co-ed? There are some super hot guys walking around here."

"Amber, are guys all you think about?"

"Excuse me, but I'm not the one living with a guy," she huffed. Bailey laughed.

"If the camp is co-ed, you are living with guys."

"Shut up! I am living with guys. I have to text Caroline with that one. She is down by the pool with Dylan. Anyway, I was calling to tell you my cheer won the contest for best cheer created at camp."

"Congratulations, Amber! I'm so happy for you."

"Thanks. I'm glad Caroline and I made up. We are having a great time at camp and I got a letter from Mathew two days ago."

"I'm glad you're having fun."

"That's not all, I get an award, and they want my parents to come, but you know that is not going to happen. Mary is gone until the end of the month, and I was wondering if you could come?" she blurted. Bailey had so much going on right now with trying to stay alive that she really didn't want to lead anyone in the direction of her sister, but she didn't have a choice. Their parents were too self involved, and Bailey wouldn't let this milestone for Amber take place without her being there to cheer her on.

"When is it?" Bailey asked.

"It's Saturday afternoon at 3 PM"

"Which camp is this one?"

"Bringelton Camp. It's only an hour drive for you."

"Text me the address, and I'll be there, Amber. I can't wait to hear your cheer."

"Oh, thank you, Bailey. I knew you would come. I love you so much." Bailey smiled.

"I love you too, Amber. Have you met a cute guy this summer?"

"You know it. He is fine. His name is Eric. He is not as nice looking as Mr. Agent, but who is?" They both laughed. He is so cute, but what I like about him is he's nice too. I'm so excited you're coming. I gotta go. They're starting a water battle, and if I don't get my phone put away it will be destroyed. I'll text you later. Love ya. Bye." Amber had hung up before Bailey got to say goodbye.

Ashton and Bailey made their way to the library. They thought maybe somewhere in there they could find something that would help them to break the spell against Adam. Some of the local libraries had been there so many years and had so many sections that maybe within its walls were the secret to setting everyone free from Perfidia. If they could take Adam out of the equation that would be one less person Perfidia could draw power from. They were looking through book after book in the library. They found nothing that would make any difference. It's not like they could go ask the librarian to help find a book on breaking dark spells. They searched for hours and never found anything. Ashton said, "We will find something. We're just going to have to search somewhere else." Bailey nodded. They decided to grab some lunch while they were out, so they stopped at a local deli. Ashton noticed a man staring at Bailey. He had never seen, nor met, this man, but he was sure this was not a human. Bailey looked up in time to see him too. When their eyes met, everything went black for Bailey.

Kilguard had been away searching for Joanne. He found her and was overwhelmed, after all the heartache and pain he had put her through, that she still loved him. She still carried his picture with her. This tormented Kilguard. He thought she had forgotten all about him and moved on with her life. He thought she may not be happily married, but in today's world who truly is happily married. Kilguard and Perfidia lived off the painful emotions of people. Kilguard never told Perfidia he had a sixth sense. He could also taste other emotions. He had never tried to drink these other emotions in, but he had been able to taste them. When he got back to check on Perfidia, hoping she was still burning because this kept her preoccupied and out of his way, he noticed she had the death spell out, and he was wondering who she was going to kill.

He didn't know how to ask without sounding suspicious, so he said, "Awe, Perfidia. Who is dying today?" She laughed a harsh laugh.

"The girl, Ashton's girl," she shrieked, her eyes casting a demented stare.

"I see," he said.

"She is the reason I am burning, and if she is dead the burning will stop."

"Who is she?"

"Just some mortal girl." That is when he noticed the pictures Adam had taken of Bailey. He saw her and said, "NO, not her!" Perfidia snapped her head around. In all the years they had been together, he had never said no to her.

"What did you say?" He didn't back down. He looked into her eyes and firmly said, "I said, no, not her!" Then he proceeded to knock over the caldron that held potions for the spell.

She screamed, "NO!" She began torturing Kilguard. She tortured him until she was sure he was dead. If he was still alive, he was hoping he was dead. It took him two days to recover enough to seek out Bailey. He was still powerful, but the torture had drained and transferred most all of what he was able to draw from Perfidia while she burned back to her. This gave her a renewal, and the burning stopped for a week before starting again. During the week she was not burning, she was trying to get together a way to kill Bailey. She decided to summon her vampires. She would send three to hunt and kill Bailey. She knew Ashton would fight a good fight, but she didn't care. The vampires would bring him to her, and she would destroy him with the blade of her father— one of only five wizard blades in the entire world. She would not let this girl take her powers. She had been High Priestess Witch for all of the United States for almost a thousand years. A mortal girl would not take this from her.

Kilguard decided to find Bailey. He had to protect her from Perfidia, even if that meant he would not survive. He would not let his mistakes be Bailey's. He owed it to Joanne and Bailey to save her. That is when he followed her and Ashton into the deli. When Ashton saw him, he knew that Ashton realized he was not human, but it wouldn't make any difference at this point. Ashton would not be able to stop what he came to do. In order to transfer his powers to Bailey, all he had to do was make eye contact and say the words that would release his powers and give them to Bailey. He would have never been able to do this if she was not his daughter. Their eyes met, and he spoke the binding words that would transfer his powers to Bailey.

"Cruentus De Intus, Ego Redono, my Imperium." Just like that, it was done. Kilguard felt weak. He had to leave. He needed to get out of there. He knew Ashton would be after him, and he wouldn't be able to fight him off. He wandered into the park and grew comfort knowing Bailey would be able to fight back. He sat down on a park bench and imagined he could see Joey in the center of the park again singing to all the children. This brought him comfort.

Ashton was in a panic. What just happened? He saw the being leave the deli as soon as Bailey went down. He knew he couldn't follow, because he had to make sure Bailey was still alive. Bailey was out for ten minutes. The deli manager called the paramedics, and they came to look her over. When she finally woke up, the look she gave Ashton let him know that something beyond this world had happened, and it took all he had to hold himself together and not pick Bailey up and run with her as fast as he could to get her away from everyone. He knew, no matter where he went, Perfidia would find them. Once Perfidia targeted someone, she could find them anytime, day or night. Ashton knew the ties that bound him to Perfidia were broken, and she would not be able to find him, but she would always be able to find Bailey, and he would always be with Bailey. When Bailey was finally released from the hospital, they were able to go home. She told him she needed the drive home to sort through everything that had just happened. She told him she would explain everything once they were within the safety of their home. When they rounded the corner at the edge of the drive, Ashton knew other vampires were watching. He felt them there. He didn't know what to do. Bailey knew they were there too.

"I know they're here. They can't come inside the house. Just get into the garage as quickly as possible," Bailey said. The vampires had positioned themselves all along the perimeter of the house. They were not going to approach in broad daylight. They were all invisible, but were told to find an opening to kill the girl. They would not be able to kill Ashton, but they could drain him of as much vampire blood as possible leaving him on the verge of death before bringing him to Perfidia. She would gain great power from the emotion of pain that Bailey's death would cause him. Bailey picked up her cell and dialed Adam's number.

"Adam? Do not come over here today! Don't leave your house, and don't let anyone inside, not even a delivery person! If you want to live, do as I say!" He didn't even want to know what horror was behind the sound of her voice, so he told her that he would not leave or let anyone inside. He closed off all doors and windows. Adam was glad the house was fully stocked, and he would be able to live there if he needed to for a good month without leaving. Of course, the thought of this made him feel a little crazy, but he didn't want to die, so he would settle for a little crazy.

When Bailey and Ashton were safe inside, she took his hand and said, "We need to talk. I don't know how to tell you everything that has just happened. I don't believe it myself."

Ashton was alarmed. "Did he hurt you?"

"No. How did you know he did something?" Bailey asked.

"I knew he was not human, and you passed out the moment your eyes met."

"I see," she said. "Well, this is a lot to deal with. How do I begin?"

"Just tell me however you need to, Bailey. You know I will believe you, baby."

"Okay. Well, a lifetime of hating my parents, not understanding why my mother had never loved me…" The tears began to flow freely. "Not knowing why my father seemed so distant to me and Amber, treating us both more or less like pieces of living furniture that he could move around and place in the best position for him to move up on the social ladder. I mean, he has the perfect family." She laughed a very hard laugh. "Looks can be deceiving. When that…man at the deli looked into my eyes, he transferred not only every memory of how he became what he is but also how that is connected to me."

"I don't understand," Ashton said.

"Let's start at the beginning. Perfidia found him more than 800 years ago. She had been a witch for over a hundred years already, but she was seeking out someone who had the ability to give her the ultimate power."

"He is with Perfidia?" Ashton asked. His face was stricken with panic.

Bailey nodded and continued, "She had searched high and low for him. She knew one day she would find him. She had been told there is nothing greater than the power of human emotion, and if someone was able to hold onto this power, they could rule the world. Legend from the dark circle of witches was that he who holds the power of true emotion holds the key to darkness, that whoever could curse him and make him a minion would be able to take in these dark emotions and feed the thirst for more power, just like a flame feeds a fire." Ashton and Bailey shuddered.

Bailey continued, "When Perfidia came to the village where Kingston lived, he was treated very differently than everyone else. Adults would not go near him. They feared the unknown, and something about him was different. Children, however, were drawn to him. Children followed him like he was a ray of sunshine. He didn't understand this. He didn't know why people would shun him, but children were drawn to him. This made him fearful. Perfidia knew when she saw him that he was the one, that the reason adults shunned him was because he could feel all the negative from them and send it back because he didn't know how to drink it in. Children, always innocent, would see the good in life and therefore what he sent back to them was lightness, not dark. They were drawn to him. Perfidia had assumed he was luring the children to him because of his true darkness. The truth was that he had that sixth sense that allowed him to feel all human emotion. If he wasn't drinking it in, then he was sending it back out toward the person that it came from. Perfidia, being the darkest of all witches of her time, only received back from him darkness. Of course, she assumed he was evil, but do not always judge a book by its cover."

Bailey continued, "Once Perfidia had Kingston under her power, she was able to drink from him the emotions of other humans she tortured. He had been under her control for almost ten years before he started to weaken. She feared he would die, and then her endless feast of human emotions would be no more. She had been able to take over almost half of the United States, and she was not going to give up on her thirst for control. She told Kingston he would have to become a wizard, and she would teach him how to drink in the dark emotions, so he would grow strong again." About fifty years after she changed him, she told him he would have died if he didn't change into a wizard. She only said he would suffer for eternity because she thought he would have chosen death over what he would become. Once the change was complete, he could now feed off the emotions of humans. She told him only to take the dark ones or he would kill the human he was drinking from. At the time, he thought maybe Perfidia was showing mercy to humans, so he agreed to only drink in the dark emotions. Perfidia didn't know he didn't need to be changed into a wizard in order to drink in the emotions. All he had to do was choose to drink them in and he could have. He could do that with any emotion, not just the dark ones. She gave him his new name, Kilguard, and he would be known as Kingston no more. Perfidia thought she would one day rule the world. Kilguard knew she was cruel, but with each drink of darkness she took, she became a beacon of pure evil.

Over the years, he grew to fear her more than death. He settled for trying to be invisible to not draw attention to himself. She didn't need him to be with her as long as the links of black light bound them together. She could feed from him wherever he was, but he rarely left the city limits. He was feeling something beyond death. He was feeling himself slip away, and even though he let her call him Kilguard, he still thought of himself as Kingston. He had to get away from her and the darkness she projected. He decided to go out for the day. He was strolling down the sidewalk when he passed her.

Something about her lured him in, but he didn't follow her. He always grew comfort from nature, so he decided to walk near the park. He turned his head in time to see her walking past him to sit down on the grass in the very center of the park. The children gathered around her as she began to play all types of funny children's songs. The laughter coming from the direction of her was so breathtaking that he had to sit down before he passed out. He felt it. He took it in. Every squeal of glee, every tickle of the tummy, every touch of a child's love, and his heart felt whole again. He wasn't thinking about what Perifdia said about not drinking in the good emotions. He had forgotten completely. He was focused on her. Once she was done entertaining the children, she got up and was walking back the way she came. He couldn't stop himself.

He said, "Hello, my name is Kingston." His smile would light up the night sky. She was under his spell as soon as she looked into his eyes. This wasn't magic. This was really love at first sight. They were destined to find one another. She was his true soul mate, and he was hers. Joanne was to be married in six months time, and she didn't know why she wanted this man to reach out and pull her to him and never let her go. She smiled.

"Hi, my name is Joanne, but everyone calls me Joey." Neither one could pull away from the other. He asked her if she would like to get a cup of coffee. She nodded. *What am I doing? I am engaged. Bill is going to marry me in six months. The wedding plans are already in place, and I just met some stranger in the park, and I'm now saying yes to coffee with him*, she thought. They walked together, and he told her how much he enjoyed listening to her music. He told her he had never seen children look so carefree and happy. She smiled as she told him about music being her true passion. She was drawn to it. She had always loved children, and making silly songs for them was just a creative way for her to combine both of her true callings.

"I see," he said.

"You know what my true callings are. What are yours?"

"I work with human emotions."

"Oh, like a counselor?" she asked.

"Something like that," he laughed.

"Oh, that is surely a calling for some," Joey said. He agreed.

"How old are you, Joey?"

"I'm twenty-two. Graduating from college in four months with a degree in music. My focus is to continue writing, and hopefully one day produce my own children's collection of silly songs."

"Wow, I'm impressed," he said. She laughed.

"You made my day today. Can I make your night?" he asked. She laughed nervously. "No, I mean…can I take you dancing tonight?" Her head was saying no no no, but her heart was saying yes yes yes. She looked at him for a long time and didn't say anything. "I'll be on my best behavior. It's Friday night, which means its dance night at the park. I think tonight is jazz night. I love jazz."

"I do too," said Joey. She was thinking how Bill was going to be gone for the weekend. He was setting up some big deal that, if all went well, would bring them so much money they would never have to worry about money again.

Before she thought about it, she said, "Yes, I would love to go." That night, they danced and danced. When the evening came to a close, they went back to Joey's, and Kingston stayed the night. When Joey woke up, he was holding her in his arms. The night had been filled with more passion and desire than either of them ever thought possible. How could she marry Bill now? She was in love with Kingston. She didn't quite understand how this had happened, but it had happened, and she would leave Bill to be with Kingston.

Kingston continued to visit her every free chance they could break away from their own lives. He was there the night she took the test—positive. Her heart was filled with love. She was carrying Kingston's child. She was going to have to tell Bill as soon as possible. He would just have to hate her. He had been her college boyfriend since their freshman year. She had thought they would truly always be together. He loved her more than life itself. She knew it, and that is why she had waited to tell him she was in love with another. She wanted to spare him the pain. Truth was, she wanted to spare herself the pain of what her betrayal would cost him.

Joey walked out of the bathroom holding the pregnancy test.

Kingston was lying across her bed. He looked like a Greek God—blue eyes, brown-blond hair that hit his shoulders. He was at least 6'2" and he was pure muscle. She was wondering how she was so lucky. When Kingston saw the test strip in her hand, it didn't register at first.

"Hey, love. What is it?" She smiled a smile that would melt even Perfidia's ice-covered heart. She was crying and laughing at the same time she was so happy.

"I'm pregnant with your child." He was thunderstruck. *He was going to be a father. Perfidia…would kill them all*, he thought. He would die for Joey, but that wouldn't be enough. He would die for the unborn child she carried in her womb—his unborn child. Perfidia would kill them in front of him in order to gain power beyond his or her understanding—a sacrifice of true love and the beauty of what that created—true love's child. He would rather die than hurt Joey, but she would die if he did not. He got up and started getting dressed.

He began, "Joey, I never said I wanted to be a father." He was breathing hard, trying to hold himself together. "I thought we both were having fun here. I thought in two months you were going to marry Bill, and we would both move on." As soon as he spoke the words, he saw her light start to fade. Kingston didn't think he would be able to walk out the door, leaving her with a look so desperate and pained that he felt his heart rip in half. It was as if he left it there lying on the floor next to Joey. What choice did he have? Perfidia was connected to him, and she would always be able to find him. If she ever found out, she would destroy anything that held that kind of emotion. Perfidia couldn't stand to be near anyone who was loved. He had to take many precautions over the four months he was able to be with Joey. He had to drink in as many dark emotions before going back to the house where he lived with Perfidia. If she tasted even a hint of happiness, he would have suffered.

Bailey looked at Ashton "Joey…is my mother." She said it like she was trying to believe it herself. "Kingston, or Kilguard, whatever you want to call him is my father. My biological father, that is." Ashton shot her a look of utter disbelief.

"Oh, babe. Are you okay?" Bailey was crying now. Ashton pulled her close, and cradled her in his arms.

"I am not…no wonder my father never could love me. He never

showed one hint of desire in wanting to love me or Amber. A father should love his daughters. He was truly betrayed. I get that, but there comes a time when you have to look at the big picture. We were just kids—kids who yearn for their parents' love, but never got it. His lack of love has caused me to be so guarded toward putting myself out there. It's not just his fault my mother did the same. Their lack of love made me who I am. Kingston abandoned us to save our lives. It doesn't change who or what he is, but there is some comfort in the fact that he knew it was the only way we would survive. It's more parenting than I've ever had."

Ashton held Bailey and kissed her hand, her forehead and finally her lips. She let him soothe her until the crying stopped. When she was able to speak again, she said, "That's not all."

"What else?" Ashton asked.

Bailey cleared her throat. "He transferred all of his *powers* to me," she said in a disturbed voice.

"What?" Ashton yelled.

"I can feel it flowing through my body. I can taste every emotion you're feeling right now, just as if I were drinking a glass of sweet tea.

"Love, fear, anger." Ashton was alarmed.

"What does this mean?" he asked.

"I don't know. I just don't know." She was thinking how love tasted like creamy, rich chocolate. Fear tasted like vinegar. Anger tasted like heat, almost like she could taste fire if that were possible. She looked at Ashton. "Right now, we have to figure out how to kill the three vampires waiting outside—one at the sliding glass door, one at the front door, the last one outside our balcony door off our bedroom." Ashton looked at her like he didn't know what to think.

"How did you know that?" he asked.

"Whatever I am now lets me feel them here. It has something to do with their emotions. From what I got from Kilguard, he could not feed off of vampires. I don't know why I can." Ashton looked at her with a clever expression.

"I do. You belong to me, and I to you. We are connected by love, thus giving you a link to the vampire world."

"Makes sense," she said.

"Do you know how to kill a vampire?" she asked. Ashton looked at her and his eyes tightened in concern.

"No, I do not," he said.

Bile rose up in his throat. *How am I going to kill three vampires while keeping Bailey safe?* he thought. She looked into his eyes.

"We will kill them together," she said.

"Bailey, you can't…*kill* a vampire. Wait, did you just read my thoughts?" he asked.

"Yes," she said.

"Perfidia can't read my thoughts," he said, amazed.

"Kilguard could read vampires' thoughts, now part of my powers. He never told a single soul. It's a lot to take in Ashton. I'm trying not to fall apart here."

"Okay, I'm here," he said, while taking her hand and pulling her in close to him.

"What do you mean we can't kill vampires?" Bailey asked.

"It's impossible to kill us. Only our creator can kill us with a wizard's blade, and there are only five in the entire world. I don't think even Perfidia has one."

"Considering I can read their thoughts, maybe we will be able to avoid them. I'm not too keen on them ripping me apart the next time I go outside. They don't know we know they're here." Ashton's eyes blazed metallic silver. Bailey tasted fire again. She ignored him.

"Bailey, vampires are natural predators. If they were sent here to kill you it's going to take a lot more than just me to keep them from you. I can't live through your death," he moaned.

"I have powers. We just have to figure out how I can use them to keep us safe," she said. Bailey's calm and sense of control made Ashton want her more. A flash of red shot across his eyes and she smiled. She could taste lust. It tasted like blood. She wondered if the emotion of lust for a human tasted the same. She doubted it. Ashton didn't know that she not only tasted his every emotion, but that his eyes also flashed red when he was lusting over her. She would tell him one day. Her new powers were blocking Ashton's ability to read her thoughts.

Chapter Fifteen

Perfidia's connection to Ashton was completely burned away from her skin. She knew she would grow strong again. She also could see the mark on her upper shoulder blade that had never been there before. It looked like two golden rings—both bound together, two never ending circles—and she knew that this was because Bailey was Ashton's true love. She touched it, and it felt like the blade of a sword was sticking into her body there. She fell back from the pain, but it only lasted seconds, and then the pain was gone. However, the mark remained. She had walked back down to the dungeon to play with a few of her humans. Torture was such a good release for her. It was like taking a bath in a warm pool of water for anyone else. It washed over her and gave her what she wanted most...power. She had only tortured two of her forty-five human playthings when she felt the abilities leave her. She couldn't taste the emotions anymore. It didn't hit her at first that the true torture for Perfidia was about to begin. The pain she felt for losing Ashton was nothing compared to losing the connection with Kilguard. Every single torture she had inflicted upon him she was receiving back ten-fold. She cried out in pain until things went black. Perfidia was out for a full week.

When Perfidia woke up, she couldn't move. She wanted to summon vampires to help her, but she didn't have the strength. Whatever happened to her that broke the connection with Kilguard had weakened her beyond her understanding. She always thought she was in control. How could she have known that turning him into a wizard and binding herself to him would result in her down fall? She didn't know how, or if, she would be able to recover. She knew the vampires she had cursed would still fear her. She could summon them to do any dirty work she needed and this might be the only way to take back what she could of her powers.

For a second she thought maybe Kilguard was dead. Maybe that is why the link was broken. How will I find another? Are there more devourers of emotion out there? She would summons as many vampires together as she could if the five she sent to destroy Bailey and bring back Ashton didn't succeed. It was her only chance of regaining control, and Perfidia would not surrender without a fight. They would have to kill her or she would kill them.

Bailey needed to check on Adam, so she called him.

"Adam?"

"Yeah."

"Are you okay?"

"No, I have just been summoned by Perfidia. I will have to go to her," he said.

"What happens if you don't?" she asked.

"She can torture me from where she is at."

"Don't leave your house, Adam. I don't think she can torture you anymore."

"What do you mean?" he asked.

"Let's just say a lot has happened today and leave it at that."

"Bailey, I need more details. I mean, she has skinned me alive on more than one occasion, so I kind of think she can do it again."

"Can you make it safely to your car?"

"Yes, it's in the garage."

"Okay, give me a minute, and I'll call you back. I need to run this by Ashton before I say anything."

"Okay, I'll wait."

"Ashton?"

"Yeah, babe."

"I think Adam should be here. I think he can help."

"Bailey, if he's here he will know vampires exist, and he will only be one more human for me to try and keep alive."

"I don't think he is safe where he is. Perfidia has summoned him." Ashton thought about this for a minute.

"Okay," Ashton said. Vampires could not enter the house, but they could enter the garage, so they would have to have everything timed right, so Adam could get inside safely. She picked up the phone and called Adam back.

"Adam, get clothes and whatever you will need to bunk here for a few nights. We have to work on a plan to defeat Perfidia, and we need your help. Pull into the garage when you get here. Don't go outside the garage. Get into the house as soon as possible. Do you understand?"

"Yes, I'll be there in five minutes." They both hung up the phone.

Bailey heard him pull in five minutes later, and she ran to close the garage door. She opened the door leading to the garage just in time to see all three vampires standing at the opening of the garage. For some reason, they didn't try to cross the threshold of the garage entrance. Adam was staring in disbelief.

"Adam, come to me," one of the vampires said.

"Adam, do not listen to them. They have no power over you now. Adam, look at me," Bailey said, panic in her voice. He took a step toward the vampire.

"Adam!" Bailey screamed. "They will shred you from head to toe. Get control!" Ashton was behind her, and then Adam regained control. Bailey didn't understand why they didn't come inside the garage. According to Ashton, a vampire could enter the garage. Ashton had swayed Adam's thoughts and took him in the direction of the house. The vampires stood there watching. Each vampire's face was filled with the hunger of a kill. One vampire leaped over the threshold, leaving the other two standing there waiting. Adam had just made it to the door leading inside the house when the vampire lunged at the door. He had not been invited in, so he burst into flames and disappeared. Bailey looked at Ashton and slowly closed the garage door.

"Adam, as you now know, vampires are real. The witch controls them, and they want Bailey dead," Ashton said.

"Why?" Adam asked.

"Because of me," Ashton said, shame in his voice

"That's not true. They want me dead because Ashton and I have a connection—a connection that could destroy Perfidia," Bailey said.

"Oh," Adam said. He was lost in thought, trying to figure out a way to save them all. He was brilliant, but his mind didn't cover the supernatural. *He then wondered what connection Ashton had with Bailey. How was this linked to Perfidia?* Bailey's voice pulled Adam back to the present.

"One down, two to go," she said. Bailey, Ashton and Adam were trying to figure out a plan.

"It's too bad we can't entice the other two to cross over the threshold without being invited," she said.

"Maybe we can," Ashton said.

"How?" Bailey asked.

"Blood," Ashton said.

"Okay, explain."

"Well, I've already told you the blood lust in instinctual. A vampire cannot resist it. We need human blood to lure them in," Ashton said.

"Okay, let's do this," Bailey said.

"Bailey, wait. I'll do it," Adam said.

"Adam, I can do it," Bailey said.

"No, I'll do it," Adam said. Ashton had a new-found respect for Adam. Adam was placing himself in danger in order to protect Bailey. Adam was thinking, *why didn't Ashton offer to lure the vampires with his blood?* Bailey was busy trying to read who was the most blood thirsty. That vampire would need to go first. The good news was that they had separated. One vampire was now at the back door, while the other was at the side door inside the garage. Bailey took a knife and handed it to Adam. He would know how to cut himself without hitting a main artery. He took the knife and dragged in down his arm, causing a large gash. Blood started pouring from the wound. Ashton's eyes went red, but he focused on Bailey's face. Bailey could taste the emotion of lust from Ashton. It tasted like blood.

Ashton opened the door leading to the garage. As soon as the vampire smelled the aroma of the blood, he was lost in blood lust. He wanted the blood so bad but knew not to cross the threshold. Bailey read his mind. He was about to retreat and find a human to kill when she lowered the door. His eyes narrowed on Bailey. Vampires are about control, and Bailey closing the door took control. This didn't bode well with the vampire. He could have so easily tore the garage door down to get out instead, he lost his restraint and forgot for a second that he wasn't invited in. He lunged for Bailey instead of Adam. He burst into flames and disappeared.

"Two down, one to go," Bailey said no hint of terror in her voice.

Since Bailey could read their thoughts, she knew their names. Bailey lifted the door and called to him.

"Tommy, where are you?" Bailey asked. Tommy was wondering what had happened to Eric, the other vampire, but they were under orders to kill the girl. Tommy was focused on Bailey…until he saw the blood. He was a young vampire. He had no self control. He didn't think for a second about the one rule he was told—a vampire cannot enter into a human's home uninvited. This would vanquish him. All of Tommy's focus was targeting Adam. Tommy lunged for Adam and was able to grab him for a second, before bursting into flames and disappearing. Bailey couldn't believe how easy it was, but then panic flashed across her and Ashton's faces.

"More vampires," she gasped.

"I know," Ashton snapped. Perfidia had sent two more just in case something went wrong.

Ashton became the animal again. He lunged at the vampire at the back door, taking him off guard. He threw him across the patio, but the second vampire jumped on Ashton and bit. Blood started pouring from Ashton. Bailey felt the ripple of power flow through her. She lifted her right hand in the direction of the vampire and light blast from her palm, engulfing him. She turned and lifted her left hand, blasting the second vampire as he tried to attack Ashton. She watched as the light of good destroyed the darkness within the two vampires, leaving nothing but their shell, which turned to ash. Bailey ran to Ashton. He was still not himself. The rage that encased him was truly frightening. Bailey would not stand back and let him calm down. She didn't want him to think she was afraid of him. She started walking toward him just as Adam made the connection that Ashton was a vampire. Adam saw the look on Ashton's face and hurled himself at Ashton, punching him across the face.

"Run, Bailey!" Adam yelled. Bailey knew this was not going to end well.

"No, Adam! Get out of the way!" Ashton picked Adam up and threw him across the room. Then he leaped onto him. He bit Adam on the arm and started drinking his blood. Bailey began to scream.

"No, Ashton. Stop!" She grabbed his face and jerked it away. His eyes were still metallic silver. Ashton's eyes now focused on Bailey. Bailey didn't flinch. She didn't run. She stood there looking into the eyes of a predator—a predator she loved.

"I love you no matter what happens. We are in this together," she said, with compassion in her voice. He snapped out of it and embraced her. Once he had calmed down completely, he healed the wounds inflicted on Adam. He then apologized to Adam for what happened. Adam was merely trying to fight a vampire to protect Bailey, so he couldn't be too mad that he punched him in the face. Besides, drinking Adam's blood had given him strength and healed the bite that the other vampire had inflicted upon him. Ashton didn't realize the elixir in his body would not heal a vampire bite. Only human blood could regenerate the body tissue destroyed by a vampire's bite. Bailey was relieved that it was over for now, so she went upstairs to get a shower. When she came back downstairs, Ashton and Adam had already cleaned up the mess on the patio, and Ashton had ordered a spinach pizza for dinner. Adam stayed to eat, and then he headed back to his beach house.

"Bailey, I don't want to leave you here alone with a vampire," Adam said.

"I'm fine. I know it's hard for you to understand, but Ashton is not like other vampires. He only did what he did tonight because he wasn't himself."

"For your own sake, I hope you're right, Bailey. Call me if you need me," Adam said.

"I will. I promise you, I am safe with Ashton." Adam's eyes widened in horror.

"I can feel Perfidia. She is still trying to summon me," Adam said.

"She can't enter the house. If you see her, don't invite her in and don't go outside.

Pick up the phone and call us," Bailey said.

"Okay," he said, and then left.

Chapter Sixteen

Bailey was lost in thought when she heard Ashton coming down the stairs after getting a shower. She was thinking about what had happened today. *What kind of power flowed within her? Were all her powers good? She hoped it was all good.*

She looked up to see Ashton as he was stepping off the last step. His hair was all wet and his body was glistening. He was so beautiful that Bailey sometimes wondered if he were real or just a figment of her imagination. Nothing real looked so flawless, and then she realized he wasn't completely flawless. He had a few scars that ran along his back. She wondered what had happened to him. Those scars gave her comfort. It was good to know that not even vampires were perfect.

Bailey looked up and said, "Well, at least that's over, or I guess round one is over." He smiled, but she could taste the fear pouring from his skin. The taste of vinegar was so strong that she thought she would have to throw up. "Babe, we got through this together. We will get through whatever Perfidia plans to do as well." He took her hand and kissed it gently. The taste of chocolate melted away the disturbing flavor of vinegar. Bailey was wearing a form fitting sleep shirt with matching shorts. Ashton couldn't help but find her attractive. He was so in love with her that the touch of her hand on his face, the feel of her lips on his, the taste of her breath in his mouth, was sometimes more than he thought he could bear.

Bailey took him by the hand and led him to the bedroom. He was used to this route. After all, he slept in her room every night. When she came out of the bathroom, he was lying on his side of the bed. He was looking at some sort of outdoor magazine. When he looked up, he was not prepared to see her standing before him wearing a slinky nightgown. He couldn't turn away. He thought she forgot he was in the room, but when their eyes met, he saw something that let him know she knew he was there, and that she wanted him. He heard her thoughts of desire, and his eyes blazed red. She could taste each emotion, the strongest being desire. It tasted of sweet, ripe cherries. Their bodies connected like two halves of a whole as the night faded into the morning.

When Bailey woke, it was midday. She could hear Ashton downstairs in the kitchen. She wondered what he could be doing. Within two minutes, he was upstairs bringing her breakfast in bed. She wondered if she would feel different after last night. She wondered if losing her virginity would change who she was. It did. She felt her life had just begun. She felt there was nothing better than loving someone and being truly loved in return. She knew Ashton completed her. They were truly each other's half, and together they made each other whole. When Ashton came into the room, she couldn't believe what he looked like. He had always been beautiful, but there was something more. Something was different about him. She couldn't put her finger on it. He looked at peace, and calmness flowed from every pore of his skin. It tasted like honey. Neither realized that the bond between them that developed last night had given all of Ashton's humanity back to him. They ate breakfast and spent the afternoon lounging by the pool in each other's arms. They were about to get up, and Bailey was going to make dinner, when the doorbell rang.

Perfidia had summoned all of the vampires she had ever changed, and they were all on their way to Perfidia's house. Kilguard was watching the house from a distance. He no longer had the powers he once had. He had transferred everything he had to Bailey, but he would not stand by and let Perfidia kill his daughter. He watched as she summoned the vampires, and he knew her plans were to attack Bailey and Ashton with them. Even though Kilguard transferred his powers to Bailey, he could still read the vampires' thoughts, so he decided he had to warn Bailey. He would have to go to her home. Bailey heard a knock at the door.

"I wonder who it is?" She could taste that it was Kilguard. "He's afraid I'll hate him, but he's also afraid for me." Ashton and Bailey went to the door.

"Kilguard," Ashton said as a gesture of greeting.

"I can go around back if you do not wish me inside your home. I assure you I wish you no harm. I have no powers. I gave them to Bailey. I want you both to survive Perfidia's wrath." Bailey nodded.

"It's okay, you can come in," Bailey said.

Kilguard started by saying, "I assume when I transferred my powers, you also got my past and how that is connected to you?"

"I did," Bailey said.

"I know you hate me. I would hate me if I were you, but I really didn't have a choice. I didn't have a choice not to fall in love with your mother. Once our paths had crossed, we could not deny destiny. I loved her more than I thought possible. I love her still. I love you, Bailey, even though I never got to be your father, hold you as a baby, bandage a hurt, hold you when you cried, teach you that sometimes we're meant to give our heart away even if we know in the end things will not end well and it will break. Life is about loving, and I can say I have lived because I have loved. I didn't get to hold her and keep her with me long, but I will love your mother always." Bailey had never known a father figure to show any emotion, and she felt everything Kilguard was feeling. Therefore, she was able to give him something he didn't expect, forgiveness. She reached out and touched his hand.

In a gentle voice she said, "I know why you did it. I know you loved my mother, and I know you sacrificed everything to keep us alive. I understand by walking away you showed true love. Sometimes when you love something, you have to let it go, and that is the reason…I forgive you," Bailey said. Kilguard was in shock. He never expected her forgiveness. He had lived so many years surrounded by hate and the lust for evil. He knew his daughter had the purest heart, and she was worth everything he had suffered. He had done the right thing in the end, and it was worth it to see who she had become.

He looked her in the eyes and said in a shaky voice, "Thank you." They both smiled through tears and hugged. "I came here to warn you. Perfidia has lost her link to me, and thus lost the power to drink in human emotion. She has summoned every vampire she ever created to do her bidding here. She doesn't know you're my daughter. It would make no difference, other than she might want to keep me around to watch you die. I could not stand by, and let this happen. I can tell you how to make it and even fight. That is going to be the only chance we have here," Kilguard said. Bailey looked at her father and then to Ashton.

"Okay," they both said. What do we do?"

"I have created as many vampires as Perfidia. After I lost your mother, I lashed out, trying to give anyone more pain than I felt. My heart was truly broken, and I didn't think about what I was doing. There's no excuse for the pain I have caused others, but at least now we have a chance."

"I don't understand," Ashton said.

"Me either," said Bailey.

"You have all my powers, along with the ability to summon and control the vampires I've turned. You're now their master." Bailey froze.

"What exactly does that mean?" Bailey asked.

"It means you can control them. It means they have to obey you, and only you," Kilguard said. Bailey looked at Ashton.

"I'm not sure I feel okay with that," Bailey said. Kilguard looked at Ashton and then to Bailey.

"Bailey, I believe if anyone had to have these powers, no one would use them better than you. I don't think you will ever turn to the darkness. You have too much light within you, but just know sometimes getting what we want doesn't always mean things end happily ever after," Kingston said. "I also wanted to tell you that you are half mine, so you were born with some powers. You just don't know what they are yet."

Bailey gulped. "What do you mean I was born with powers?" she asked.

"I don't know what powers you have taken from me. I didn't realize I had powers until Perfidia came to seek me out all those centuries ago. Looking back at my childhood, I now realize the power of magic was passed to me from both my mother and father. I didn't realize it was magic at the time. I guess I was oblivious to the truth. My father could control the weather. That is how we lived so well. He could produce the best garden because he could make our crop live while others didn't. My mother's ability was different indeed. She could talk to animals and control them. It's all very strange. As for my abilities I could drink in human emotions and draw power from them, and now you will be able to do so, along with whatever powers you were born with."

"What if I don't want this?" she asked.

"You can't help what abilities you are born with, Bailey. Life is about learning who you are and being the best person you can be. I didn't go down the right path. I should have fought Perfidia long before now. Now, I leave it to my daughter to fight that fight. I'm sorry to burden you with this."

Bailey sighed a long sigh, "I choose to protect what is mine. I will not let her take from me what I have been born with, nor Ashton, who is attached to my very soul. The power of light will prevail over the power of darkness."

"I hope for all of our sakes that you're right," Kilguard said.

Perfidia was able to get 452 vampires of the 500 she had turned. The other forty-eight were dead. Once summoned by their master they could not refuse the pull. This made her angry. Who had killed forty-eight of her vampires? She knew five of them went down trying to kill Ashton and Bailey, but what happened to the other forty-three vampires? She asked one of her strong vampires named Samson.

"The leader of the Light Fairy Bien Faire had been working with vampire hunters and taking out as many of us as possible. She has approached all of us, wanting us to surrender, so we can be destroyed. She claims we are taking too many human lives, and she will stand, even if alone, to defeat all who uphold the murder of innocent people. She said we were not meant to exist, and if there was a chance she could save us too she would, but that didn't seem to be the case," Samson said. Perfidia was livid. She wanted Bien Faire to die for this. She wanted to torture her and drink every ounce of her life away, but she couldn't do that anymore. She knew her powers were weak, and she could be destroyed very easily if she didn't have her vampire army.

"I have but one command for you today, my children. You have to seek and destroy a mere human. She is with Ashton, and he refuses to follow orders, so he must pay the price." They all looked at one another. How can Ashton refuse her if she commands him to do something? This didn't make sense. They couldn't refuse her. How could he?

A few days had passed and Bailey was still trying to understand how she was going to control vampires. She didn't want to be a master to vampires. She didn't want any of this really. All she wanted was to live in peace, with Ashton by her side. She was picking up a new outfit to wear to Amber's cheer camp event and then home to change. Ashton was going too. He didn't want her to go anywhere alone, but she talked him into letting her go to the shopping center. There would be too many people around in daylight for Perfidia to try anything. Bailey picked out a whimsical sun dress. It was baby blue—simple, but everything about it screamed fun. She would wear her ankle-strap, wedge sandals—not really something she wears all the time, but she would make it through the day, and Amber would be proud of her clothing choice.

When Ashton got back from hunting, he walked upstairs. He was going to change into some dress pants and a polo shirt—something for summer that would look nice. He walked into the room just as Bailey was walking out of her dressing room. His eyes flashed red.

"I like that dress," he said. Her shoes elongated her legs, and Ashton noticed that too.

"Nice shoes. You look beautiful," he said. She smiled. He wrapped his arms around her, and they began to kiss. It wasn't long until all of their clothes were on the floor. Bailey was so happy. She didn't think she could ever love anyone as much as Ashton. Her phone rang.

"Hello, Amber," Bailey said, breathless.

"Hey, have you left yet?" she huffed.

"No, not yet," Bailey said.

Amber made a grumpy noise. "You're going to be late," she whined.

"No, we will not," Bailey said in an irritated tone. "We will be there in an hour we're leaving now."

"Okay, thanks again for coming. Did I tell you I have a boyfriend?" Bailey laughed. Her sister could jump from one subject to the next without knowing it.

"No, you didn't. Who is he?"

"Eric. He plays baseball, as well as cheers."

"Oh yeah, you did say something about him the last time we talked. So, Amber, are you a virgin?"

"Shut up, Bailey."

"See how it feels?"

"Yeah, I do. Sorry. By the way, yes, I am still a virgin."

"I know we'll see you soon."

"Love you. Bye," they both said. Ashton and Bailey had to pull themselves away from each other in order to get up and get dressed. They finally got up and dressed as quickly as possible. Ashton was holding Bailey's hand when they arrived at the camp. He got out of the car and walked around to open the door. Bailey didn't really care so much about the door stuff, but Ashton thought it showed a level of respect for his lady, and she couldn't argue with him. If he wanted to open doors for her because he loved and respected her, then who was she to stand in his way. He took her hand just as Amber came up and gave her a big hug.

"Bailey, you made it on time." Amber knew as soon as she saw her sister that she was not a virgin anymore. Now that Amber was experiencing a relationship, she knew not to cross that line in front of Ashton. She would get details later. Amber walked toward the front of the stage while Ashton and Bailey went and sat down with the other parents. Most of the kids there had their parents. Bailey saw a few grandparents and one possible nanny, but she was the only sister there replacing someone's parents. She sighed.

"She's happy you're here. I'm sure more happy than if your parents were, so don't think about it," Ashton said.

"Thank you, babe. You're right. I've been more of a parental figure to Amber than our parents have, so what others see in that should not matter." She held her head high and clapped and hooted as Amber walked onto stage to say her cheer with all of the cheer camp there to say it with her. The presenter then said that the cheer was created by Amber Evans, and on behalf of Bingleton Cheer Camp, he honored her ability to bring it on. They presented her with a trophy, and everyone cheered. Amber was smiling. The smile reminded Bailey of lazy summer days when she and Amber would hang out and just be sisters. For everything her parents didn't give her emotionally, they gave her everything she could ever want in her sister—someone to share childhood with, to pretend with, climb trees with, blow bubbles, dance, have water balloon fights…sometimes real fights. They were sisters forever, through and through. Each and every memory of her childhood was wrapped around Amber, and the tears began to flow. She was so happy for her sister, and grateful they would always have one another. They stayed for a while after the ceremony. Amber still had two weeks left at camp, and she showed them all the cool things they got to do there. Amber also introduced Eric. He was an attractive boy. He was very respectful, and Bailey liked that. They said their goodbyes, and Bailey told Amber she would see her in two weeks. Amber said okay, and then she looked directly into Ashton's eyes.

"Break her heart, and I will break your face. Oh yeah, and take care of her please." She smiled and walked away. Ashton liked her. She had spunk. He thought, *if she only knew she just picked a fight with a vampire*, and he laughed. Bailey laughed too.

They got back to the house, and everything seemed quiet. She didn't understand why she hadn't heard anything from Kilguard, and Perfidia had not sent anymore vampires. It didn't make sense for her to summon and then not send them. She didn't want to do it, but she had summoned Kilguard's vampires, her vampires now, before they left. It would be interesting to see how this worked out. They hadn't been back more than an hour when she started feeling their presence.

"Ashton, they're here," she said.

"I know," he said. He looked at her, anxiety written all over his face.

"They will not listen to me. You're their master, so be firm and demand respect. They're different from me, Bailey. I have been able to resist killing humans. Each and every vampire out there now has killed numerous humans. They have no humanity left, and no soul left either. It's all about the blood for them." She took a deep breath, and somehow from within herself she drew courage to open the balcony door. She then stepped out onto the balcony, head held high. There were hundreds of vampires staring up at her from the pool level below. They were all thinking, *she is not Kilguard.* She knew if she didn't show she had authority here, they would eat her alive. They were already thinking that she smelled half human. I bet she tastes good. Bailey wanted to flinch away from them, but she didn't move. She raised her voice and in a confident tone she said, "Kilguard is no more. I have taken his powers. You are now mine." All trains of thought from the vampires, were now completely focused on Bailey.

"Did she just say she took his powers?" They were skeptical that she could have overpowered Kilguard. The Kilguard they knew was almost as bad as Perfidia when it came to torturing. He preferred to torture vampires rather than humans. Bailey spoke up then, speaking without giving them a chance to see that she was shaking a little.

"Perfidia is seeking to kill me and Ashton. I ask you not to let this happen. I am in love with a vampire." They were shocked. They didn't think a human could ever love a vampire. It had never happened before. The blood lust was too strong. The possibility that she was the chosen one who could undo the curse on Ashton, which could lead to them learning how to reverse the curse on themselves, was worth the risk. There were legends among vampires. Legends that claimed that a vampire could be released from the blood lust if he found his true soul mate. They looked at one another.

"Okay, we're in," they said. She stopped them by raising her hand.

"Before you say you're in, you have to know Perfidia has her own army of vampires. I do not wish to bring death among human nor vampire. I realize you have to eat to live, and I am trying to show mercy here, but you are forbidden to kill another human. This has been dictated by your master," Bailey said. One of the strong vampires spoke then.

"But we will grow weak, and even though it will take time, we will die."

"Ashton lives without killing humans. You can drink the blood of humans if you sway their minds and take only what you need without hurting them. Ashton can help you with this. I doubt any of you can think back to what life was like before the curse. If there is anyone among you who can remember, remember what it was like to lose your life and have someone else in control. Imagine what it's like to have a being drink from you until your life is no more." Something about her humanity was washing through the other vampires. They began to remember life before becoming what they had become. They no longer had the desire to kill. Oh, they desired the blood, but not the kill. She could taste the atmosphere. She thought, *maybe there was hope after all.* They made plans to be ready to fight when Perfidia showed up.

Bailey had told the vampires that they could leave, but they were to stay close. She didn't know when Perfidia would strike. Ashton and Bailey spent the evening trying to relax. They watched a movie and ate enchiladas for dinner. Ashton had really taken to Mexican food now that he could really taste it. He liked the spicy stuff—it seems the spicier the better. They went to bed that night holding each other and not wanting to think about what could happen if things went wrong.

Chapter Seventeen

Ashton had been up for hours. He went for a swim, read an entire book on ocean life and was now making Bailey some breakfast. Bailey heard her cell phone ring. She didn't get up in time to get the phone, but she noticed she had a message.

"Bailey, it's Amber. I've been taken, and I'm scared." Amber's voice was stricken with panic. "Some lady named Perfidia said you have something that belongs to her, and she wants it back. Holy crap, Bailey, what do you have of hers? Is it Ashton?" Amber was breathing hard, her voice cracking. She swallowed hard and continued, "She said for you to meet her at the Lakers' farm off of County Road 231. She said the family has gone away for the summer. She said to be there within 24 hours or you won't ever see me again." Amber was crying when the message cut off. Bailey was crying. She listened again. She began to scream.

"No, No, NO! Why is this happening to me? I can't lose my sister, please!" Ashton was upstairs as soon as he heard her scream.

"Baby, what's wrong?" Bailey could barely speak. She whispered to Ashton.

"Amber just called and left a message. Perfidia has her." Bailey's voice broke, and she lost control of her emotions. She was crying hysterically. She handed him the phone, and he listened to the message.

"I know where this is. Get dressed. Summon the vampires," he said. Bailey got dressed as fast as she could. She was so thankful that Ashton was there. She didn't think she would be able to even get dressed if he had not been there. She summoned the vampires and told them where to go. She told them to stay invisible until she called for them. If they didn't have to die for her, she wouldn't put them in danger. They respected her. No other being—mortal or not—thought enough of a vampire to not want to risk his life to save her own. They would not stand by and let Bailey die. She was a true leader—their master—and they would die to save her.

When they arrived at the farm, all was quiet. There didn't appear to be a vampire in sight. This chilled Bailey to the bone. She could usually sense their presence. They must not be close enough yet. What was going to happen here? She only had her own life to exchange for her sister. She could never exchange Ashton for her. She didn't know how she was going to get through this, or if she would. She reached out and touched Ashton's face. "I love you more than life itself, but I can't lose my sister. I want you to know," Bailey said.

"I know, Bailey. The time I've had with you has been worth my existence. I will always love you no matter what happens. Please know that," he said. She nodded. They both knew there was a great chance that neither would make it out alive. They stepped out of the car as it was getting dark. They waited for about ten minutes before Perfidia stepped out from the blackness.

"Hello, Bailey. I see you have brought me Ashton in exchange for Amber." Perfidia's voice sounded like ice. Bailey glared at her. Bailey had been about to fall apart just minutes ago, but fire erupted from inside and she had the courage to speak. She felt the powers that were passed from Kingston to her, but she had something he never had. Bailey had all of this love to put with her powers. This made her stronger than anyone could know. She also knew Perfidia was not going to live after tonight.

"Exchange Ashton for Amber, Perfidia, I think not." Bailey's voice was filled with confidence. Perfidia was not going to let her see that this affected her.

"Oh then, I guess you want to exchange Ashton for Kilguard, your father?" She then saw Kingston, lying in a pool of what appeared to be his own blood. He was moaning painfully, but she could tell he couldn't move. It appeared he had major bones broken. It was possible they were crushed. From the looks of his bruised body, he had major internal damage. Bailey winced at the sight of him, but tried not to lose her focus. That is the first time she had noticed Amber. Amber was looking at Bailey like she didn't understand. Amber was crying. She had been crying awhile. You could tell Perfidia had hurt her. She had a gash on her leg, but the blood was now dried there. Emotions were flowing from every pore of Bailey's skin, giving her power she didn't know how to use against Perfidia.

"I will not exchange Ashton for anyone. You are going to give me my sister, and I might let you live," she hissed. "You are also going to let Kilguard go. He is no longer your slave, and his name is Kingston." The power that rolled off of Bailey was truly unbelievable. Ashton just stood there trying to understand.

"You see, Perfidia, you can never take love away. You might take the person, but the love will live on forever." Bailey spoke with a calm conviction. Perfidia stepped back, shaken by her words and the power that she held within her body. "I warn you again to release them and go. I'm not saying I won't come find you one day. I'm saying for now, you can live one more night." For once in Perfidia's life, she was scared. She didn't know how Bailey thought she was going to save everyone, but her confidence—and the talk of love—petrified Perfidia. Bailey tasted it too. It tasted like vinegar and rot. The rot was hatred. She hadn't tasted that one before.

"Enough of this nonsense, I am the one who makes the rules in this world, Bailey. You are but a mere child," Perfidia hissed. She raised her hands and all 452 vampires stood around her. Bailey didn't have to raise her hands. She didn't have to speak. All 460 of her vampires were around her. For a moment, Perfidia was taken off guard and it took her a second to collect herself. "How do you have these vampires? Are they loyal to your father, Bailey? They will eat you for dinner." She laughed a hard laugh. "Oh well, they might just do my job for me. It would be a pity though," she drawled. "I do like my fun."

Bailey spoke each word building her confidence and giving her more power. "These vampires belong to me, but here and now I set them free. I am your master no longer. You can choose to walk away from this fight.

You can choose to go to the other side. You are just as human as you were the day you were cursed. You just have to find your heart. I know it's there." She raised her hands and said, "I release you." Light started to flow from every vampire. The bonds that had held them captive for centuries were broken, but not one moved from his position.

The vampires on Perfidia's side knew Bailey was the one who could break Ashton's curse, and the thought of being human again flickered through their vampire minds. Blood was no longer all they were thinking about. They turned toward Perfidia.

Samson said, "Perfidia, you are our master no more. We choose to be free. You changed us for power. You loved us not. We will not fight against the light. You are the darkness we had to become, but we will not continue this, even if we all perish here and now."

Perfidia was livid. The old Perfidia would have ripped Samson's head off right there, but Perfidia was weak. She barely had any powers left. She needed her army to win this fight and now all she could do to get some sort of revenge was to kill Amber and Kilguard. "Fine, then go, but the girl and Kilguard die," Perfidia snarled. Ashton lunged for Perfidia just as she was about to slice Amber's throat.

Bailey screamed, "NO!" Amber frantically ran to Bailey. When Perfidia got up, Ashton was on the ground, blade through his heart. Bailey looked at Ashton and screamed out in pain. The other vampires surrounded Perfidia and would not let her move an inch. They couldn't kill her because the dark magic protected her, but they would not let her hurt Bailey. Bailey ran to Ashton. She was crying and screaming his name. "Ashton! Ashton! Get up…please!" Bailey wailed.

Perfidia laughed, "You will never win. I always win. The wizard's blade has pierced his heart. He will *die*," she shrieked, like someone who had gone mad. There was nothing human left in her. She was completely filled with wickedness. Bailey stood and faced Perfidia with a vigor that she didn't know she had. She centered her emotions and pulled from her core every ounce of good she could remember—every moment of laughter with her sister, every second spent with Mary nurturing her inner child and, more importantly, every kiss, embrace and feeling of overwhelming love she had for Ashton—and thrust the emotions like a ball of fire toward Perfidia.

Perfidia's eyes flashed in horror a second before the power of love hit her. She was crying out in pain and thrashing about. She couldn't stand this type of torture. She would take the burning again any day and love it. In the minutes in took for her body to try and resist the love, Bailey got to see Perfidia's past of how she became what she was.

Perfidia's mother was human. She was a beautiful, loving woman, who cared for Perfidia with all the love and heart a mother has for her child. She spent every waking moment pampering her child. Perfidia's father left before she was born, and her mother never spoke of him. Perfidia always resented her mother. She considered her perfect and loved by everyone. Perfidia didn't understand why she was drawn to darkness, but from the time she could remember, all she wanted was to cause pain to others, including her mother. Any chance she could torture her mother by pretending to be hurt, or really hurting someone else, she would. The agony on her mother's face was like laughter to a normal child. Perfidia spent sixteen years of her life with her mother, causing her as much pain as she could.

When Perfidia's father showed up on her sixteenth birthday to ask Perfidia to join him, she was elated. Her mother stood in front of her daughter to protect her and told her father to leave. She would not allow him to take her daughter.

Perfidia's father laughed a cruel laugh and said, "It is not up to you." He spoke directly to Perfidia and said, "Perfidia, I am your father. I am a dark wizard. Your mother is nothing but a human weakling. You can join me in ruling the world. Or, you can stay here with your mother and pretend you don't desire the dark powers that await you."

The look on Perfidia's face was filled with evil. She glared at her mother. "I am going with my father," she hissed, with a scowl on her face. Her father laughed.

"You must complete a task first to make sure you're worthy of me, Perfidia," he said, his voice like velvet, but the darkness that surrounded his words were pure venom.

"Anything, father," Perfidia said, her voice hungry for darkness and longing for her father to accept her as his own partner to take over the world. He looked directly at Perfidia's mother.

"You must kill your mother," he said, his eyes filled with amusement. Perfidia's mother's eyes flashed with panic and grief so strong that it fed Perfidia's father.

"Don't do this, Perfidia. I love you. He is using you. You are better than this. You can resist the darkness. I knew it was there…from the time you were born, but I still loved you and will always love you," she pleaded. Without even thinking Perfidia picked up the blade her father had placed on the table and stabbed her mother through the heart. Her mother died, while Perfidia laughed with pleasure. Perfidia then joined her father in his quest to rule the world. She killed her own father about five years later with the same blade. She gained all of his powers by killing him, and this gave her the title to overtake what is now known as the United States. His eyes, too, flashed with panic and fear right before she cut off his head.

Bailey finally pulled out of Perfidia's past in time to see the feeling of love that overtook her body. It was too much for her to take. Darkness had ruled her life for so long that it only took minutes for her to give in to the light. The love was ripping her apart. Every part of her was trying to resist, but the love was too strong. She exploded into pieces and disappeared, but a dark, translucent cloud emerged from her and hovered above where her body had stood. It hovered for about ten seconds before it took off toward another destination. The love had destroyed Perfidia, but what was the blackness that came from her body, and where did it go? Bailey didn't have time to consider what this darkness was. She had to get to Ashton. Bailey ran to him.

"My love, please don't leave me. I need you to be okay." Ashton looked into her eyes like he was touching her very soul.

"I love you, Bailey. I knew I loved you the first time I heard your thoughts about wanting me to want you, but sometimes things don't always end happily ever after," he said, as his eyes closed.

"NO!" she wailed in agony. "Please don't leave me. I love you, Ashton. Please, don't give up!" Ashton was no longer making any noise, and he was not moving. Bailey screamed. "Ashton, I give everything to you—my heart, my soul, my life." She took the blade from his heart and sliced her wrist, holding it to his lips. The blood that flowed from her veins was filled with golden light. It was as if her blood was the gift of life. The blood drizzled into his mouth. At first, there was no reaction, but then Ashton started to drink. She could see the emblazoned blood weaving around the wound in his chest. He was taking in short breaths now. He didn't understand why her blood tasted so different than other humans' blood. Bailey's blood tasted like sunshine, earth, rain, fire, ice and the strongest flavor, love. Her blood was a million flavors, but it had emotions that charged and ignited each hint of flavor. Finally, the wound around his heart was closing up, and he raised his head and kissed Bailey. Light shined from within him like a covering of love. She knew when their lips met that he was no longer a vampire.

The most miraculous thing happened. As soon as Bailey's blood had touched his lips, every single vampire there began to feel his humanity and soul returning. They were crying out. "She broke the curse." Bailey just assumed they were talking about Ashton. Then, she looked and saw the humanity; light and love start to grow over every single being there. It was so beautiful. Each vampire radiated a fire-like glow that spread over his entire body. Ashton just held her in his arms while they watched. Once every vampire had been transformed back into a human, they saw the light—the most spectacular ray of light with wings—coming toward them. She was the most phenomenal being that Bailey or anyone there had ever seen. Her body was like a billow of liquid cloud. She was translucent, and light burned from within her. She reminded Bailey of a walking star, if that were possible. Once you set your eyes upon her, a feeling of good spread throughout your entire body. Her eyes looked like two mini suns set inside a moon almost like an eclipse with just the outer edge showing the rays. The inside revealed a soul so pure there was no mistake that she was filled with magic from centuries long ago. They all bowed to The Leader of Light, Fairy Bien Faire.

"Hello, it seems you have all been given the gift of life. Now, we will all be friends and fight no more. I, too, have a gift to offer. Even though your humanity and soul have returned, the memories of who you were before the curse and who you became during the curse shall always remain. I am afraid this will weaken your soul very soon, and life would not be what you deserve for it to be—a gift of a new life. I can give you each this gift, but the choice for once is yours."

Samson spoke up and asked. "What is the choice?"

"You may leave here today as you are. You will live out the remainder of your human life. Or, you may leave here a different way. You can be reborn into a human life. You will be an infant again and start life anew. If you choose to be reborn, you will truly be reborn. You will have no memory of your life before, during or after the curse. You have an hour to decide," Bien Faire said.

Bailey looked at Ashton. She couldn't live without him, but maybe he had endured so much pain that he would rather be reborn into a new life—a life without the memory of what he had lost. She looked into his eyes with an expression of great loss and sorrow. "If you love something, sometimes you have to let it go. If you want to be reborn into a new life, I understand." Tears were flowing down her face. He smiled and wiped her tears away with his finger. He then ran his finger along her jaw line, cupping her face in his hand.

"Bailey, I have already been reborn. I was reborn into a new life the day I met you." She smiled at him and continued to cry.

"I feel like I was reborn the day I met you. I love you so much," she said.

"As I love you," he stated.

"What is going on here? Why are there so many people here? What is that thing with wings? Why did the lady explode and disappear?" Amber asked, sounding delirious. Bailey looked at Ashton.

"I think you should sway her mind," and then she remembered he couldn't. "I forgot," she said.

Fairy Bien Faire spoke and said, "I can take care of the child. I will sway her memory. She will fall into a deep sleep. This will give you time to get her back to cheer camp before she or anyone else wakes up."

"How did you know about that?" Bailey asked.

"I know everything about you, Bailey. I have heard of your pure heart and know no one greater could have such powers. You have not even begun to realize your powers yet. I will tell you this. You are known throughout the circle of light as the one who delivers from the darkness, for you have been able to bring light back into each vampire, delivering each of them from the dark. You were Ashton's true soul mate. You released him from the curse. When you sent the loving emotions to Perfidia, it killed her. The purity of your love was too much for her darkness to bear. Her death brought about the release of all those she had cursed, but it only took effect when you gave a sacrifice of your blood to Ashton.

It even brought about the release of the vampires Kilguard had cursed, because Perfidia transformed him. Kilguard will be able to start life anew as well. Or, he can remain from this day forward and seek a new life. From what I feel from him, he plans to remain, in the hope you will one day call him father. He also desires to seek out your mother and beg her forgiveness. He has longed for that day since he walked out the door," Bien Faire said. She then looked at Ashton.

"Ashton, you may offer a gift to your true beloved for setting you free. You may remain human together and live out your days here on earth. Or, you may both become immortal and spend all of eternity together. I will give you until tomorrow night to decide."

"Thank you, Bien Faire," Ashton said.

"I will come to you tomorrow. For now, I bid you well. I must go. It seems every person here that was once a vampire, with the exception of you, has decided on rebirth. I will be very busy tonight indeed," Bien Faire said. They smiled at her as she walked away. Ashton picked up Amber and took her to the car. The swaying of Amber's mind didn't take effect for the first ten minutes, so it was like she was drunk. She scowled at Ashton.

"Man, I'm going to kick your ass. I told you not to hurt my sister. I saw you drink her blood. That was gross." She hesitated, looking at him sternly, and said, "God… you're pretty." She then fell into a deep sleep. Ashton and Bailey started laughing at her reaction to what had taken place. They were able to get Amber back to cheer camp without anyone realizing she was missing. Once they were back in the car, they started talking about the future.

"Bailey, I am fine with remaining human. I have longed to be human for over a hundred years," Ashton said.

"Okay, I understand that, but I need to know if these powers I hold will affect my life span. Kingston is over 800 years old, and I can't live without you," Bailey said. "

"Ah, yes. But he was a wizard. He was transformed into the darkness. The drinking in of dark emotions kept him young and extended his lifespan. You will more than likely outlive a human, because you carry such light within you. We can ask Bien Faire if that will make a difference for you," he said. Bailey nodded.

"It will make a difference. I can't imagine living a single day without you, much less hundreds of years," she said. He sighed.

"I think it comes down to this. No one knows when life will end.

You can only choose to live life to the fullest. Only those not of this world live beyond the boundaries of it. I want nothing more than to live with you in this world," he said.

"I will do that with you, Ashton. Can I give up the powers?" she asked.

"They were gifted to you by your father. Only you can pass them to our children," he said.

Did he just say our children? Oh my, I can't be a mother. He can't hear my thoughts anymore, thank God, she thought.

Bailey, I can hear your thoughts, he thought.

"What? How is that possible?" she asked.

Because we are connected in ways that other couples are not, he thought.

"Did you just say that or think it?" she asked.

I thought it. You are reading my mind right now, he thought.

"Well, at least we won't fight over keeping secrets," Bailey said. They both laughed. Bailey thought about the fact that she could pass this down to their children. There might be a reason to keep her powers.

"You think about it, baby. No matter what you decide, I'll do what you think is best," he said. That night, as Ashton was holding her in his arms, she thought about the sacrifice he had made to save her sister. She thought about life, love and truly living. She didn't want to live life where everyone she knew would die. Immortality is worth nothing if you lose the ones you love. Bailey loved Ashton, but he was not the only person in her life. She loved her sister and Mary, her old nanny who seemed more like her mother. She also wanted to get the chance to know her father, Kingston, and maybe truly know her mother, Joanne. She had people in her life that it would hurt to outlive by a single day, much less hundreds of years. She didn't know in the end what she would decide.

The next evening when Bien Faire showed up at her door, she invited her inside.

"Good evening," Bien Faire said.

"Good evening," Bailey said.

"Have you made your choice?" she asked.

"I have a question, if that is okay?" Bailey asked.

"Yes, Bailey?" Bien Faire said

"I want to know if these powers will extend my lifespan beyond Ashton's." Bailey asked.

"The light within will linger always. It will never burn out. You will be able to pass it down to the next generation. It doesn't work like the dark light. The bearer of the dark light holds on to it, preventing her from aging. Therefore, they become immortal, but the bearer of the light of life passes it down when they are ready to move on to the next life. I do not believe Kingston was a true bearer of black light. If he were, he would have been too selfish to pass along the powers to you in order to save your life," she said. "Your years will be different though. You will age one year for every ten years you live," Bien Faire said. Bailey was horrified.

"So I will remain young, and everyone around me will get old?" she asked, her voice stricken with panic. Bien Faire smiled.

"No, child, the light within you can be passed along to others, not just your children. You have already passed it to Ashton when he drank your blood. He will age the same way you do. If you choose to pass along the light to another loved one, it can be passed using your gifts. You will have to figure that out on your own. It is against the rules to tell you how," Bien Faire said. Bailey nodded.

"So, I can pass it along to other people I deem worthy?" Bailey asked.

"Yes," Bien Faire said.

"Why should I have this power to choose who lives and who dies?" Bailey asked.

"We can't help what gifts are given to us, Bailey. We can only choose to use them for good or evil. I must tell you, Bailey. You shared so much of yourself when you gave Ashton your heart, soul and life that you will not outlive him if you remain human. The powers that protect you will protect him. You are two halves of a whole, forever connected in this world and the next. Your children will be bound to you as well by blood, so they will have some powers before you transfer your own to them," Bien Faire said.

"Thank you, Bien Faire…for everything." Bailey didn't like this power. She didn't like the overwhelming responsibilities it placed upon her. She had always been the grown up, and just when she thought she could focus on herself and have a simple life with Ashton, she was now coming to understand that life for her would never be simple. Bailey looked at Ashton, and he smiled at her with such love she knew all she wanted was to give him the life he wanted…and that life was the life of a human.

"I think Ashton and I will remain human, for it's a great gift," she said, while returning Ashton's smile.

"Goodbye…and remember to always stay in the light," Bien Faire said. With her parting words she was gone, just as if someone had blown out a candle.

Chapter Eighteen

Two weeks later, Bailey went to pick up Amber from cheer camp. Amber was so happy to see her that she gave her a big hug. Bailey was surprised that Amber didn't say anything about the events with the vampires that happened two weeks earlier. When they got back to the beach house Ashton was already gone.

"Where's Ashton?" Amber asked.

"Ashton flew out this morning. He's on his way to Texas," Bailey said.

"Did you guys break up?" Amber asked with a pout on her face. Bailey laughed.

"No, he's going to sell his cattle ranch," she said.

"Oh, well I never could picture Mr. Secret Agent living on a cattle ranch. What a waste to hide away where no one can see him." They both laughed. Ashton had thought he loved living on a ranch. The fact was, it was what he had to do in order to subsist. It was truly a lonely life. Now that he had Bailey, he no longer wished to live that way. After spending the summer on the beach, he found he had a passion for ocean life. Something about it reminded him of another world, and he decided he would pursue a career in marine biology.

Bailey was excited that she and Ashton would be attending college at the same time. She was glad that in the end they had made the choice to stay human together. Bailey and Ashton's love was beyond this world, and they both knew it. Some people go a lifetime and never find someone to love. Ashton knew he had gone a human lifetime without love, and now he was getting a second chance at a life filled with love.

Bailey and Amber had fun the last week of summer. They spent most of their days out by the pool or swimming in the ocean. They had a sisters-only shopping trip on Wednesday. That is when they ran into Adam. He looked the way he did the first time they met. In a way, Bailey was sad for Adam. He had lost so much and, unlike her, he didn't have a happy ending. Bailey decided that after all they had been through, they should remain friends. She hoped he would want to. She was hoping he would find the right girl one day. The way Amber was looking at him, if he waited another five years, he just might have Amber. Adam promised to keep in touch. He had plans to head back to college too, so he could finish up his medical training. Adam had thought that, after finding out about Perfidia, his passion for being a doctor would not be as strong. His passion for saving human lives had only grown, and he knew one day he would make a difference in the world. He would save people who no one else would take the time to save, and that would be his happy ending.

The week went by quickly for Bailey and Amber. They were so happy to be able to get to spend some time together. Bailey had spoken with Ashton every night for over an hour after Amber went to sleep. She missed him so much. She could tell he was missing her too, and this made her happy. She wanted him to need her. After a lifetime of parents who didn't need her, having someone who longed to be with her gave her peace—a lifetime of being at peace with who she was and who she decided to be.

Mary came by on Saturday afternoon to pick up Amber and catch up with the girls on what had been going on over the summer. Since Mary wouldn't accept text, it was hard to keep in touch with her over the summer. They all had fun finding out what had happened to each other—Amber finding a boyfriend and having the best cheer at camp, Mary realizing just how much she adored Jack and how happy she was that she was going to be able to continue working at the Evans home. She loved the girls. They would always seem like her children. Bailey found out just how strong she really is. Of course, she didn't go into details about her summer. It's not like she could say, "Found out my dad was not Bill, but a wizard controlled by an evil witch who wanted to kill me because I fell in love with a vampire she had cursed, which could in turn set all vampires free and kill her." She settled for, "I spent a lot of quality time with Ashton and found out we are true soul mates." Mary and Amber had to get back to the house. They had so much to do tomorrow with school starting on Monday. They hugged goodbye. Even though Ashton would be back soon, Bailey felt sad to say goodbye to her family. She was truly grown up now, and it would take time to adjust to it.

Ashton returned late Sunday night. Bailey picked him up from the airport. They were so happy to see each other. They embraced. The heat between them in that moment would have melted an iceberg. That night when they got back to the loft, they spent some time making sure everything was in place the way they wanted it. Bailey had a surprise for Ashton. "Close your eyes," she said. She was thinking, *don't think about it. Don't think about it.* Ashton laughed. They were surprised to find out that they could still read each other's thoughts, and Bailey's new powers allowed her to read human and non-human thoughts as well. They walked toward the back of the apartment. Bailey had a room set up like an art studio—a place where she could be creative—and she wanted Ashton to have a place to be creative with his passion. His creative space was set up with row after row of ocean specimens and book after book on marine biology. In the corner, she had a space with a leather chair and his guitar, along with a book on how to write your own music. A smile spread across his face so wide that Bailey felt dizzy from it. He was so beautiful, inside and out. He was the man of her dreams before she knew she even had a man of her dreams.

A month later, Ashton and Bailey were both so enthralled in their classes that it seemed each day held a new adventure, with the nights holding nothing but the desire and passion they had for one another. It was Sunday morning. Bailey ran to the coffee shop on the corner to pick up a surprise breakfast for Ashton. He slept more now that he was human, so some days Bailey got up before him. She noticed a lot of people talking about an article in the paper. She purchased a paper but didn't read it, because she needed to get back in time to surprise

Ashton. He smelled the coffee not to long after she came in the door. He no longer drank it black. He liked it with milk and sugar. He got up all smiles as usual and kissed her with such intensity that her knees went weak. He had to hold onto her to keep her from falling over. When they finally were finished kissing and ready for breakfast, Bailey turned, "I need to see the paper." She picked it up and started reading the headlines. "Mass pregnancy in Los Angeles," she said. She scanned the article and a smile spread across her face. Ashton's eyes flashed with delight as he read her thoughts. "Bien Faire apparently completed her task of rebirthing all 912 vampires." Bailey began explaining the high points of the article to Ashton. "According to the article, doctors at a local chain of fertility clinics were stunned to learn that 912 of their patients have the same due date. All 912 women had been trying to get pregnant for years. The article says that only 40% of women who undergo fertility treatments become pregnant. It seems that all 912 women became pregnant within the last two months. Doctors are still trying to figure out how this happened."

"Just another thing science cannot explain. I would love to see their take on vampires," Ashton said. They both smiled and were glad that so many got a happy ending. They knew they had been given the gift of sharing their lives together, for they were true soul mates.

Chapter Nineteen

It had been exactly one month since Perfidia was destroyed and exploded into a puff of smoke vanquished by the love that connected Ashton and Bailey. Perfidia was the High Priestess Witch who has ruled over the United States since its existence. She cursed people who would not follow her and made them vampires. Those who did follow her were made into human minions to be used when needed. When she was destroyed, all of her vampires were released. Bailey was a true witch—not like the witches you see on television that wear robes and carry wands. A true witch's powers flow within her. She can summon her powers and control them, just like working another muscle in her body. Bailey has yet to discover all the powers that flow within her. That kind of power can sometimes make a person turn evil without any understanding of what's happening.

Kingston went back to the house he shared with Perfidia and set free all of the human prisoners. Bien Faire swayed their minds to remember nothing of what had happened. Some of these people had been missing for years. Families were reunited, and life seemed to be getting back to normal for everyone involved. Kingston was set to leave within the next two days. He knew Joanne was in Hawaii with Bill. Kingston was going to get her and bring her back with him. He had to tell her he loved her, and he needed her to know why he had left.

Bailey agreed she would help explain everything to Joanne if he could get her to come back here. She couldn't leave her classes or Ashton. Tonight was the first full moon since Perfidia had been destroyed. Kingston no longer wished to remember the night of the full moon, for most bad magic happened on this night. Now that he no longer had magic in him, he had to do things the old-fashioned way. While packing his bags, he heard a loud noise coming from the hallway. He went to explore and noticed the painting that Perfidia had once deemed her most treasured possession lay on the floor, broken in half. He looked around, trying to see what had happened, but didn't see anything out of the ordinary, so he turned and went back to packing. As he finished up his packing, he heard laughter coming from the hallway. He didn't understand what was going on. He wondered if some children, thinking the place abandoned, had broken in to goof off.

When he rounded the corner of the hall, he saw the picture on the floor, radiating light. Then, one by one, children started stepping out from the painting. As the children started to be released from the picture, he noticed with each release the light grew less bright. He counted forty-eight children in all. He knew Perfidia had worked in the orphanage for ten years, but he never knew she had trapped the children in the picture.

He had always wondered why she had been so fond of that picture and now he knew. He now understood that each time he had passed the picture, and assumed he was going mad because he would see different faces, that Perfidia had enchanted the painting when she had trapped the children in it. The children stood looking at him, each with a curious look on his face.

Finally, one spoke up. "Hi, my name is Jackson. Can you tell us what has happened? We've been trapped in that picture for years. Is the witch dead?"

"Yes, she is dead. You are now free," Kingston said.

"How will we find our brothers and sisters?" Jackson asked.

"I don't know," Kingston said. He was thinking that most of these children's siblings wouldn't understand how they had not aged. He would have to contact Bailey for help on this one. He didn't have any magic to fix these problems.

"Is everyone okay?" Kingston asked.

"Yes," they all responded."

Jackson spoke again, "You're not going to be able to find our older brothers and sisters are you? I mean, we have been gone for too long." His face was sad. Jackson was one of the oldest children Perfidia had trapped in the painting. He had been the leader, the protector, all of these years.

Kingston looked at each of the children.

"I promise you, I will do my best to make this right, but I don't know if you are going to be able to return to your families. I don't know how long you have been away. I'm sorry," he sighed.

"It's not your fault. We thank you for your help." Jackson paused. "Do you think we can get something to eat?" Jackson asked.

"Of course, I will be right back. Everyone sit down," Kingston said.

He came back with crackers, cheese and some fruit. He didn't have anything other than water to drink, but he told them to eat up and he would get them something else to eat. He needed to call in some help. They all said thank you and started eating. He didn't fully understand how they had lived in the painting. He wondered how Perfidia had done this darkest of magic without asking him for help. She had been the director at the orphanage, so it would have been easy for her to explain the children's absence by saying they had been adopted or transferred to another orphanage. She had transformed the chosen children and trapped them in the picture in order to gain power over another wizard. He picked up the phone and dialed Bailey's cell phone. She answered on the third ring.

"Bailey?" Kingston asked.

"Yes?"

"It's Kingston. I have a problem. I can't talk about it over the phone. Can you bring Ashton and get here as soon as you can? It's an emergency!" Bailey didn't hesitate. She knew that the world she lived in held all kinds of secrets and, from the way Kingston sounded; this was one of those secrets that needed her attention.

"We'll be there in twenty minutes," Bailey said.

"Bailey, can you bring about twenty cheese pizzas?" Kingston asked. Bailey wondered what this was about but didn't ask.

"Sure. But it will be longer if we have to pick up pizzas."

"Thank you, Bailey. I'll see you here as soon as you can make it," and he hung up the phone.

Bailey went to Ashton's creative room and knocked on the door. He had been working on discovering a new species of fish and was trying to figure out what to name this one. Before she ever knocked, he knew she was coming. They could read each other's thoughts. He was still focused on what he was working on and hadn't taken the time to realize that she had some anxiety in her thoughts.

"Come in, babe," he said. Bailey looked at him with so much love that he truly wondered how he had gotten so lucky. He then noticed her face.

"What's wrong, Bailey?"

"Kingston called and said we need to come over as soon as possible. He also said to bring twenty cheese pizzas. He sounded very strange," she said.

"Okay, let's go," he said. She smiled at him. She loved that he would go without having to question her, just as she would go to Kingston without questioning him. She had been able to get to know her father a little more and, even though she didn't call him dad, she still trusted him. She knew he wouldn't bother her unless it was an emergency.

When they arrived, Kingston came to the door. He took the pizzas and asked them to wait on the porch. Bailey and Ashton could hear children's laughter coming from the house, and this caused them both a little unease. Kingston came back to the door and started explaining what had happened.

"Perfidia had this picture of children playing on a playground. It was her most prized material possession. I didn't understand why until today. She had enchanted the picture and trapped forty-eight children inside it, all from the orphanage she worked in years ago." Bailey gasped.

"How do you know this?" Ashton asked.

"About two hours ago, the picture broke in half, and the children were released from it. I am assuming they were released because she is dead, and tonight is the first full moon since her death. There is a great possibility that her other curses will be reversed. I don't know. I have never experienced anything like this," Kingston said.

Bailey looked at Kingston with an animated expression on her face.

"The children are inside right now?"

"Yes," Kingston said. Bailey pushed through the front door and ran into the room where all the children waited. Each face lit up when she walked into view. She looked at each face and smiled.

"I'm looking for Blake and Mark," Bailey said. Two small boys stood up. They were in the back of the room. They looked exactly like Adam—blue eyes, bleach-blonde hair. She started to cry.

"I'm Blake, and this is Mark. We are brothers. How do you know us?" Blake asked.

"I know your older brother, Adam," she said. Blake smiled, and then his face fell.

"We haven't seen him for a long time. We have missed him so much. Do you know where he is?" Blake asked. Bailey smiled

"I do know where he is, and he is going to be so happy to have found you."

Ashton and Kingston had been listening to the conversation. Bailey looked at Ashton, and he knew she was so happy to give Adam his happy ending. Bailey took full control of the situation. "I need each of you to tell me your name." Bailey found a roll of masking tape and created name tags for the children, so she could call them by name. "Do any of you remember the names of your older brothers and sisters, so we might be able to find them?" Bailey knew Perfidia had only trapped those children who had strong older brothers and sisters. It was their pain she drew from. Their grief fed her power. A child's grief gave her maximum power. Bailey didn't waste any time calling Adam. Adam answered on the fourth ring.

"Adam?" Bailey asked.

"Yeah, this is Adam."

"It's Bailey. How are you?"

"I'm good," he hesitated. "How are you?" Adam didn't know why Bailey would be calling him. He had been through so much because of her, and he was finally starting to put his life back together again. He could sense from her voice that this was not a social call. He waited.

"Adam, I need to see you as soon as possible. Can you come to Perfidia's old house?" she asked. She knew this might be hard for him, but she needed to get him there, so he could see that Perfidia did not destroy his world. She wondered how he was going to be able to deal with all of this. She knew she would help him any way she could.

"Bailey, do you know what you are asking of me? I mean…coming to Perfidia's house." He shuddered as he spoke her name. "That is a lot for me to have to do," he said.

"I wouldn't ask this of you if it were not important. I promise you, this time when you leave her house you will have a happy ending," she said.

"Okay, Bailey. I'll be there in twenty minutes," Adam said. He then hung up the phone. They were able to see that, out of the forty-eight children, thirty of them were brothers or sisters, each having one older sibling that they were taken from. The other eighteen children had a younger sibling that they were taken from. Everyone assumed that she only took the youngest kids, because the older children could endure more suffering, but that was not the case. With some of the kids, she took the younger ones, who brought her more power, for they could endure more suffering than their older sibling. When Adam arrived, he was nervous. He didn't understand why he was doing this. He knew Bailey wouldn't hurt him, but he was still not comfortable going back to the place where he had endured so much torture from Perfidia. Perfidia had made Adam a minion in order to distract Bailey from Ashton. When Adam failed her in any way, she would torture him with the feeling of being skinned alive. Bailey met Adam at the door and took him by the hand, leading him over to a chair on the front porch.

"Adam, I have good news for you. I know it's going to be hard for you to believe me but…I need you to listen before you make a decision on how to move forward from here." Adam simply nodded in agreement.

"Adam, when Perfidia died because of the pure love Ashton and I have for one another, it broke the curse she had set on many people. You thought she had killed Blake and Mark when you were told they had died in the orphanage, but she didn't kill them. She trapped them inside the painting that you saw in her hallway. When she died, the enchantment on the picture was broken, and all the children she trapped there were set free. Both of your brothers are in the house right now. I know this is a lot to take in, but they have not aged at all. Blake and Mark are still five and three years old," she said.

Adam was in shock. He couldn't wrap his head around the fact that his brothers, whom he thought he lost fifteen years ago, were a few feet away, behind the walls of Perfidia's house. He smiled at Bailey.

"Can I see them now?"

"Yes, of course."

Adam and Bailey walked inside, and she called to Blake and Mark to come here.

She had already explained to them that their brother had not been enchanted inside the picture, so he had aged and was now twenty-one years old. She really wasn't sure they understood, but as soon as they all saw each other, she knew the fact that Adam was fifteen years older made no difference. They still saw their older brother there, and they ran and jumped into his arms. All three were crying. Bailey was crying too. Ashton wrapped his arms around Bailey and held her close to him.

Ashton whispered, "Adam gets his happy ending too." Bailey looked at Ashton and smiled.

"Yes, he does," she said with tears streaming down her face.

Kingston was trying to figure out if there was going to be any way to get the other children to their brothers and sisters, but he didn't think it looked good. Adam was in on the secret about the world of dark magic, but he didn't think the others would be. They were going to have to call in help from Bien Faire to get her thoughts on this matter. He didn't know how to contact people when he didn't have magic to do so. He would have to depend on Bailey to contact Bien Faire. All he really wanted right now was to hold his Joey, but he knew now that trip would have to be delayed. Ashton, Bailey and Adam had stayed over, trying to figure out how they were going to make this better. It was midnight when they heard what sounded like an explosion coming from the dungeon.

Chapter Twenty

Ashton was the first one to make it down to the dungeon. When he saw her, he thought he was dreaming. Those beautiful brown eyes—Elizabeth's eyes—were staring directly into his. Bailey reached him just as Elizabeth threw her arms around him and kissed him full on the mouth. For once, if her eyes could have changed to metallic silver, they would have. She didn't know who this woman was or where she came from, but they were about to have a few words. Then she tasted the emotions rolling off of Elizabeth and Ashton. It was chocolate, the taste of love. Kingston and Adam were making their way downstairs too. They both wanted to know why Ashton was making out with this woman. He couldn't pull himself away from her. Bailey was hurt. She ran out of the room crying. Adam followed. Kingston stepped in and pulled Elizabeth and Ashton apart.

"What is going on here, Ashton?" Kingston asked.

"I don't know. This is Elizabeth. Perfidia killed her to get to me. I don't know how she is here right now," Ashton said.

"Well, Bailey saw you kissing her. She ran upstairs crying," Kingston said.

"What? She's crying?" he gasped.

"Yes, she is. This is not good, Ashton," he said. Ashton nodded.

"Can you stay with Elizabeth while I go explain to Bailey?" he asked.

"Yes, I can," Kingston said. Ashton looked at Elizabeth—his Elizabeth—and he didn't understand why every seemingly unimportant emotion was magnified and meant everything to him.

"I'll be back. Stay here with Kingston," he said.

"Okay, Ashton. I will," Elizabeth said.

Ashton ran up the stairs to find Bailey. She was sobbing so uncontrollably that he didn't know how he was going to get her to calm down. She had given him everything, and he was in love with this woman downstairs. How could he have loved another? She didn't love another. She could never love another. She was past being comforted.

He heard Adam saying, "It's not what you think, I'm sure. Think about all that has happened today. We don't know what is going on. Let's hear what he has to say, Bailey. It can't be that bad."

"Oh, but it is that bad. I could taste the emotions from them. They both love one another. I don't know how, or why, this is happening, but things are not okay," she cried.

Ashton walked into the room. He poured off the emotion of sorrow. He was confused. She tasted that, too. He was so afraid Bailey would hate him. She really wished she couldn't taste his every emotion tonight. Tasting his emotion meant knowing he loves another woman, knowing he feels bad about it, confused, not knowing what to do.

He looked at her and said, "I'm sorry. It's Elizabeth." Understanding crossed her face, and she looked at him and then at Adam. Adam knew who Elizabeth was as well. She saw the pity on Adam's face, and she wanted to scream. She looked back at Ashton with a hurt so deep in her eyes that he thought he would rather be blind than have to see that look on her face.

"What does this mean, Ashton? Do you love her more than me?"

"I don't love her more than you. I don't know what it means. Bailey, I'm sorry. Please, she kissed me. I was in shock. She was my first love, and she was taken from me. I'm trying to deal with all of this. I don't want to hurt you, baby. Please, don't hate me," he moaned. She wanted to run and let him wrap his arms around her, but she wasn't sure after tonight if he would ever do that again. She didn't want to put herself out there, not knowing if he would choose Elizabeth over her. He saw it on her face, and he tried to read her thoughts, but unlike him, she could block him if she truly wanted to–one of her many talents that she had learned over the past month. Adam wanted to leave the room, but he could tell Bailey needed him to stay.

"Bailey, what do you want me to do? I'll do it," Ashton said.

"I don't want you to do anything. You are going to have to figure out who you want to be with here, Ashton. I have no power over that. I can't force you to choose me. I don't know how this is going to play out...It really scares me," she said.

It broke his heart to have to see her so upset. Her eyes were all red and puffy. Tears streaked down her face. His beautiful Bailey was not sure he loved her more than Elizabeth. He had thought he knew for certain that he loved Bailey more, until Elizabeth kissed him, and now he didn't know. If it had not been for Bailey, none of this would have even been possible. How could he even think about loving someone else? She was the one who loved him beyond the natural world, yet Elizabeth came back beyond the natural world for him.

Adam spoke up, "I think it best if we find answers to how this happened.

Elizabeth died. If she is here now, something is not right."

"How can you say that after your brothers have returned?" Ashton asked.

"Because they were not killed. They were trapped inside a picture," Adam said.

"Adam is right. Death is something even magic is not supposed to be able to fight," Bailey said.

"Are you saying we should be worried about Elizabeth being evil?" Ashton asked.

"I'm saying nothing is impossible. We all know this," Adam said.

Bailey agreed.

"We'll see if she knows what happened to her. We will find out where she has been all of this time," Ashton said. Bailey didn't like the feeling of how defensive Ashton was toward Elizabeth. He had been her protector, and now he was protecting Elizabeth from her.

They went downstairs to talk to Elizabeth. Bailey noticed the light that had always linked her to Ashton was not there in the presence of Elizabeth. This was very eerie to her. She didn't like this at all, and she knew Elizabeth's return was not a good thing. She could sense it, but how could she explain it to anyone else without seeming jealous? She was going to have to be on guard at all times. She would protect her loved ones with her life. She loved Ashton, even if he was blinded by Elizabeth. He had endured her dating Adam while she was getting to know him. How could she not offer him the same courtesy with Elizabeth? If he chose Elizabeth in the end it was not meant to be between them. Maybe what she sensed with Elizabeth was a result of her emotions of jealousy. She couldn't be sure, so she would have to deal with it the best way she could.

Ashton looked at Elizabeth and asked, "How did you come to be here?"

"I don't know. It was like I was asleep and just woke up," she said in an innocent voice.

"You're saying you have been asleep for over a hundred years and didn't know it?" Bailey blurted.

"No, I don't know. A hundred years?" she gasped. "What is she talking about Ashton?" Elizabeth asked.

Bailey tasted guilt from Ashton. She read the thoughts undulating through his mind. He felt he let Elizabeth down when Perfidia killed her, and now guilt for causing Bailey pain. She also tasted a new flavor from Elizabeth—one she had never tasted before. She was trying to get a handle on it when Elizabeth started crying. This blocked the unknown emotion. Bailey didn't like it at all. Elizabeth was hiding something—something dark and not right. She didn't know what it was, but she was determined to find out. Elizabeth ran to Ashton and put her arms around him, continuing to cry. Ashton didn't know what to do. Bailey could hear his thoughts again. *Should I hold Elizabeth? Should I hold Bailey? Why do I always hurt those I love? I love Bailey. Why is this affecting me this way? Elizabeth was supposed to be my wife, my wife if Perfidia had never touched our lives. We both would be long dead by now. How can I walk away from her when she doesn't even know what the world is now?* Bailey decided she needed to push her feelings aside and take control here.

"Elizabeth, I know this has got to be very confusing for you, but we need to know what you do remember." Bailey said, in a soothing tone. Bailey felt a hardening of Elizabeth's emotions. She was blocking

Bailey from tasting her emotions. Bailey had gotten so used to being able to taste emotions that she thought it unnatural. With Elizabeth blocking her, she knew for certain she was hiding things now. If she thought Bailey was going to step aside and let her take her soul mate, she had better think again.

"I'm sorry. I don't remember anything. The last thing I remember is Ashton asking me to marry him." She looked at Ashton with innocent doe eyes and said, "I said yes." Elizabeth then looked at Bailey giving her a peculiar smile of triumph.

"Okay, so you can only remember what happened to you the night you…died,"

Bailey stated firmly.

"I died?" she asked.

"Yes, you did, and we need to know if you feel different than you did before you died," Adam said.

"Different how?" Elizabeth asked in a child-like voice.

"Why are you blocking me from reading your emotions, Elizabeth?" Bailey snapped. "What are you hiding from us?" Bailey asked.

"I'm not hiding anything. I just learned I was dead and now I'm not. You also told me that I have been dead for over a hundred years, but Ashton has not aged a single day. I'm trying to understand all of this, and you're yelling at me because I can't answer your questions. I am not blocking anything. I don't understand what you're talking about, reading my emotions," Elizabeth snapped back.

"Maybe it would be better if we all get some sleep and talk about this in the morning," Ashton said.

"Yes, that is best. The kids will be up soon. We have to figure out how to deal with them," Kingston said.

Bailey was still glaring at Elizabeth. She watched as Elizabeth took Ashton's hand. Bailey had to restrain herself from crossing the room and ripping off Elizabeth's head. Ashton stood there, staring at Bailey. He watched her look at their hands and then at his face. He watched as Bailey's face grew cold and hard, her jaw tightening like a vice and a glaze covering her blue eyes to shield her soul. When he didn't remove his hand from Elizabeth's, she turned and walked upstairs alone, leaving everyone in the dungeon. Her heart was breaking. The Ashton she knew would have followed her upstairs. Bailey and Ashton would have worked through this and figured it out together. *Did he only pretend to love me, so I would set him free from being a vampire,* she thought. The rage sweeping through her body was so strong that it scared her. The powers she now controlled could be used for good or evil. These powers could get rid of Elizabeth for good if she wanted to. Her dark side was coming to the surface, and she wondered if keeping Ashton would mean using dark magic. If it did, would she resist or would she use it to her advantage? A few moments later, she heard a knock on her door.

"Bailey?" Ashton whispered.

"Can I come in?" he asked. She didn't know if she wanted to see him now—the man of her dreams who existed in Elizabeth's dreams as well. She stayed silent.

"Bailey, please. We need to talk," he pleaded. She walked over and opened the door. She didn't make eye contact with him. She knew if she met his eyes she would burst into tears, so she turned around with her head down and walked over and sat down in an overstuffed chair, never taking her eyes off the floor. His heart was breaking. He knew she had endured so much pain from people not loving her the way they should. Now, he was making her think he didn't love her, because he couldn't walk away from Elizabeth.

"Bailey, I…" he paused. "I love you. I'm sorry this has happened. Elizabeth is sleeping downstairs in one of the guest rooms. I'm here because I want to be. She asked me to stay. I will tell her about us, but right now I'm trying to understand how she is here at all. I won't lie to you, Bailey. I thought all my feelings for her were gone. Somehow, with her here, they were brought to the surface. It doesn't mean I love you any less. It just means I'm going to have to figure out things about myself," he said.

"So you're saying you might not know who you want to be with?" Bailey asked, her voice shaking.

"Bailey, it's not that simple. Of course, I love you. But something is pulling me toward her, and I don't understand it. I have never felt this for anyone other than you, and now it's like I'm being pulled in half, both of you wanting me…" he hesitated. He finally finished saying what he really didn't want to say aloud. "And there is a part of me that wants both of you," he blurted.

"I can't believe after everything we have been through you would feel this way. I don't understand it. Once I found you, my life was complete. Now you're saying you feel drawn to her—like half of you belong with her, and the other half belongs to me. I gave you every part of me, Ashton. Do you understand what that meant for me?" Bailey made a disgusted sound in the back of her throat. "No, of course not. It doesn't matter. While you're trying to figure out what you want, you should sleep somewhere else. I can't be in the same room with you right now," she snapped.

"Bailey." He reached for her, but she pulled away.

"No," her voice was sharp. Ashton was not used to Bailey being so angry. "You can't have it both ways, Ashton. You can't love me while still feeling you love her. You need time, and I will try and give it to you. However, I will not let you hold me and kiss me while doing the same with her. If you decide you want her, I will try and walk away. If you decide you want me, I hope after all you are putting me through I will still love you. I need for you to go now," she said in a defeated tone.

He nodded. He wanted to say so many things in that moment, but he thought it best if he just left. He was upset, too. Bailey had never sounded so crushed, nor had she ever sounded so menacing. He didn't believe the powers within her would change her, but now he wondered, if by losing him she would lose herself. He shuddered.

Bailey spent the rest of the night crying and trying to block the images of how to kill Elizabeth from her mind. She thought about how different her life would be when Ashton chose Elizabeth. It also scared her that the powers within her were saying that she could stop it and have Ashton all to herself again. All she had to do was make sure this time that Elizabeth didn't come back when she killed her. Bailey shuddered. Where are these thoughts coming from? This is not who I am. She didn't like the feeling of losing herself to the darkness. She wondered why it seemed so easy to just want to let her powers take over in order to win Ashton back, instead of Ashton fighting the darkness within himself. This time, it would be Bailey who would have to fight against the dark magic that wanted to consume her very soul. This time it would be her who would have to choose between the good and evil that flowed within her very blood. All she could do was hope that she was strong enough to walk away…when she didn't win.

The next morning, the kids were up running around the house.

They paired off the children into three groups. Kingston was in charge of the first group, Bailey was in charge of the second and Ashton was in charge of the third. Adam was helping Bailey, and Elizabeth was helping Ashton. Bailey couldn't dwell on what was going on with her and Ashton right now. She had to find homes for these children. She told Adam to hold down the fort and she walked outside to the backyard. She was going to call on the elements a power she only recently discovered. She called on air, water, fire and earth to send a message to Bien Faire that she was needed at Perfidia's house as soon as possible. She released the powers into the wind, and they rolled off to summon Bien Faire. Bien Faire was the Leader of the Light Faerie. She ruled over all that was good within the world of magic. She helped to maintain the balance of good and evil and that meant hunting and killing vampires in the United States before Bailey had freed them. She still hunted in other countries, but the United States was now free of vampires. She didn't know how long it would last. Word would spread, and soon others would come to take over this territory, the territory that Perfidia had ruled for almost a thousand years. Bien Faire had hoped Bailey would stake her claim here and defend it. Bailey didn't know she was the chosen one who could change everything. She didn't understand the powers that flowed within her. Bien Faire knew Bailey would rule with the light, and this was going to affect the world on many levels.

They were able to find the older siblings of over half of the children. They were waiting on Bien Faire before deciding how to move forward. Bailey had decided the only way to keep the dark thoughts from her mind was to not focus on Elizabeth. She was keeping her mind busy with what to do with the children. Bien Faire finally arrived and they explained everything that had happened. Her solution was simple. The children could not go back to the siblings. It was unfortunate, but they could not be put in danger.

"It's simple really. We cannot risk the human world knowing of our existence. The only way to protect them, as well as us, is if they don't know we are here. I will have to sway the children's minds. They will remember only the brother or sister they were trapped with inside the painting. They will remember nothing of where they have been all of these years. That is the best I can do for them, and us," Bien Faire stated.

"I must keep my brothers!" Adam exclaimed.

"Adam, how will you care for them? Are you not in school?" Bien Faire asked.

"I am, but I know of them, and they of me. I thought I had lost them. I cannot go back pretending they died fifteen years ago. Please, don't take them from me," he pleaded.

Bailey spoke then, "Bien Faire, I think it reasonable that Adam keep the boys. I will offer my assistance to him as much as possible. I think, after what Perfidia did to him, he should be allowed to keep his brothers. I also think we need only take the memories of Perfidia from the boys' minds. Let Adam keep his memories. I may need him in the future, and it's always good to have a friend who knows who you truly are."

"Bailey, by letting Adam keep the boys you are now taking full responsibility for them. Letting them know of our existence will put them in danger, but if you think it's best for them to stay within our world, I will allow it," Bien Faire said.

"Thank you, I will watch over them. I give you my word," Bailey said.

Ashton didn't like this. He didn't like this link that would forever keep Adam in Bailey's life now. He couldn't argue with her though. Here he was not knowing if he was in love with someone who died over a hundred years ago, so he stayed quiet. Bailey sensed his unease with this subject, but she pushed his feelings out of her mind. She had to take care of herself. Bien Faire noticed the light that had connected Ashton and Bailey had been disconnected by the presence of Elizabeth. She could also feel the powers shifting within Bailey. Bailey was fighting against her dark side, trying to keep the black light from taking over her mind…as well as her actions.

"Bailey, I would like to speak with you in private," Bien Faire said.

"Okay," Bailey said.

"I understand that you are having problems with Elizabeth and Ashton's relationship. I feel your fight between the black and white light. Bailey, are you going to be able to handle this?" she asked.

"I will do what I have to do to remain in the light of good. I won't lie…it's not easy. Every part of me is fighting not to kill her. She is taking from me what I love most." Bailey's voice cracked as she said,

"It's not my choice. It's Ashton's. If he chooses her..." Breathing hard and shaking, Bailey paused, not wanting to say what she felt she had to say. Bailey regained control, and the malice in her voice was clear. "You may have to kill me, before I go over to the black light. I don't know if I will be able to stop it. He is my world. Without him, I have nothing," Bailey said, tears rolling down her face.

Bailey didn't block her thoughts, because she didn't think Ashton was close enough to her, but he heard every word, and he moved away from Elizabeth. Elizabeth looked at him with hurt in her eyes. He thought, in that moment, he would go mad. Trying to keep both of them safe was beyond anything he felt he could do. How could he love them both and keep them safe?

"Bailey, you're stronger than you think. You will never choose the dark light. Everyone fights between what is right and what is easy. You will choose light over dark and, in the end, survive no matter what choices Ashton makes. I believe in you." Bien Faire stated this as fact. Bailey smiled

"Thank you. I hope you're right," Bailey said.

Bien Faire started swaying the children's minds and setting up where they were going to be taken. Bien Faire was able to get each of the children into a good home—a home in which they would be able to grow up and be loved. Once each child had been placed, she was ready to depart and get back to keeping the world safe from dark magic. She told Bailey to contact her if she needed her and then she left.

Bailey decided to take Adam, Blake and Mark to find a place to live. Kingston offered to let them stay at his house, but it held too many negative memories for Adam. Bailey figured she would put them up in one of her family rental units. There was one unit available close to campus, and it was a two bedroom. The boys could share a room and Adam could have his own space. She was also going to help Adam find a nanny. That way, he could continue his pursuit for a degree in medicine. Ashton stayed behind, trying to figure out where to go from here with Elizabeth.

Elizabeth made every attempt to push herself on Ashton. Part of him knew this wasn't right, but he still couldn't admit something was off with her. Bailey had told him she was getting Adam set up today and then going back to the loft. She had class this afternoon that she couldn't miss. He too needed to get back to his classes, so he told Elizabeth he would show her around the neighborhood, and he would come back after class to check on her. When Elizabeth was alive, they didn't have the technology that they have today, so around every corner something scary lurked. She didn't know what cars were, and buildings looked like monsters. Ashton had to show her how to use the indoor plumbing, so she could use the restroom and get a shower. Things we take for granted she didn't even know existed.

Kingston said he would stay there and watch out for her until he got back. Ashton didn't know what he was going to do. Did Bailey even want him back at the loft? He wasn't sure. She had made herself pretty clear when she told him he couldn't be with her while thinking he was in love with Elizabeth. He couldn't worry about this right now. He had to get to class. He told Elizabeth that Kingston would be there if she got scared or needed anything. He would check on her later, and then he left.

He went to class and found that route so easy to step back into. Everything that had happened with Elizabeth seemed more like a dream. He also found that when he was away from her, the need to be with her and care for her faded. However, the need to be with Bailey returned and magnified. He then realized something dark was happening. Magic was causing him to need Elizabeth when, in fact, he didn't love her.

He was afraid because he didn't understand why this need felt so urgent in Elizabeth's presence. He needed to speak with Bailey. She had to forgive him. He didn't want to go back to see Elizabeth now. He knew that whatever was causing him to feel he loved Elizabeth might grow stronger over time. He needed to find out why and how this was happening, so he could stop it. When he got back to the loft, Bailey wasn't there.

He waited at the loft for over three hours for Bailey to come home, but she never did. He knew he was going to have to go check on Elizabeth, and he didn't like this. He didn't want to be sucked back into the overwhelming need he had to love her when in her presence. He decided to call Bailey to ask when she would be back at the loft.

When he called, she didn't answer her cell phone. Her phone rang five times and went straight to voice mail, so he called again five minutes later and the same thing. His chest tightened. What if he had already lost Bailey because of Elizabeth? He had to find her. He had to find her and fix this. In that moment, he didn't care Elizabeth was waiting for him to show up. In that moment, he needed to hold Bailey and let her know he loved her more than life itself. But why didn't she answer her phone? He thought he would go insane if she didn't call him back soon, so he sat down in the living room and waited. While he was waiting for her to come home, he fell asleep in a chair.

Chapter Twenty-One

Bailey was over at Adam's apartment helping him get the boys settled. They had gone to IKEA and gotten all kinds of household stuff, so Adam could take care of the boys. Bailey was so glad she didn't spend all of the money in her bank account on Mary's wedding right now. Mary was Bailey's old nanny, and she loved her like a mother. She had paid for her wedding in the summer and spent over $300,000 on the wedding and honeymoon. But she still had a pretty good nest egg left. Plus, her parents continued to add a $3000 monthly allowance to her account.

She had never used any of the money on herself before Mary's wedding, but she had used some of it for living expenses while in college. She intended to help Adam with monthly bills, as well as paying for a nanny. Blake and Mark already loved Bailey. She had attempted to leave earlier, but the boys would not let her. She helped give them a bath and read them a story before tucking them into bed. When she walked into the living room, Adam was sitting on the sofa studying some medical book.

He looked up and said, "Bailey, how can I thank you enough?"

"Adam, you don't owe me anything. I am glad I could help you. After everything I put you through, it's the least I can do," Bailey said.

"Mary is coming over tomorrow to help out with the boys until I can find a nanny," she said.

"Thank you so much, Bailey. I could have never done this without you," he said.

"You're welcome, Adam. I am glad you get your happy ending, even though it seems my happy ending is over," she said.

"Bailey, he loves you. There is something not right about Elizabeth. Somehow, I can feel it. Can you feel it?" he asked

"Yes, Adam. I can feel it, but I don't know how he is going to see it. Whatever she is doing to him is bringing feelings for her to the surface. He must truly love her. I was just a stand in until she returned," she cried.

"That is not true, Bailey. You need to talk to him. You need to tell him everything you're feeling, and what you have sensed about her. If you guys are meant to be together, you have to be honest with one another. Talk to him, Bailey," he insisted.

"I will try. I need to get back to the loft. I have to interview several nannies tomorrow. I will call you if anything is promising. Call me if you need anything. Mary will be here first thing in the morning. Get some sleep. You're going to need it," she laughed.

"Goodnight to you too, Bailey. Talk to Ashton," he said as she was getting into her car.

"I will. Bye," she said as she pulled away from the curb. She was dreading going back to the loft—the loft she had assumed would be shared with Ashton until they graduated from UCLA. Her heart grew heavy at the thought of going there now and sleeping in the bed she had once shared with Ashton, while he was asleep somewhere else dreaming of Elizabeth. She was crying when she opened the front door. She put her purse and keys away and walked into the kitchen to get a glass of water. When her eyes glanced over to the living room, she saw him asleep in the chair. Her heart fluttered, and for a second, she felt faint. He opened his eyes to see her looking at him. He could tell she had been crying. He didn't like how, whatever darkness this was, it was hurting Bailey. He had to fix it.

"Bailey?" he asked his voice full of sleep.

"Yeah, it's me," she muttered. "What are you doing here, Ashton?" Her voice sounded broken. "I thought I had made myself clear. I can't be around you while you have feelings for Elizabeth. My heart can't take this, Ashton," she exclaimed.

"I am here because I don't have feelings for Elizabeth. Something is happening to me when I'm around her that makes me believe I love her, but I don't. I don't know what to do. After leaving her earlier today, it was like a fog lifted from my mind.

Everything was clear again. It was like I was disconnected from my feelings for you. I don't understand it. I believe you and Adam were right. Elizabeth is not the same person she was before she died. Something is different—something about her is missing.

Does this make sense to you?" he asked. Relief washed through Bailey. She ran to Ashton and jumped into his arms, throwing herself around him. She was crying and kissing him. He was kissing her back with a passion that let Bailey know there was no one else.

"I believe you, Ashton. I just didn't think you would believe me. You were blindsided by her. I couldn't reach out to you. I felt lost," she wailed. "I know something dark is going on here. I just don't know what it is. I had tasted a very eerie emotion from Elizabeth, but I couldn't put my finger on it. She then started blocking me from tasting her emotions. I didn't know how to tell you. Something about her was bringing out the darkness within me. I wanted to kill her, Ashton. It scares me how bad I wanted to kill her," she said menacingly.

"It's okay. We will figure this out. You will never go to the dark light, baby. I know you," he said.

"Something else upset me about her. In her presence, the light that connects us to each other disconnects and disappears. I can see it now though," she said.

"What? The light disconnects and disappears? What does that mean?" he asked, taken aback.

"I don't know what it means, but it can't mean anything good," she said.

"I agree. That light connected us from the moment I met you, Bailey. If she is causing it to disconnect, then there is darkness within her. Should you contact Bien Faire?" he asked.

"I think if I summon the power of love whenever we have to be around her, the binding of love will protect us from anything dark. It will give us time to figure out her plan. She has to be up to something.

I know it's hard for you, Ashton, because you did love her once, but that is not the Elizabeth you loved. The Elizabeth you loved is dead," she said.

"I know that now. I'm sorry for everything. I didn't have control over my own mind. The weird thing about it all is I knew I never loved Elizabeth like I love you. This desire to be with her scared me. It's not real, just like she is not real," he said.

"Wait, do you think Perfidia could have cast a spell to bring her back somehow?" she asked.

"Maybe, it was Perfidia's plan to break us apart," he said.

"I don't know, but I don't like it. I don't like how I feel around her either. I feel like she is pulling you away from me, and I have no control over it," she said.

"I think we should go see her tomorrow and find out, if she lets anything slip," he said.

"I bet with the binding of love protecting us that she will not be able to block me from tasting her emotions," Bailey said. They both headed upstairs to go to bed. They were exhausted from the mental turmoil this had placed on both of them. They fell fast asleep, holding each other as tightly as possible.

When they arrived the next morning at Kingston's house, the house looked disturbing to Bailey. It had and aura of darkness cast around it that only she could see. She tried to explain this to Ashton, but he couldn't see it. Ashton knocked on the door, and Elizabeth answered. They were both taken aback at how haggard she looked. She had looked so beautiful the day before, and now she looked like she had aged twenty years overnight. Her eyes darted around, looking between Bailey and Ashton.

In a possessive voice, Elizabeth hissed, "Where have you been, Ashton?" Bailey could feel the pull she was trying to have over Ashton, but she had called on the elements to protect their minds, bodies and spirits. Elizabeth couldn't take hold of him like she did that first night, and she was losing her composure.

"Elizabeth, I'm sorry. I had to go back to the loft and talk things over with Bailey," Ashton said.

"Talk what over with Bailey?" she hissed.

"You being here, for one. Second, she is my life. I'm sorry, but I'm in love with her," he said.

"You mean you *were* in love with her. Now I'm back, and we are getting married," Elizabeth said through clenched teeth. Bailey really had to hold herself back and let Ashton deal with this. If she stepped in now, there would be a fight, and poor Elizabeth would lose some body parts. And even though Elizabeth looked liked crap, Bailey was certain Elizabeth would probably prefer to keep all of her body parts.

"Elizabeth, I'm sorry if I gave you that impression. It was hard to see you after all these years. I did love you long ago but, unlike you, I lived, over time, moved on. I hope you will find happiness here with the new life you have been given. I realize there is a lot for you to learn, and I will be happy to find someone to help you, but it cannot be me. It's not fair to Bailey," he said.

"Ashton," she said with panic now in her voice. "I still love you. Please, don't do this. We can just be friends. Please don't walk away from me. I'm scared," she pleaded.

Bailey could taste it now. Elizabeth could not hide her emotions now that the elements were protecting them. She tasted several emotions—one she couldn't name and then rot, which was hatred directed not only at her, but also at Ashton. This came as a shock, but she played it cool and continued to taste Elizabeth's emotions. The other was deceit, and it was a mixture of bitter and sour.

The last emotion, the one she was focusing on trying to figure out, was a very unpleasant taste. It didn't taste like rot. It tasted worse. She finally realized it was not an emotion she tasted. It was a feeling of blackness, of being consumed by blackness. It was like being buried alive and slowly suffocating. It was death. What did this mean? Bailey didn't know, but she knew Elizabeth was not back from the dead out of luck. She had returned for revenge. She wasn't sure if it was for her own revenge or Perfidia's, but someone was going to pay the price for her pain.

Bailey continued to taste her emotions and tried to feel anything from her that would help them. But all of a sudden Elizabeth's eyes narrowed on Bailey, and they tightened with loathing. Then, the wall went up and Bailey couldn't read Elizabeth's emotions anymore. Bailey didn't know how she was going to deal with any of this. What were they going to do with Elizabeth? She started to notice that the haggard look Elizabeth had when they arrived was slowly fading, and her face was youthful again. Bailey didn't know what this was about either. She had so many questions without any answers.

Bailey and Ashton sent word to Bien Faire about Elizabeth. They decided they needed help watching over her. They wanted someone to stay at Kingston's with Elizabeth because Bailey and Ashton didn't feel comfortable, yet they didn't want to leave her alone. Bien Faire decided she would stay with Elizabeth and help her get acclimated to her new environment. Bien Faire didn't like Bailey's unease about Elizabeth, so she decided she would stay with her. Bien Faire's powers allowed her to see what type of light was within Elizabeth. There were no signs of white light. However, she didn't show any signs of black light either. It was as if Elizabeth didn't exist.

Bien Faire had been there less than twenty-four hours when she felt the shift in her powers. She couldn't get a hold on her longing to destroy. Bien Faire had a desire for blood. She didn't want to drink blood, but she wanted to see it. She wanted to cause pain to others. She was fighting hard against the overwhelming wish to seek out and obliterate Bailey. She called on all the powers within to deny this malicious craving to spill every ounce of Bailey's blood. By doing this, it weakened her to the point of exhaustion. She didn't want to go to sleep. She felt she should contact Bailey, but she had no strength to do so.

Chapter Twenty-Two

Kingston had left that morning on his quest to find Joanne. Kingston was finally able to seek her out. Joanne and Bill were still in Hawaii. He knew it would be a great shock for her to see him, for he had not aged a single day since the day he left her, but she had aged over nineteen years. He knew that his body would start to age now that he was human again, no longer taking in dark emotions. He really didn't care about getting older. All he wanted was to hold her, kiss her and love her again. She was the one person in this entire world he would no longer live without. He honestly didn't understand how he was able to stay away from her for all these years. He knew that, in order for her to stay alive, he had to stay away. She was lounging by the pool with her personal assistant, Lily, when he first saw her. Lily was really her babysitter. She was someone Bill paid to watch over Joanne to make sure she never betrayed him again. Bill kept a tight leash on Joanne. Her betrayal had cost them both the light of their spirit. Joanne looked up and saw Kingston across the courtyard. At first, she thought she was hallucinating again. This would not be the first time she thought she had seen him. She had envisioned him so many times in her mind that he was imprinted in her brain. She smiled at him. She did this sometimes when her hallucinations seemed so real. She thought the alcohol she drank today must be helping her illusions be more life-like. He didn't want to approach her with Lily there, so he just sat down across the courtyard from her, never taking his eyes off her.

She watched him, too. Her hallucinations normally didn't last this long. They would fade out after about five minutes, but she had been looking at him now for about thirty minutes. Joanne's face grew more delighted with each passing moment. Finally, Lily needed a bathroom break. Lily also needed to go get lunch for them both, so she said she would be back soon. Joanne wasn't really hungry. She didn't eat much these days. She was feeling sick a lot lately and didn't know why. She assumed it was stress related. She hated every part of her life. She hated who she was now. She wondered who she could have been if life had taken a different turn and Kingston had never left her. When Lily asked her what she wanted to eat, it distracted her from Kingston. When she finally looked to where he had been, he was gone. Her face fell in despair. She closed her eyes, because she knew she would see him as soon as her eyelids were closed. She smiled again, thinking and picturing him in her mind.

"Joey, it's been so long. So very long," Kingston said. She didn't open her eyes. She thought, "*Wow! Now I can hear his voice. I've got to remember what I was drinking today.*"

"Joey, can you open your eyes, please? I need to talk to you. I need to explain why I left. I didn't want to leave," he said, sorrow in his velvet voice. This brought her back into reality, so she opened her eyes, expecting the picture would disappear. Instead, Kingston was there, standing no more than two feet from her. Joanne gasped.

"Kingston," she sighed, letting out a deep breath. "Kingston, are you real?"

"Yes, Joey, I'm real, and I'm sorry." Joanne tilted her head to the side.

"I don't think you're real. You look the same as you did when you left, and it's been nineteen years, two months, five days..." she paused, looking down at her watch. She continued, "...four hours, twenty-two minutes and thirty seconds since you walked away from me." Tears were streaming down her face, and his control was slipping. Kingston had to fight to keep from reaching out and pulling her to him then and there.

"Joey, my love, I'm really here. I know I haven't aged. It's part of why I left. I have loved you since the day we met. I have loved you, missed you and longed to be with you every second since I was forced to walk away."

"I don't understand," Joanne said.

"I know. I can explain if you will let me," Kingston said. Joanne sighed a vulnerable sound.

"Lily will be back, and I will not be able to talk to you then."

"Can you come with me now, before she gets back?" Joanne didn't think. She grabbed her things and got ready to move. Kingston took her hand and led her to his room. When they got to his room, it was lush and just as nice as the room she was staying in with Bill. Over the years, the black magic had given Kingston just as much wealth as Bill had acquired. He didn't really need it, but he had it, and it came in handy now that he was human again. Joanne was looking at him like someone who had won the lottery. Every desire she had ever had for him was brimming at the top of the pot, ready to boil over. Kingston wanted to make sure she was fully aware of everything before he started discussing it in details, so he handed her a cup of coffee and took her hand in his.

"Are you coherent?" he asked. She laughed.

"I doubt it. First, I'm seeing you, and you look so good, by the way. Better than all the times I imagined you in my mind. I doubt you're really here and telling me you didn't want to leave me, that you've loved me all of these years. You still love me. I mean who would believe that?"

"Believe it, Joey. Loving you was the best thing I ever did in my life."

"Loving you was the only thing I ever did right," she said, her voice cracking.

"I'm sure that's not true. You have Bailey and Amber. They both are great girls, by the way."

"Okay, now I know this is not real, because you wouldn't know them."

"But I do know them. That is part of what I have to explain to you. Bailey said she would help me if I could get you to come back to Los Angeles."

"I'm not going to be able to leave here. Bill will not let me go," Joanne said in a pathetic tone. Kingston didn't like how beaten Joanne had become. She had lost every ounce of her own identity. He knew it was because of him. He would not let her continue to live her life this way. The woman he loved would be set free from the burden of pretending to live. She would truly learn to live all over again, and he would walk with her every step of the way.

"I hate to tell you this, Joey, but when did you ever let someone tell you what to do?"

"A lot has changed since I saw you last," she said, her voice broken and defeated.

"That just means a lot is about to change for the better for you, Joey. You're no longer going to do things the way someone else wants it done. Your life means your choices."

Joanne couldn't believe she was about to walk away from Bill and go with Kingston. She couldn't go back to pretending anymore. She was going to leave Bill for good, no matter what it cost her and him. Maybe it would be best for them both. Either way, she had to find Bailey and see what all of these secrets were about. She still trusted Kingston, even though he had left her. She still loved him with every fiber of her being. So, she told Bill she was filing for divorce, and she got on a plane.

When Bailey called to check on things with Bien Faire, all seemed normal. Bien Faire had been staying with Elizabeth for a week, and nothing seemed out of place. She didn't understand any of this. She was relieved at the possibility that Elizabeth wasn't bad. Ashton and Bailey continued the regular route—going to classes and spending what free time they had together. Bailey had to go help out with Blake and Mark, but Ashton would come along. She was surprised at how well he interacted with the boys. Mary was filling in as nanny until Bailey could find a suitable replacement. Life seemed to be pulling itself out of the nightmare created by Elizabeth's return. Bailey would text Amber daily to make sure things were good. So far, it was nice to live a normal life. But, she was careful not to forget the calm before the storm.

Unlike Bailey, Amber didn't go to an all-girls school. She had fought hard to be at a school with boys. Joanne, her mother, had decided it wasn't worth the fight to make Amber go to an all-girls school, but she did force her to attend a prestigious academy that would give her a great education—and also offer her the company of boys.

On Amber's first day back at school, everyone was abuzz about the new kid. The girls were all going crazy trying to get his attention.

Caroline came up to Amber and said, "Have you seen him yet?"

"Seen who?" Amber asked

"The new guy," Caroline said, with a dreamy look on her face. "He is beautiful. I can't believe he is real. Everyone wants him!" Caroline exclaimed.

"Hmmm, sounds interesting. I'm sure Holly will get him before any of us have a chance," Amber laughed.

"I wouldn't be so sure, Amber. He doesn't seem to be interested in any of the girls here," Caroline said.

"Well, maybe he doesn't like girls. Maybe he would rather be with Brian," she laughed.

"That would be a waste," Caroline huffed.

"Have you seen Mathew around this morning? He sent me one letter this whole summer. I'm kind of pissed at him," Amber said.

"No, I haven't seen him. I heard he moved away over the summer to live with his dad."

"What?" Amber asked a little frustrated. "He never said anything in his letter." Amber's mind was wondering now, thinking about Mathew and the friendship that had developed over last year. She missed him a lot more than she wanted to admit.

"Besides, you have Eric now," Caroline said.

"Yeah, I hate to tell you, but that was over before it even got started. He texted me to say he couldn't do long distance. I'm so glad I didn't truly fall for him," Amber said.

When Amber and Caroline walked into History, the new kid was in their class. Caroline cleared her throat and looked in his direction. Amber's face flushed with heat. He was so beautiful. He had brown hair with some blond streaks. His eyes were gray- blue. He was tall. His skin was sun kissed perfectly. He was toned and ripped. He had major muscles underneath his clothes. Amber was truly wishing she had done something different with her hair today—not that it would make a difference. Guys like that always go for the Holly's of the world—blonde hair, blue eyes and big boobs. Amber sighed. This year was going to suck it. Having to see him and knowing he would never be hers was misery.

Caroline and Amber sat down and turned their history books to the pages dictated by the teacher. He was lecturing on the Civil War, and Amber was taking notes. She noticed from the corner of her eye that the new kid was watching her. She glanced over at him, and he smiled at her. Her heart leaped. *Was he smiling at me,* she thought. She looked around and noticed that no one else was looking at him, so she smiled back. Her stomach was churning, and she was really wishing she hadn't eaten that breakfast burrito Mary had forced on her this morning. *He's only being nice. I'm sure girls have been smiling at him all day. Try not to look like a retard,* she was thinking. She slowly turned away and continued writing in her notebook. When class was over, Caroline said, "I'm starving, can't wait till lunch. I'll meet you in the student lounge after math class."

"Okay," Amber said. She went to pick her books up off the desk, but they were gone. She looked up to see he was holding her books.

"He smiled and said, "Hi, Amber."

"Do I know you?" she asked

"Yes," he said, with the most adorable smirk on his face.

"What is your name?" she asked her voice unsure.

"James," he said.

"I don't know a James. How do you know my name?" she asked, her eyes narrowing on him.

"I would never forget you, Amber," he stated, and Amber's heart fluttered underneath her ribs.

"Can we sit together at lunch today?" he asked.

Amber was thinking, *Okay this is a truly weird day.* She shrugged.

"Yeah, if you don't mind Caroline," she said.

"Okay, if dealing with Caroline is the only way to spend time with you, then I guess I'll endure it," he laughed. "Caroline said she was meeting you in the student lounge. Is that right?" he asked.

"Yes, I sometimes sit outside with a friend, but I don't know where he is. Besides, we're really not supposed to sit out there," Amber said. James gave Amber a look that made her think he wanted to say something, but decided not to.

He gave Amber her books back and said, "I'll see you there." And he walked away. Amber didn't know why this guy wanted to talk to her, when every girl in her school wanted him. This was going to be a very interesting lunch. The next class dragged on and on. She was dying to get to lunch to see if she could figure out who this guy was. When class was over, she bee lined for the lounge. When she got to the lounge, Caroline was already there. She walked over, placed her stuff down and saved a seat beside her for James. Caroline noticed she saved a seat, but Amber was already gone to grab her lunch before she could ask who it was for. Amber returned to the table with a slice of pizza and a bottle of water.

Caroline raised one eyebrow and asked, "Who did you save the seat for?"

"A friend," Amber said in an I'd-rather-not-say tone. Before Caroline could push the subject, James walked into the lounge and every girl's head turned now focusing on James. He saw Amber and smiled. He proceeded to walk right past her. She thought,

Yeah so much for sitting with me. I knew it was not happening. She shrugged. She was wishing she was sitting outside with Mathew at the picnic table that became her haven last year. *Where the hell is Mathew,* she thought, frustrated? A minute later, James was back with a slice of pizza and a bottle of water.

"Amber, did you save me a seat?" James asked, with that smirk on his face again.

"Yeah," Amber said, as she removed her stuff from the seat beside her. Caroline's eyes narrowed on Amber.

"Amber, I didn't know you knew the new kid," she said. She introduced them.

"James, Caroline. Caroline, James."

"Hello, Caroline. It's nice to meet you," James said.

"It's nice to meet you, too," she said. Then, Caroline started in with twenty questions. Amber poked her in the ribs and whispered for her to stop asking him questions. Caroline did.

"Amber, did you have a good summer?" James asked.

"I did, other than a friend of mine decided not to tell me he was moving. How about you?" she asked. Caroline was bored now. She decided she would move to the next table over to talk to Jessica. Amber knew Caroline was a little jealous now, but she didn't care. She wanted to talk to James without others taking his attention away.

"Why do you think he didn't tell you?" James asked.

"I don't know. I thought...never mind. What about your summer?" she asked again.

"I had a great summer. I went to visit my dad in Colorado, and a lot of things changed for me this summer," James said.

"Like what?" Amber asked.

"Well, apparently my looks," he laughed.

"I don't understand," Amber said.

"Amber, I have been going to the same school now for two years and this is the first time ever that seemingly every girl in this room wants my attention," James said.

"Oh, well...I really am sorry. But I don't know a James," she said.

"I didn't say I always went by James. I decided I needed a change, and that included being called by a new name," James said.

Amber's eyes tightened in on James, taking in his face, trying to figure out who he was. She couldn't place him. He didn't look like any kind of guy she would have ever known. He was just too pretty. In fact, it made her a little jealous that he was prettier than her. At least, she thought he was.

"James is my middle name. If I told you my first name, you wouldn't see me in the same way," he said. "And I don't want that," he stated.

"Why is that?" Amber asked.

"I don't know. I believe anyone can change for the better. This summer, I focused on becoming a better person and, by doing that, the new me was born. I didn't want to come back with the old name that had represented me all my life. With my old name comes the stigma of me not being good enough for you, Amber," James said.

"What? Good enough for me," she said, shaking her head. "I'm nobody special. Why do you think you have to be good enough for me? You seem like a really nice guy. I'm sorry if your school life has been crappy. I get it, sometimes peer pressure sucks," Amber said.

"Sometime peer pressure does suck, and sometimes you find someone who doesn't care so much about what others think. A person who puts herself out there to take the heat off of someone else. A person with a truly good heart. I never thanked you for that day on the bus or the first day Holly saw you eating lunch with me. I do thank you," James said.

"Day on the bus…lunch? What?" Then she realized what no one else knew—the new hot guy was Mathew, the one everyone thought was a loser, but she didn't. He liked her for her. She could tell he was nervous that this information would change the way she had been looking at him five minutes ago, but it did not. She believed everyone had the ability to change, to reinvent themselves, so she looked at him and said, "You're welcome, James." She smiled at him. He smiled back and took her hand. Every girl in the room froze, staring in utter jealousy. *This year was not going to suck it after all*, she thought.

Chapter Twenty-Three

When Kingston and Joanne arrived at Bailey's loft, all was quiet. Kingston assumed Bailey and Ashton were in class, so he decided to take Joanne around the corner to their park, the place where it had all started. The place…they fell in love. There was a light breeze that made the trees sway like they were dancing to the beat of an unknown song. The flowers blossomed, reaching up toward the sky as if they were trying to kiss the sun. Children were running carefree, and laughter spilled over from their lips. They strolled through the park for hours just holding hands. Joanne didn't realize how much of herself she had been holding back. A better definition would be how much of herself she had locked away in a sunken chest—a chest so deeply buried in sand that each time you tried to dig it out, more sand covered it, causing it to sink deeper into the earth.

Joanne hadn't truly smiled in nineteen years. She raised her face to the sky, letting the sun shine upon her. Kingston took in two short breaths, like the sight of her was taking the very breath from his lungs. He could no longer resist her. He reached down, cupping her face with his hand. Gently, he positioned her face within inches of his own. Once their lips met, time stood still. In Joanne's mind, she was a girl again—the girl who had loved Kingston with all she had, the girl who wanted to give back to the world and not take from it, the girl who had aspirations to make a difference, the girl who was truly a force to be reckoned with. Joanne didn't pull away. She clung to him like he was the blood that kept her heart beating.

Ashton and Bailey had just gotten out of class when they decided to take a stroll in the park before heading back to the loft. The day was just too beautiful to hide away inside. Everyone dreamed of living in California because ninety percent of the time the weather was perfect. When they got halfway across the path, Bailey stopped, staring in absolute disbelief.

"Bailey, what's wrong?" Ashton asked, suddenly concerned.

"Nothing, really. I'm just a little shocked. My mom…" she hesitated, "is making out with Kingston over there," she said, pointing in their direction.

"Oh, well this should be interesting," he said.

Bailey scowled at Ashton and said, "Indeed it should."

They walked over and stood in front of Joanne and Kingston. They stood there for a few minutes before Ashton finally cleared his throat to get their attention. Bailey was just trying to figure out who this woman was. Her mother wouldn't even kiss Bill in front of her or Amber. At that moment, she was making out with Kingston in a public park in broad daylight.

Bailey thought, *who is this woman and what did she do with my mother?* Ashton chuckled in response to her thoughts. Kingston and Joanne both looked in Ashton's direction. Joanne's face flushed a shade of red. Kingston took Joanne's hand, holding it with the utmost care. Bailey and Joanne looked into each other's eyes as if they were strangers.

"Hi," Kingston said, "I convinced Joey to come to Los Angeles, so we could explain."

"Oh well, I guess that's good," Bailey said, her voice a little icy.

"Maybe we should continue this discussion back at the loft," Ashton said.

"I agree," Bailey and Kingston said at the same time. Kingston stood and gently helped Joanne from her seat. He guided her toward the direction of the loft. Bailey was lost in thought. She had never seen her mother look so…different. She finally figured out that for the first time in her entire life, her mother looked happy. She looked alive. Bailey thought it sad that she didn't know her mother, that her mother had chosen to lock herself away and conceal not only her life from her children, but also who she truly was. Bailey was trying to find some form of sympathy for her mother, but her mistrust of her mother wouldn't allow her to hope. When they made it back to the loft, Ashton walked everyone into the living room.

"Can I get you both something to drink?" Ashton asked.

"Tea would be great," Kingston replied.

"Tea for me as well," Joanne said.

"I'm good, honey," Bailey said. Joanne eyed Ashton with a sudden understanding of who he was to Bailey. *I wonder how long they have been living together*, Joanne thought. "*I wonder if he comes from a good family. He looks really good. He looks like a movie star or something. Well, this is L.A. I wouldn't doubt her finding love with an actor, just great.* Bailey was hearing her thoughts and getting more agitated by the second.

"Kingston, I think it best if you explain everything to her," Bailey said. Kingston frowned.

"Okay, Bailey."

"Joey, when we met over nineteen years ago, I was…" he paused, looking at Bailey with pleading in his eyes. "I don't know how to explain this to you," Kingston said.

"Joanne," Bailey said.

"Yes, Bailey."

"The world is different than what we believe it to be. There are things that exist that people perceive as fantasy…" Bailey paused, "or fairytale, but these things are indeed real. Kingston was once a powerful wizard. He was born with magic. That is why he has not aged. A lot has happened over the past month, but he is no longer a wizard, and he will start to age and grow old just like any other human," Bailey said. Joanne's face twisted with confusion.

"Is this a joke? I mean, how long have you been plotting this revenge on me, Bailey? How did you even find out about Kingston? Where did you find this…ACTOR?" She snapped.

"What? You think I'm trying to seek revenge for my crappy upbringing. Please, I have far bigger fish to fry than a mother who doesn't love her children and a father who didn't have to love me but should have at the very least loved his own biological daughter," Bailey snapped back.

"How dare you. We have given you everything you could have ever wanted," Joanne spat back.

"Really? How could you know what I want? You have never been in the room with me longer than twenty minutes at a time," Bailey said. At this point, Bailey and Joanne both were fuming. Bailey then started to read Joanne's thoughts, and her heart softened a little towards her mother. *How could I love you? You have his eyes, his hair. You are the spitting image of your father, the only man I have ever loved. It hurt to be around you. I wanted to be your mother. I wanted to be the best mother to you and Amber, but I couldn't. I gave my heart to Kingston, and when he walked away, he took it with him.* Joanne's eyes were filled with tears and pain.

"Why are you thinking about wanting to be a good mother to me? Why don't you say the words out loud instead of thinking them and keeping it to yourself? Maybe we both could heal and move on," Bailey said.

"What? How do you know what I am thinking?" Joanne asked. Bailey rolled her eyes.

"My father was a wizard. I was born with powers. In order to save my life, Kingston transferred all of his powers over to me a little over a month ago," Bailey said.

Joanne's eyes narrowed on Kingston.

"Kingston, you were a wizard?" Joanne asked.

"Yes, I wanted to tell you. There was a witch who helped transform me back over 800 years ago. She would have killed us all if she found out I was in love. She would have grown very powerful from the pain both of your deaths would have caused me. I had to walk away, so you both could live," Kingston said, sorrow seeping through his masculine facade.

"Okay, what exactly does this mean for Bailey?" Joanne asked.

"It means I have powers now. It means I will not age the same as you. It means I have responsibilities now beyond your comprehension," Bailey said, her tone even.

"What do you mean *responsibilities*?" Joanne asked.

"It's better if you don't know. I only agreed to this for Kingston. He truly loves you. I would know, I can read his thoughts, even the ones he tries so desperately to hide. You both were meant for each other. I'm sorry your life didn't turn out the way you wanted. I guess that's my fault. It's possible you both would have been able to be together if it were not for me."

"Bailey, don't think that for a minute. I'm sorry, too. I wanted so desperately to be your mother, but I had nothing left to give," Joanne said, tears rolling down her face. She wiped the tears away and continued, "It was selfish of me not to try and be a mother to you and Amber. Basically, I have to admit, I have been dead inside since the day Kingston left." She paused for a minute, as if putting her thoughts together, "I grew accustomed to pretending." Joanne smiled a clearly-fake smile, "It was my life. All I had to do was get up every day and pretend. I pretended to love a man that has resented me for the past nineteen years. I pretended that I was normal. My life's focus was being the socialite Bill wanted me to be. My world was made up of nothing but superficial filler. This filler kept me busy and my thoughts away from why I hated every part of who I had become. I was afraid to walk away. She hesitated, with a look of despair flashing across her face. "You see, if I had walked away, I knew I wouldn't have to pretend anymore. The thought of reality being able to seek its way back into my life was, in my eyes, appalling."

"Why?" Bailey asked.

"It would have been a living nightmare to wake up each day, knowing part of my soul was lost and would never return," Joanne said. Kingston took in two short breaths, filled with the miserable realization of the hell he had put her through. Joanne touched his face and smiled. Bailey was trying to take in every word. She couldn't believe her mother was laying everything out on the table. It was like opening a closed book reading it, finally understanding the world hidden within its folds.

Joanne turned back to Bailey and continued speaking, "I had to keep doing the same things in order to merely exist. Staying away from you and Amber was a given. You look so much like…Kingston, it pained me to be in the same room with you, Bailey. I'm…sorry. I was the adult. I should have pushed my feelings aside and loved you for the beautiful, smart, funny, strong-willed girl that you are, but I didn't. Instead, I used Bill's business to push myself to stay away. Of course, I would have been able to see Amber more, but I knew that would raise questions as to why I was avoiding...you. If I was just a negligent mother all the way around, it would cause no one to take a closer look—a look that would show I was just a shell of the girl I had been." Bailey's eyes suddenly softened.

"I can only offer you three words—I forgive you," Bailey said.

"What?" Joanne was crying and unable to comprehend how Bailey could forgive her.

"We all make choices in our lives, some we are proud of, others not so much. I can't blame you anymore for not being a good mother. I can understand what it's like to think you've lost your soul mate. I can't begin to imagine what that would have been like long term. If I were in your shoes and this happened to me, I can't say I wouldn't have done the same thing. It had to be a never-ending nightmare. The good news is, now you can move forward together," Bailey said.

Joanne was wondering how Bailey ended up being such a wonderful person. She guessed Mary had made the difference. She knew it wasn't her. For a second, she thought Bailey had inherited some of her traits, and she realized Bailey was the girl she had been before Kingston had walked out the door. This fact gave Joanne great comfort. She had not helped raise Bailey, but Bailey was truly part of her.

They both hugged and were able to walk away with a better understanding of who the other person really was. Ashton and Bailey made dinner together. Tonight was grill night. Ashton still enjoyed his meat practically raw. Well, it was cooked on the outside, but still pretty red on the inside. Bailey had grown so used to this that it didn't faze her anymore. She too had a small steak, but she required that hers be fully cooked. She had made baked sweet potatoes and a dinner salad. They decided it was just too nice outside to eat dinner inside the loft, so they sat on the balcony, watching the sun go down as they ate.

Bailey really loved the loft. It was as if she were meant to exist there. The neighborhood was hip and eclectic. Bailey liked that it was such a happening neighborhood. There was always something going on—art shows, coffee house poetry readings, or someone selling handmade art on the street corner. It seemed every inch of this district held part of her creative soul. It was the first time Bailey felt like she belonged somewhere. She felt at home, and she was looking forward to what the next four years would bring. That is, before Elizabeth stepped out of her grave and back into the world of the living.

Ashton and Bailey were trying to keep their distance with Elizabeth. Bailey watched Ashton's face closely whenever she mentioned Elizabeth. She would also listen to his thoughts as much as possible. She didn't want to pry, but a part of her was still afraid he loved Elizabeth. Ashton had shown no signs of thinking about her, other than when Bailey brought her up. This put her mind somewhat at ease. She knew she was overreacting, but jealousy will make one not only do strange things, but also have strange thoughts. She worked hard to keep herself in check, not letting reality bleed into non-reality.

It had been over a month since Amber and James had started hanging out. Amber didn't want to admit that she was having major feelings for James. They spent a great deal of time together, but she tried to keep it on the friend level. Caroline drove her crazy asking her why she wouldn't make a move to let James know she was interested. She didn't know why she didn't make a move. First of all, she didn't know how to make a move. Second, part of her was scared because James had become a really good friend to her. Amber didn't want that line crossed in a way that couldn't be undone. If something went wrong on the romantic side of the line, it would destroy their friendship.

She decided she would push the crazy feelings she was experiencing for James aside. If he had been interested in her as more than friends, he would have already made a move.

Amber was in the locker room getting dressed after cheerleading practice. Amber was popular, but she was one of the popular girls who wouldn't hurt people in order to move up the social ladder in high school. She knew life would eventually move beyond the walls here on campus. Amber chose to see people for people, not for the artificial façade the popular girls displayed. As she made her way from the locker room, to her surprise James was waiting. He had an unusual expression on his face, and she wondered what was wrong.

"Hey," James said.

"Hi, what are you doing here?" Amber asked.

"I came here for you."

"Uh." James chuckled in amusement.

"I wanted to talk to you. If that is okay."

"Okay, it's cool. What's up?" Amber asked.

"Can we go grab something to eat? We can talk then," he said.

"Sounds good. I'm starving. I should have known to eat more lunch today with Mrs. Bonds now in charge of the cheerleaders. She pushes us to the verge of blacking out before she lets up on the exercise end of being a cheerleader." James thought this was funny for some reason, and he laughed again.

"Exercise is always a good thing. Keeps your heart going. We definitely want to keep that working right," James said. Amber was a little aggravated by that remark.

"You don't do any form of exercise, but you're telling me I need to exercise? Nice. That is just another way of saying you think I'm fat." James frowned.

"Not true. Man, you really do get grouchy when you're hungry."

"Shut up! I need a milkshake," Amber said.

Amber hopped into James' car, and they headed for their usual hangout spot—a diner with excellent burgers and shakes. The diner made milk shakes so thick you could turn your cup upside down and the shake would remain inside the cup. The diner was known for their burgers, too. Amber was not one of those girls who didn't eat. She ate whatever she wanted, but it was all about quantity control. If she ate a hamburger, fries and a milkshake tonight, that would mean salad for the next two nights. It was worth it sometimes to splurge and have really yummy, but fatty, foods. They sat down in the usual booth and ordered.

Amber got a cheeseburger, fries and strawberry milkshake. James got the same, except he wanted a chocolate shake. The diner had been built in the early 60's and, over the years, it had run down. About ten years ago, two brothers purchased it and refurbished it back to its golden day state. Ever since then, it had been a happening spot for local teens. It had the traditional red vinyl booths, along with a soda shop counter where you could sit and eat. It had a huge jukebox that had been restored and played not only oldies, but also an array of modern day alternative music. It was just an overall cool hangout for kids. James smiled at Amber for a minute. It was nervous smile. Amber thought he looked indecisive, like he was trying to decide whether to say something or not. She was getting so annoyed that she finally looked at him and said, "Spit it out already."

"What?" James asked.

"Whatever it is. You know you can tell me," Amber said. He opened his mouth to speak but hesitated again, closing his mouth tightly. James felt so uncomfortable in that moment that his face flushed. Amber's eyes narrowed on him.

"Is it that bad?" Amber asked.

"Depends," he said.

"Depends on what?"

"How you react."

"Okay, for me to react I have to know what it is," Amber said.

"Caroline asked me out," he blurted. Amber's face flushed with jealousy. She was mad. How could Caroline do this to her? Did he want to date Caroline? James watched Amber as her face grew more frustrated with each second that passed. He thought that maybe it flashed with jealousy for a second or two, but he couldn't be sure.

"Okay." Amber paused before blurting. Do you want to date Caroline?" Amber asked anger fully visible on her face now.

"No."

"Are you afraid to tell her no?"

"No, I already did," James said, with a knowing look on his face. "Caroline said she only asked me out, so you would wake up and see we were meant to be together," James said. Amber's face froze in surprise. She didn't know what to say. She decided to push it back on him.

"How did you respond to that?" she asked. James' face showed a glorious smile.

"I told her that I agree," he said, clearly happy that he had finally had the courage to speak it aloud.

"What? You think we should date?" Amber asked.

"Oh, I think we should do more than that," he teased.

"Funny," she said.

"I'm serious. It has taken me this long to get the nerve up to ask you. I want nothing more in this world than to be your boyfriend." Amber's entire body flashed with heat, and she decided that sometimes you have to take a leap of faith in order to truly live. She was jumping feet first, but she was going to jump.

"Ground rules then." He laughed so hard that his eyes watered.

"There are ground rules to dating you?" he asked.

"Of course. Hello, do you think I'm stupid? Everything that is worth anything has rules."

"Okay, what are your rules of engagement?" Amber rolled her eyes.

"If we do this...and things don't work out..." Amber hesitated. "I don't want to lose you as a friend." James thought about it for a minute and then answered.

"Deal," he said, still smiling cunningly. Amber couldn't help but smile, too. James looked like a guilty cat holding a bird between his teeth. When they left the diner and were walking to the car, James took Amber's hand.

Chapter Twenty-Four

When Bien Faire awoke, she found herself locked inside a steel cage located in the dungeon. Faeries are weakened, and sometimes destroyed, by being close to steel, much less being surrounded by it. It could also burn them if they touched it. Bien Faire was lying on a bed. The cage had been set up to allow her to live there forever, if her captor intended her to. It was the largest cage in the dungeon. It had a chair with a lamp sitting on a side table. The bed was a twin with green bedding. The room also had a small sink, shower and toilet. Bien Faire noticed a pile of clothes lying on the chair, along with a pair of shoes. Bien Faire had taken human form while staying with Elizabeth, and she would need to keep every part of herself covered in order to keep the steel away from her skin. Bien Faire didn't know how long she would be able to maintain the glamour of being human while inside the steel cage. If she stayed there very long, it would be her tomb.

Bien Faire was trapped within the cage, and her magic was useless. She didn't know what was happening. She remembered wanting to hurt Bailey. She found the courage within herself to overcome that desire, but it drained her of all powers, causing her to pass out. Now she was under the control of Elizabeth. For the first time in Bien Faire's existence, she was alarmed as to what Elizabeth was going to do with her. Elizabeth could use Bien Faire to destroy the world, if she knew how. Bien Faire was trying to figure out how she could prevent this from happening. Bien Faire decided she would use Plan B as her last option. Plan A was to figure out Elizabeth's plan and stop it. She was thinking about every angle of evil that could come at her, when Elizabeth walked into the dungeon.

"I see you're awake," Elizabeth hissed.

"Yes. Why am I in here, Elizabeth?" Bien Faire asked in an even tone.

"You rallied against me with Bailey in order to take Ashton from me."

"That is not true."

"Yes, it is," Elizabeth shrieked. "But I have better plans than to sit here and agonize over Ashton. He took my first life away. He will not take my second."

"Perfidia took your life from you, not Ashton." Elizabeth glared at Bien Faire, and she reached through the cage bars with a steel prod and touched Bien Faire's arm, causing it to burn. Bien Faire screamed.

"I have the power now. You will do as I say, or you will die." Elizabeth then prodded her again with the steel, and Bien Faire shrieked in horror. She looked into Elizabeth's eyes and they were hollow, as if nothing existed behind them. Elizabeth's eyes had turned black as coal, and they appeared to be filled with evil. She watched as Elizabeth walked over and pulled a very large book from underneath a hidden nook. The book itself was terrifying. It was made from human skin. The front of the book looked like the torso of a child, the grooves for each rib clearly visible. Bien Faire couldn't tell if it was a male or female. There was a lock on the front that had another hand that linked around front, the back like the hand was holding the book. The thumb and first finger were made to lock into one another holding the book tightly shut. The binding was made of ten little hands—children's hands—each a different shade of human. Elizabeth said three words that Bien Faire couldn't understand, and then the first finger released its hold.

Elizabeth opened the book and scanned it for a spell. She started gathering up potions from Perfidia's mass collection and throwing them into the large black caldron. When she was finished, she walked over to Bien Faire and said, "In twenty-four hours, you will be binded to me for all of eternity. Every task I command of you will come to pass. You will not be able to deny me anything, including transferring all of your powers to me." Elizabeth glowered an evil glare and laughed a wicked snicker.

"Elizabeth, don't do this. You are better than this. You can live a happy life here."

"You don't know what I'm capable of," Elizabeth hissed. "I am not Elizabeth anymore. I am something different now. Whatever brought me back didn't bring every part of me. I think it only brought my body. My insides seem to radiate death. It's a darkness that is sometimes suffocating, and can cause me to age. In order to keep it at bay, I must focus on drawing other life forms' spirits into mine. At first, I thought I only needed to be around Ashton. He seemed to keep it away, but he decided he didn't love me," she said, her voice pained. "He loves her... Bailey." She said her name like it was a disease. "She will pay the price for his betrayal. He will watch as I slowly kill her, and he will suffer just as I have suffered for his lack of love," Elizabeth snapped. "As I slowly pull the very life from her body, I will laugh with joy at the torment this will cause Ashton."

"Elizabeth, we can help you. We can try to remove the death from you, or at least free your mind from it. Release me, and I will do everything to help you." Elizabeth's death eyes narrowed on Bien Faire, and chills shot through her entire being.

"The only way you're leaving here is by death. Don't think you have any power to sway me. I have no heart, no soul, no emotions whatsoever. I feel nothing but death. I can make that happen for you... death, I mean...after I take away your powers, if you like. It will more than likely end that way. I do not get attached. After I'm done using you, you will die."

Bien Faire was overwhelmed. Deep down, she thought it might come to Plan B, and she was not looking forward to it. She had noticed the metal shavings in the corner when she first woke up. It must have been from the previous prisoner trying to slowly break free from the bars. When Elizabeth left the room, Bien Faire gathered up the metal bits, and they burned her hands. She knew doing what she was about to do meant Bailey was the only one left to rule over the light and make sure good triumphed over evil. She had lived millenniums, and now her fight against evil meant ending her own existence.

Bien Faire went to the bathroom sink and got a glass of water. She picked up the pile of tiny metal shards, flinching away from the scorching pain burning her hand. She then placed them in her mouth and chugged back the water to wash them down her throat. The burn was searing her throat so bad that she grabbed the sink basin to keep herself from thrashing about. She didn't want Elizabeth coming down to check on her. She needed time for the metal to kill her. She feared Elizabeth would try to retrieve the shards from her core and heal her with some spell from Perfidia's book. The metal bits needed to be inside her for at least fifteen hours to poison her system.

For Bien Faire, it would mean dying a very slow, painful death. The pain was like having hot bits of lava slowly burning her away from the inside out. It was utter torture. She tried to keep from crying out in pain, so she dragged herself to the bed and bit down on the corner of her pillow, trying to stifle the sounds demanding to escape from her lips. All she wanted to do was leave this world in her natural form. She feared that Elizabeth would know what she was doing, so she would have to leave this world in a disguise—her human disguise.

Bailey had a strange wave of unrecognizable fear wash through her. She knew something was wrong, but didn't know what. She picked up the phone to call Kingston to see if he was back at his house and to check on any updates with how Elizabeth was adjusting to her new life. Kingston picked up the phone on the second ring.

"Hi, Bailey," he said.

"Hi. Are you back at Perfidia's house?"

"No, your mom and I are staying at the beach house."

"Oh, okay. I was just checking. I have tried to call there, but no one answers."

"Bien Faire is probably showing her the area."

"Do you think Ashton and I should go and check on them?"

"If you call back and can't get them by tomorrow, I will go check on them," Kingston said.

"Something just doesn't feel right," Bailey said.

"Do you want me to go check today?" Kingston asked.

"That would be great. Call me as soon as you get there."

"Okay, Bailey. I will." They both hung up the phone. Bailey had to get to class. Ashton was already at class. He took an early morning surfing class. Bailey loved how he had taken to living in Los Angeles. It was like he was destined to live there. She went to class with mixed emotions. Part of her wondered if she shouldn't skip class for once and go check on Bien Faire and Elizabeth, but she just hated having to see Elizabeth. She decided Kingston would call if he needed her.

School was closed at lunch for teacher conferences, so Amber and James decided to hang out at the beach. He took her to his favorite surfing spot. It was a short distance up the Pacific Coast Highway, and Amber was excited to be spending the afternoon with him. They had now been dating for two weeks, and life seemed perfect. James did a complete 180. He was now in advanced classes with Amber. He also had his own alternative rock band. They had even gotten some gigs at some of the eighteen-and-under clubs. When they got there, Amber slipped off her shorts and t-shirt to reveal a two-piece bikini. James' eyes widened with excitement. Amber laughed.

"Don't get any ideas," she said.

"Too late for that," he said.

"Remember, we are here so you can teach me to surf." A frown crossed James' features.

"Are you sure that's why we're here?"

"Well, to hang out, too."

"How about I teach you to surf, and you teach me to kiss?" Amber rolled her eyes.

"I know you can already do that. You have already taught me a thing or two," she said. His face shined with delight.

"I'll be happy to teach you a lot more if you like," he said.

"Learning to surf will be fine for today."

James made a low grumble and said, "Fine, take all the fun away." Amber laughed.

"Boys are so predictable. They only have one thing on their mind," Amber huffed. James didn't seem to like this remark, so he picked Amber up and ran to the water, throwing her in.

"Would you still say I'm predictable?" he asked.

"I would say you're a jerk. This water is freezing."

"Oh, don't be such a baby," James said.

"Baby? I'm not a baby," Amber said, with a sour look on her face. James jumped in the water and tried to catch Amber, but she swam away faster than a fish.

"Okay, I give. You're not a baby. Will you please come back?" he asked.

"If you're truly sorry I will." James' eyes tightened. He didn't want to say he was sorry. After all, she was the one that said boys were predictable, but he didn't want to end the day bad.

"Fine, I'm truly sorry," he said. Amber swam over to him. When she reached him, she wrapped her arms around him and kissed him.

"Remind me to make you mad more often, so I have to say I'm sorry," he laughed.

Amber rolled her eyes.

"Okay, teach me to surf."

"It's better to start out on land, so you can get a feel for the board."

"You're the teacher," Amber said, swimming toward the shore. They spent the next hour going over the best ways to stand up on the board. They finally made it into the water, and Amber was a natural. She was surfing like she had surfed her entire life. James really liked how athletic she was. He was really impressed. She surfed better than he did, and he had been surfing for three years.

When they were finally tired of surfing, they made their way back to James' Jeep. James loaded up the surf boards. He pulled a picnic basket out of the back, along with a blanket. He then started a fire. They sat around the beach fire and ate. When they were done, they both lay back onto the blanket and looked at the stars. James reached out and held Amber's hand. The day had been perfect. Amber was so glad she had taken the jump from friendship to something more. James reached over and looked into Amber's eyes.

"Thanks for such a fun day," he said.

"Thank you for teaching me to surf," she said.

"You surf better than I do now," he said. Amber blushed.

"Thanks." She reached over and kissed him softly on the lips. They lost track of time as they laid there kissing each other.

Chapter Twenty-Five

When Kingston arrived at the house, all was quiet. He unlocked the door with his key and took Joanne by the hand. He didn't want to bring her along, but she insisted she was never going to let him out of her sight again. He was glad that the main level of the house looked like any other. The kitchen had every modern-day technology—stainless steel gas stove, dishwasher and refrigerator. The kitchen was very large, and the living room was just off the kitchen, so everything connected into one big open space.

The living room was furnished with a very nice sofa and two custom made chairs. The chairs had a table and lamp sitting in between. A cushioned coffee table-ottoman combo was in the center, bringing harmony to each piece. The sunroom was to the left of the living room. It had a jungle feel to it. One would think a tiger could pounce at any moment when sitting in the sunroom.

The dining room had a beautiful crystal chandelier that looked like it was over a hundred years old, but it was in perfect condition. The dining room table could seat twelve. It was larger than any Joanne had seen. Joanne could tell the house was furnished with antiques. Some of the items had to be centuries old.

The outside of the house was beautiful, too. She had not expected it to be so up to date. The outside looked like it needed minor repairs so she had assumed the inside would also need repairs. Perfidia had always taken pride in keeping up her image. She was actually able to glamour herself and be friends with a few of the neighbors. It was all part of her plan to fit in and not bring too much attention to herself. Once a year, she would throw a huge party. She would use this time to see if she wanted some new play toys. If she took notice of someone at one of her parties, they would become her human minion within a week, or she would turn them into a vampire. It was amazing that no one was ever suspicious, considering at least one person in the neighborhood would move away within three days after the party. They moved because they were turned into a vampire and had to. She would usually pick single people, so families wouldn't file a missing person report.

Joanne was scanning her surroundings with a feeling of wonder. Kingston didn't like how quiet everything was. He knew this time of day Bien Faire and Elizabeth should be at home. It was about that time that Elizabeth came walking up from the dungeon. Her eyes narrowed on Joanne. Kingston didn't like the look on her face. It was a look of evil. He had seen that look before, but this time was different. This time the death glare behind the evil horrified Kingston. He grabbed Joanne, trying to leave, when Elizabeth spoke.

"Don't leave. Let's…play."

"I just wanted to show Joanne the house, but we need to be getting back," Kingston said.

"I don't think you will be going anywhere today," Elizabeth said. Kingston lunged for Elizabeth and yelled at Joanne. "Joey, run! Get Bailey!" Elizabeth darted out of the way before Kingston could take hold of her. He knew her movements were unnaturally fast. He was trying to see every angle, hoping for a way out. If he couldn't escape, Joey had to.

"Are you trying to ruin my fun, Kingston?" Elizabeth asked. "I'm afraid you and Joey will not be going anywhere today."

"She has nothing to do with this. Let her leave. She can just go home," he pleaded.

Joanne spoke then, "I'm not leaving you again!" Her tone was harsh.

"See, it's settled then." Elizabeth started speaking a spell, and

Kingston screamed in rage. He was human now, so he could be changed into a vampire, and so could Joey. He threw Elizabeth across the room. When she stood up, she aimed her torture at Joey. The feeling of being buried alive and slowly suffocating started to seep through every pore of Joey's skin. She started to scream but couldn't, for she didn't have the oxygen to do so. Her eyes glazed over, and her face was frozen in terror.

"You're Bailey's mother, right?" Elizabeth asked. "Well, you'll regret the day she was ever born."

" *Vomica cruor...*"

"Elizabeth, please take me instead! I will do anything if you let Joey go," Kingston begged.

"You'll still do anything I say, for you have no powers to stop me." Kingston sprang for Elizabeth, but before he could take hold of her, she had him in the death stare, his life draining from his body. Kingston began to age and Elizabeth grew more beautiful. He looked to be the same age as Joey now, so Elizabeth released him, and he fell to the floor. Elizabeth glared at Joey and spoke the spell that would transform her into a vampire.

"*Vomica cruor phantom ex lux lucis, vas of obscurum, forever a lamia.*" Then Joey collapsed. Kingston screamed and, while he looked at Joey's broken body on the floor, his mind went back nineteen years ago when Joey's broken body lay on the floor, along with his heart, as he walked out the door—that pain too was caused by a witch. The rage bubbled up inside him like lava ready to spill from a volcano.

He grabbed Elizabeth this time before she could move. He twisted her neck until he heard it break, and every bone in her spine crunched as if they were crushed. Then he dropped her to the floor. Her body hit the ground with a loud clump of broken bones. It rattled like broken pieces of glass in a jar. He thought if she was dead the curse would be broken. He ran to Joey and held her in his arms. He picked up his cell phone and dialed Bailey's number. Bailey didn't answer the phone as quickly as she normally did.

"Hey," Bailey said.

"Bailey...I need you! My Joey!" he wailed. All she could hear now was his heavy breathing and cries.

"Kingston, what's wrong?"

"Help me, Bailey. I can't go through this. Please! I should have just left her alone," he said.

"Are you at Perfidia's?"

"Yes," he said. Then the phone went dead. Bailey tried to call Kingston back, but no one answered. She dialed Ashton's number next. He picked up on the first right.

"Hey, love. How was your day?" he asked.

"Not good. Something is wrong at Kingston's," she said. "I think Elizabeth has done something to my mother. We need to get there fast! Can you meet me there?" Panic filled Bailey's voice.

"Yes, Bailey. Do not go inside without me!" he pleaded.

"Okay, just hurry!" As Bailey pulled out from her parking deck, Amber was a few cars back coming to visit. Amber reached down to pick up her cell phone to call Bailey, but noticed her battery was dead. She decided she would follow Bailey, and maybe they could hang out together. Amber had meant to call before coming but forgot. Besides, a sister is supposed to be able to drop in without being announced. Amber followed Bailey for about fifteen miles. She was wondering where Bailey was going.

When Bailey pulled into Kingston's driveway, the house that had only had an aura of darkness before was now totally consumed by darkness. She knew no one else would be able to see it. To Bailey, it looked like a storm cloud had rolled in and wrapped itself around the house, keeping it protected from intruders and sending out a message of power to anyone who happened to see it. Within a few minutes, Amber was pulling up behind her. Ashton pulled up two seconds after Amber did. Bailey, Ashton and Amber got out of their cars and approached one another.

"Hey guys. Who lives here?" Amber asked.

"A friend of mine," Ashton said.

"Oh," Amber said.

"Amber, why are you here?" Bailey asked.

"What? A girl can't see her sister?" she asked.

"No…I mean…how did you know where this place was?" Bailey asked.

"I followed you. Duh…I was coming to visit, and I saw you leaving the loft. I tried to call, but my cell phone battery is dead," Amber said.

"Okay, I need you to leave," Bailey said.

"No way. Besides, I could never find my way back to the main freeway from here."

"Amber, this is not a game. I need for you to trust me and leave." Amber looked into her sister's eyes and knew she was hiding something from her. She knew Bailey was hiding something very important, and it irked her that she didn't trust her enough to tell her what it was. Amber was mad now, so she decided she would pretend to leave.

"Okay, I guess I'll try and find my way out of here," Amber said.

"Good. Once you get out of the neighborhood, go left at the red-light and that should take you back to the freeway," Bailey said.

"Got it," Amber said. Bailey could read human and non-human thoughts, but for some reason she had never been able to read Amber's. Her thoughts were all jumbled together like a heavy metal rock video, so Bailey didn't realize Amber planned to stay behind and follow them inside.

When Bailey heard the phone go dead, it was because Kingston ended the call by accident. He was in shock, watching a very disfigured Elizabeth pull herself up from the floor and twist and turn her body to get everything back in the right position. Kingston could hear each vertebrae slowly popping back into place. The sound was so unnatural that Kingston shivered. He then watched as Elizabeth eyed him with such fury that he knew he was going to die. Instead, she started torturing him. He felt the suffocating feeling of death overwhelm him, and he thought for a minute that maybe he would prefer dying to the feeling of being consumed by death while still alive. Kingston gasped for air, and then his eyes glazed over with terror.

Bailey and Ashton waited for Amber to drive away before they approached the front door. When they got to the door, it was cracked, so Ashton stepped inside first. He made sure to check every available space for trouble. It was at a time like this that he missed being a vampire. He missed the strength. As a vampire, his eyes missed nothing. As a human, they missed things and this concerned him. He also had excellent hearing and that too was gone. He wouldn't trade being human for his soul though. He loved being human again. He loved the emotions of truly feeling every part of being in love with Bailey. When they reached the living room, they found Kingston and Joanne both lying on the floor lifeless. Bailey was frantic. She ran to her mother first and checked her heart. Bailey heard her mother's heartbeat, but realized it was faint. She checked Kingston next, and his was beating wildly. Suddenly, he opened his eyes and flung Bailey across the room. Ashton ran to her. She was a little dazed, but okay. Kingston realized it was Bailey then.

"I'm sorry. I thought you were...Elizabeth," Kingston said menacingly.

"What happened here?" Ashton asked. Bailey was still trying to gain her composure. Bailey shook her head from side to side, trying to dislodge the swimming in her head.

"Elizabeth..." he hesitated, "cursed Joey." Kingston was barely audible when he said it. Bailey snapped out of it then.

"Cursed her how?" Bailey asked. Kingston locked his eyes on Joey and then looked back at Bailey.

"Bailey, she turned her into a vampire. She will become a vampire in three days. There is no way to stop it." Amber gasped out loud then, and Bailey turned to see her sister right before she fainted. Bailey went to check on Amber. She appeared to be fine, but she was so pissed at her for not going home. Bailey realized the meaning of her entire existence was in this room. Fear shot through Bailey.

"Where is Elizabeth?" Bailey asked.

"I don't know," Kingston said. "She tortured me, and I passed out."

"When she dies, the curse will be broken. She has to die now," Bailey said.

"Bailey, she is nothing like Perfidia. Elizabeth is a mixture of evil and death. She is here for revenge, and she is not going down easy...if at all," Kingston said.

"Where is Bien Faire?" Bailey asked.

"I haven't seen her," Kingston said.

"She could be dead. But I would check the dungeon first to see if she is there," Kingston said.

"Okay. Ashton, I need you to stay with Amber and my mother. I will go and see if Bien Faire is still here somewhere."

"Bailey, I don't want you to go alone."

"I'll go with her," Kingston said. Ashton nodded. Bailey and Kingston starting walking toward the doorway that led to the dungeon. As soon as the door was opened, a smell so strong hit their nostrils that Bailey turned and threw up. It was a scent like nothing she had ever encountered, and she didn't know what awaited them at the end of the stairwell.

From halfway down the stairwell, she spotted Bien Faire lying on a bed within a steel cage. She ran to her and yelled to wake her, but she didn't move. Bailey saw a key on the shelf halfway across the half-lit room, so she picked it up and ran back to unlock the cage door. When she unlocked the door, Bien Faire opened her eyes. Bien Faire had always been beautiful. She had placed a glamour on herself that made her look human. Even with a glamour, in her human form she looked unworldly. She was such a natural beauty. The light of life within her was of good, and the natural glow was an aura so beautiful—no matter what form Bien Faire took. When Bailey looked down at her, she cringed. Bien Faire looked like a skeleton with skin. Her face was gaunt. Her eyes sunk in so much that she looked almost alien to Bailey. Bien Faire realized it was Bailey and reached out and grabbed her arm.

"I have to tell you before it's too late," Bien Faire whispered.

"Bien Faire rest. We will get some help."

"There is no help for me, Bailey. I have ingested steel in order to prevent Elizabeth from bonding me to her for all of eternity. She only wanted to take my powers, so she could destroy you and who knows what else. I didn't have a choice." Bien Faire was breathing hard, and Bailey could tell she was fighting to stay alive long enough to say what she needed to say to her.

"This is all my fault. I should have stayed here," Bailey wailed.

"Bailey, you are everything I knew you could be," Bien Faire said. "We don't have much time. Before my light fades to nothing, I have to transfer my powers to you. I am not sure my powers will help, but if I don't pass them along, they die with me." Bailey was crying. A creature as kind hearted as Bien Faire was dying while the death shell of Elizabeth walked free on this earth. Tears rolled down Bailey's face.

"I have lived a good life. I have lived for thousands of years, and I hope I have let the white light shine from within me each and every moment I have been able to exist, but now I pass the light to you. My power is different from the powers you were born with. I don't know if there will be any side effects," Bien Faire said. Bailey nodded. "One more thing, when he comes tell him I'm sorry. I was wrong, and I will love him always." Bien Faire paused for a moment and a single tear escaped her eyelids. "Light within, I pull from my core. I release to Bailey, for I am no more." Bien Faire transformed back into her natural state and, just like that, Bien Faire's light slowly dimmed. Her entire being dissolved and vanished.

Bailey was overwhelmed. Bien Faire had died, leaving her the only one to fight against the black light. Its only passion was to consume everything good in the world. She was concerned about her mother now. Her mother would be a vampire in three days, and Elizabeth would have some sort of control over her. She could cause her to attack anyone Bailey loved. If her mother did this, she might have to destroy her. The thought of losing her mother now, after finally understanding her, was something Bailey couldn't bear.

Bailey picked herself up off the bed with a self awareness she had never known before. She would fight against the black light with her last breath. She would kill Elizabeth if it was the last thing she ever did. She would destroy her for causing Bien Faire to take away her own existence in order to prevent Elizabeth from having the powers that now flowed within her. Bailey closed her eyes, feeling the powers ripple within her. When she opened her eyes, she could see everything so clearly. These powers gave her a different view of the world. Everything was crisp and clean. She could see that Kingston had an aura of white light that shined from just under his skin. She wondered if everyone would have this new glow to them. She could refocus and turn it off if she needed to, but it was a good way for her to tell whether a person was good or not. She started looking around the room.

"Kingston, I think we should see if there is anything here we should take with us, so Elizabeth doesn't have it."

"Bailey, we are not going to be able to leave here. Your mother is going to be a vampire. We are going to have to prevent her from hurting people. She can kill any one of us," Kingston said. "She won't be able to stop. The blood lust will rule her life now."

"You're her soul mate. You can change everything."

"How do you know I'm her soul mate?"

"You were always meant to be together. You just have to offer her a sacrifice of your blood. I won't lie. It's dangerous. She could still choose the blood over you and kill you before I could stop her. It will have to be your choice to try this or not."

"I'll do anything for my Joey."

"Okay, we will bring her down here and place her in the steel cage when it gets closer to the time for her to wakeup. I know she could break free easily, but I'm hoping it will buy us enough time to convince her that she loves you."

"It's worth a try..." he hesitated, his voice clearly miserable. "I should have left her with Bill. At least she would still be human," Kingston said.

"Human...depends on your definition of what a human is, I guess. My mother has not been human since you left. When you came back... so did she," Bailey said. Kingston nodded.

"Now, I just have to figure out what I'm going to do with Amber," Bailey said.

"I think you should tell her...everything," Kingston said.

"I agree," Ashton said, standing at the top of the stairwell.

"Okay, I guess she has a right to know," Bailey said.

"It looks like Elizabeth left in a hurry," Kingston said.

"Why do you say that?" Bailey asked.

"She left the book right beside the keys to Bien Faire's cage."

"What book?" Bailey asked.

"Elizabeth was going to take Bien Faire, but she must have realized Bien Faire poisoned herself, so she couldn't take her. She must have been infuriated to forget the book...Perfidia's book of spells. Without this book, all the potions in this room are worthless. I know she can use different powers from Perfidia, but she needed some of these spells. I'm sure of it. I never knew where Perfidia kept that book. I would have destroyed it long ago."

"I don't need it. Let's burn the book," Bailey said. Kingston laughed.

"I know you don't need it, but we cannot destroy it with fire. When I said I should have destroyed it a long time ago, I meant I would have needed you to do it with magic. The book has nothing but dark magic in it. You just need to focus on it with the white light within. It should cause it to explode."

"Okay, I'll give it a try," Bailey said. That is when Bailey saw the book for what it was. She flinched away from it. Bailey was trying to regain her focus, but she couldn't help but wonder who had died in order to make the book she was about to destroy. Bailey centered herself and pulled from her core the white light within. She took both of her hands and touched her palms together as if pulling the light to them. She then raised her hands toward the book, and the light flowed from her palms, touching the book's cover first. The book shuddered and shrieked like it was alive. Bailey watched as the ribs on the torso rippled like waves in the ocean. Bailey maintained her focus and continued to let the flow of white light stream from her palms, but she put more force behind the light now. The stream intensified. The book jumped and jerked from side to side as if trying to escape the light that had it bound.

The book leapt onto its side, and the tiny hands that made up the binding started creeping toward Bailey. Bailey's focus grew more intense and the book started spurting a dark liquid. At first, Bailey thought it was blood. After taking a second look, she realized it was ink. The light was cutting into the book like a serrated knife cutting into bread, and the book was bleeding ink instead of blood. Finally, a loud shrill erupted from the book until it made a gasping pant and exploded. Shreds of paper, the skin book cover, along with tiny fragments of bone and ink were clinging to everything within a few feet from where the book originally lay. Kingston looked at Bailey and smiled. Bailey calmed the light flow from her hand until it ceased. Bailey didn't realize what all she could do yet. The powers that flowed through her were never-ending.

Chapter Twenty-Six

Amber finally came to, and Bailey was there holding her hand. She looked into Amber's eyes and told her everything. It took Amber a while to fully understand that this was real and not a joke. When Bailey told her the truth, the memories of what happened when Perfidia kidnapped her, along with the night at the Laker Farm, came crashing back to her mind, and Amber started to panic. Bailey slapped her swiftly across her right cheek, and Amber finally regained some control.

"I'm sorry, Amber. I didn't want you to have to know about this world…or live in it."

"It's not your fault."

"I should have protected you more."

"I can take care of myself. Stop treating me like a baby."

"Okay, Amber. The best thing for us to do right now is for you to go back home and not let anyone know of this world. It will protect you as well as them. I mean it, Amber. You cannot tell anyone. First of all, they wouldn't believe you. Second, it's dangerous for humans to know of the existence of witches and vampires."

"Are you a witch, Bailey?" Amber asked.

"I haven't really thought about a title for myself, but yes, I am a witch. I was born a witch. I just didn't know it. Also, I have been given more powers than any one witch has ever controlled. It's a little scary for me."

"I would be scared too," Amber said. Bailey smiled at her sister.

"I will be okay. I learn something new about myself every day, just like you. It's just that I learn how my powers grow and change to fit the needs set before me. Sometimes it's good things and sometimes bad, but it's all me."

"Hmmm. Do you need my help, Bailey?"

"The best way to help me is to get out of here and go home. Please take care of yourself and don't come visit me until I call and tell you everything is okay."

"Okay, Bailey. I will try and listen this time." They both laughed and hugged as they walked toward Amber's car. Amber got in and waved goodbye as she drove away. Bailey was relieved that at least Amber was on her way back to safety. She dreaded the thought of what the next few days would bring.

Elizabeth billowed around the perimeter of the house. Bailey seemed to notice the blackness, but she didn't realize it was Elizabeth in her other form. Elizabeth could transform from her human façade to her true self, which was liquid darkness. Elizabeth discovered she could travel in this form. If she surrounded a human with this darkness, the darkness would cause their true nature to come to light. Sometimes, the human would resist the darkness. She found that if she confined them to it and they resisted…they died. She had killed five humans in the past week. Elizabeth grew more beautiful with each death. Those who didn't resist eventually went crazy and wandered off from their families and day-to-day life. They were soon lost to the world of the living.

It seemed Perfidia grew strength from the torture of humans, but Elizabeth grew her strength from their death. Elizabeth watched as Amber got into her car and drove away. She wanted to follow her, but Bailey had this new glow of white light that shined from within her, and Elizabeth knew Bien Faire had given Bailey her powers, so she shrieked out a maddening cry.

Bailey heard it, flinching a little, and looked around to see if her new sight could shed any light on where the sound had come from. It was as if the sound came out of the darkness that surrounded the house, but she knew it sounded like Elizabeth, and this made Bailey edgy.

She didn't want to drag the people she loved yet again into this battle of good versus evil, but she would have to. Ashton wouldn't leave her, and she knew asking him would only cause a fight, but she was going to ask him anyway.

"Ashton, can I talk to you for a minute?" Bailey asked. Ashton eyed Bailey with a sudden alertness. Bailey could tell he was trying to read her thoughts, but her magic far outweighed his now, so she had more control over what she would let him see.

"Sure," he said with a curt expression on his face.

"Ashton, the next few days are going to be crazy, so I want you to go back and stay at the loft."

"You're kidding, right? There is no way I'm leaving you here alone."

"You're not a vampire anymore. Elizabeth can hurt you. I can't live through what happened with Perfidia. What if something happens to you that I can't fix?"

"It won't. We have to stay together."

"No, I don't want you here." Ashton's face was pained. This hurt him, and she knew it would, but she had to get him to leave.

"I won't go," Ashton said.

"Why not?"

"Because I can't let you face something alone that is in your world now because of me."

"Don't feel like you owe me anything. This is your chance at a human life. Elizabeth could curse you again, and I won't be able to turn you back. You could lose your soul forever."

"Bailey, if I lose you because I wasn't there to help, my soul will mean nothing. You are my soul."

"You are my soul too, Ashton, and that is why I need you to go. I have powers now that I'm going to have to use in order to save us all. I can't do that if I'm afraid for your life.

"I can't do it, Bailey. Please don't ask me to do this. I will be fine."

"I can make you do it," Bailey said. Ashton was mad now. He knew Bailey could cast some sort of binding spell that would not let him leave the loft, and the thought of how controlling that was pissed him off.

"But you won't. That would be taking away my choice. Going home is my choice, not yours." Bailey glared at Ashton and stormed out of the room. She knew he was right. She knew they would fight over this, and he would win because he wouldn't leave. She wouldn't leave him either if the roles were reversed. She would never use magic to force him to do something he didn't want to do, but the thought was tempting.

Right now, she was frustrated. How could she be expected to fight against Elizabeth if she could easily curse Ashton? Bailey was going to have to draw on her new-found powers to find the self control in order to fight with Ashton there. She had no other choice. She would have to be strong enough to protect herself, Kingston, her mother and Ashton.

When Ashton found Bailey, she was pacing in the backyard. He thought she looked very attractive when she was mad. He smiled at her, but she continued to glare, so he tried to hide the smile, but it was a lost cause. He couldn't refrain the chuckle that slipped through his lips. When Bailey looked at him very angrily and saw the playful look on his face, she could no longer stay mad. She started laughing too.

"I guess you win this round," Bailey said.

"Don't worry. You put up a good fight. Very entertaining," he said.

"Humph."

"Don't be mad. It's going to take all of us to get control over Elizabeth."

"If that is possible," Bailey said.

"She has a weakness, just like Perfidia. We just have to find it."

"That is the problem, figuring out her weakness before she figures out mine."

"What is your weakness?" Ashton asked.

"You." His eyes tightened in concern.

"Me?"

"Ashton, I will protect you at all cost. I know it, and it scares me."

"What do you mean *at all cost*?" Ashton's mind was racing with the thoughts of how Bailey could sacrifice herself for him.

"I mean...no matter what it costs me; you will walk away from this." Bailey knew she would freely give her life for Ashton. She also knew that the chances of both of them getting out of this a second time alive was impossible.

"Bailey, we both will walk away. Promise me you will not do anything stupid to keep me alive if it will cause your death."

"I can't promise you that."

"Bailey, I can't live without you. Don't put me in this situation."

"Don't put me in this situation. Don't get me wrong, I am grateful you saved my sister, but your sacrifice taught me something. I can't live through thinking you're dead again. I won't do it."

"You're scaring me, Bailey. What exactly does that mean?" he asked.

"I don't know." Ashton reached out and pulled Bailey to him. He loved her so much, and the thought of her dying for him made him angry.

"Promise me, Bailey."

"Promise you what?" she asked.

"You're not going to get yourself killed trying to save me."

"Okay, I'll promise that when you do." He glared at Bailey, so she glared back.

"Why are you so stubborn?" he asked.

"I could ask you the same thing," she stated. He frowned in frustration. He reached down and kissed Bailey very aggressively, as if he could will her to do what he wanted.

"Nice try, but this is not going to make me not want to keep you," she laughed.

"Okay, how about we promise each other to keep ourselves out of Elizabeth's path as much as possible."

"You know I can't promise that. She is targeting me and my family. I've got to stop her and fix my mother."

Ashton made a low moan and gave up trying to convince Bailey to not put herself in danger. He knew he would have to keep her out of trouble. He only hoped his attempt at keeping her safe would be enough. For once in his life, he wished he were still a vampire—after all the years of not wanting that fate. Yet he knew now that a vampire's strength, sight, hearing and ability to go invisible could have made a difference in this fight, and he wished he had the ability to use them to keep Bailey safe. He could only hope he would be able to save her. He knew that if it came down to her life or his, he would give his life in a heartbeat to save her. Her powers would give her the advantage in offering herself first, and this terrified Ashton. He knew as soon as her heart stopped beating, so would his. They were forever connected—two lost souls bound together in love.

Amber was trying to get a hold on her new reality. She had tried so hard to stay sane in front of her sister—her sister the witch—but it was all so surreal. How could it really be true? How could her mother become a vampire in less than three days? She wanted to tell James so badly, but she knew Bailey was right. He would think she was insane. Bailey also said it could put whoever she told in danger, and James was someone she didn't want in any kind of danger. She was in love with him. She didn't know if she would ever have the courage to tell him. He had never said he loved her, so maybe he didn't. Falling in love was so frustrating. Finding someone she couldn't live without—someone who complements who she is—was not something she thought would happen so soon. It was like a flash of light, bright and eye opening, Amber thought. Amber heard a knock on her bedroom door. She let out a scream because it frightened her.

"Are you okay, Amber?" James asked.

"Yeah, you just scared me. Come on in."

James laughed, "You're such a little chicken."

"Humph, not a good way to start…if you want to hang out."

"I didn't come here to hang out," James said, a little smug. Amber raised one eyebrow.

"Then why did you come, James?" Amber asked, annoyed.

"To make-out," he said smiling. Amber rolled her eyes.

"Yeah, good luck doing that by yourself."

"Oh, come on. Don't be so crabby." Amber didn't know why she wanted to talk about their relationship at that moment, but she did. She was tired of assuming he was with her to make-out, while she was falling head over heels for him. It frustrated her that James seemed so casual about their relationship. She had never seen him jealous or show the least bit of concern that she might like someone else. She had guys approach her all the time, and he had not once tried to mark his territory. It was so frustrating. She would have clawed someone's eyes out if they came after him. James seemed to take their relationship one day at a time…like if it were here today and gone tomorrow he would be fine. Amber frowned.

"Is that all you want from me?" she asked.

"Huh?"

"Making out…is that all you want from me?" James' eyes tightened.

"What does that mean? Where is this coming from?" he asked.

"I want to know why you're with me." Amber asked. James didn't answer. He just watched Amber with curious eyes.

"Can you just answer the question?" James still said nothing. He was watching her like he was waiting for some brilliant answer to pop into existence right in front of him. Amber sighed. "Just forget it," Amber said, shaking her head. Her phone rang, so she ran to grab it, anything to help take her away from this tension-filled situation.

"Hello," Amber said.

"Hi, Amber."

"Hi. Who is this?"

"Adam." Amber's face flushed red. James' eyes narrowed on her conversation like he was taking in every word.

"Hi, Adam. What's up?"

"Bailey gave me your number. I was calling to see if you would like to do some tutoring for me?"

"What kind of tutoring?"

"Well, I have my brothers now. I don't know if Bailey told you, but they are 3 and 5. They have fallen behind in preschool and need some help catching up. Their nanny is helping some, but I thought it would be more fun for them if someone younger and more fun could teach them. What do you think?"

"I'd love to help you, Adam. I can help on Tuesday and Thursday afternoons after school."

"Perfect! Thanks, Amber. I'll text you with more details. I'll see you on Tuesday."

"Okay, bye." Amber hung up the phone. She was smiling from ear to ear. She forgot how much she liked Adam. He was so beautiful and smart. She shook her head from side to side smiling. When she turned to look at James, the expression on his face was not happy.

"What?" Amber asked.

"Who is Adam?" James asked in a stern, almost parental voice.

"A friend."

"Someone we go to school with?"

"No...he's in college."

"You're talking to some college guy?"

"Huh?"

"I don't want you going over to some college guy's house, Amber."

"He's friends with my sister. That is how I know him. He wants me to help tutor his two younger brothers. That's all."

"Sure, that's what he says," James said, clearly jealous and annoyed.

"Are you jealous?" Amber asked. James' face went beet red.

"NO!" he said, too loud and much too quickly.

"You are," she laughed. "You're jealous."

"So what. You would be, too. What if I was going to some college girl's house to tutor her sisters?" Amber decided she could get her answers now about their relationship.

"We're just having fun, right? Making out...nothing serious...so why does it matter if I'm going to a college guy's house?" James' face fell.

"Nothing serious," James muttered. "Right, I gotta go. I'll talk to you later," he said.

"Wait, you're clearly upset...Why?"

James sighed, "I don't know. Maybe because the girl I'm madly in love with just said our relationship is nothing serious. We're just having fun, right?" Before James could move, Amber threw her arms around him and kissed him passionately on the mouth. His eyes widened in surprise.

"I love you, too. I thought you didn't think we were serious. I thought you only wanted to have fun. Somewhere along the line, I have fallen in love with you. I was mad because you don't seem to ever get jealous when other guys give me attention, and I wondered why."

He laughed, clearly relieved. "I know you, Amber. You are not interested in any of the other boys in school, but this college guy made you blush, and it made me mad."

Amber laughed, "Oh, I see."

"So, what does he look like?"

"Typical blond hair, blue eyes, about six foot two."

"So he's nice looking then," he said.

"Not too bad on the eyes," Amber said, smiling.

"Well, if he looks good, he must not be smart. What is his major?" Amber was having a little fun now.

"Medicine…he plans on being a doctor. Oh yeah, he's also a very good surfer." James' eyes tightened with annoyance, and his face was flushed with heat. Amber couldn't help but notice him stiffen when she said that Adam was going to be a doctor and loves to surf.

"You have nothing to worry about, silly. I just told you point blank that I'm in love with you," Amber said.

"True, but…" Amber stopped him from protesting when she placed her lips on his, and the kissing began.

It was Tuesday afternoon, and Amber was on her way to Adam's house to help tutor Mark and Blake. She was happy to be seeing Adam again, but she felt bad for leaving James alone this afternoon. He was clearly unhappy that she was going to Adam's house, but he was determined not to be controlling. She could tell it took a lot of effort on his part to be supportive with this venture. Amber was nervous because she knew at some point today her mother would wake up as a vampire. She still couldn't wrap her head around it. If someone had told her a week ago that her sister is the most powerful witch in the world or that her mother would be cursed into a vampire, she would have thought they were crazy.

Witches and vampires don't exist. That is fairytale crap that writers make up to sell books and make movies. She just couldn't believe it was really true. She wondered why no one had ever linked the vampire world to the world of magic. It was very interesting to her that a witch or wizard made a human a vampire by cursing them. She wondered if Bailey could curse people into becoming vampires. This world scared her, but it also lured her in, just like a gulper eel lures its prey with a glowing light, so the prey thinks it's going to receive its own meal. Amber was lured in by what the world of magic could offer her. Amber knew she was lost to the world that existed for her sister and mother, and part of her was jealous.

Amber thought it would be cool to have powers and be able to control the world she lived in, but she didn't fully understand the consequences of that responsibility and what that meant for Bailey. She didn't realize that Bailey would live every second of her life in fear of losing someone she loved to the world of dark magic. She would have to constantly stand guard and never be able to live her life the way she wanted. She was guardian now of Bien Faire's world, too. Too much to place on the shoulders of an 18- year-old girl.

Amber finally made it to Adam's house. Adam had texted her directions, and she knew the neighborhood. She knew that her parents owned this entire building, and she guessed Bailey was helping Adam with the bills. Bailey was so giving of her allowance. Amber didn't blow all of her money, but she was not like Bailey when it came to being responsible. She loved being a cheerleader and being popular. Amber and her best friend, Caroline, were kind of in the middle group until James came along, catapulting them to the upper level of popularity.

No one knew James was really Mathew, and he didn't seem to want anyone to remember him by that name, so Amber never told a soul. Amber was not cruel to the other kids like the rest of the popular people, but she did have a problem with saving her money. Her parents put the same amount of money in her bank account every month as Bailey's, but Amber would usually spend most of it. She would purchase clothes and accessories. She was always downloading new things to her IPod Touch. Amber didn't give much thought about saving any of the money. However, there was one thing she did that no one knew about. She took $1000 of her money every month and donated it to various soup kitchens and shelters, just whoever she thought needed the money for that month. She may have been a little shallow, but she was a really good person.

Adam was waiting at the door when she drove up. She blushed and was hoping he didn't see her. She had forgotten how utterly gorgeous the boy was. He was every girl's dream. She thought he was better looking than that secret agent boyfriend of Bailey's. She got out of the car and walked up to the front door. Adam stood there smiling a smile that made her heart flutter. She had to get control over this. After all, she was in love with James.

She smiled and said, "Hello, Adam."

"Hey, Amber. Thanks so much for doing this."

"No problem. What do the boys need to work on?" she asked.

"Everything...Mark needs to work on learning his alphabet. He also needs to work on his numbers. Blake needs a refresher on that too, but he needs more help learning to write his name and recognizing the letters on his own."

"Okay, let's get started. Where are the boys?" Amber asked.

"They're outside with the nanny right now. Why don't we talk for a minute about what you think you will need to work with them?"

"What do you mean?" Amber asked. Adam laughed.

"Well, for one, what type of materials do I need to get for you and, second, what kind of fees are you going to charge me?" he asked. Amber rolled her eyes.

"I don't need money, but thanks for the offer. I'm doing this as a friend. Now, as far as materials, I'll go get what I need from the Parent Teacher Connection off of Candlewood Street tomorrow after school."

"Thanks, Amber. Let me give you some cash for the materials." Amber watched as Adam opened up his wallet, and she noticed he only had sixty dollars in there. She decided this month's donated money would go to Adam and the boys.

"Don't worry about it. I tend to go overboard with stuff, so it's best if I purchase what I need. Besides, this could be my new calling," she said and smiled. Adam looked at her and knew that she was being kind to him by offering to pay for everything. He realized she was trying to let him keep his dignity while still giving him a handout, but at this point he needed all the help he could get.

"Thanks. You're a life saver," he said.

"You're welcome." The boys came inside, and Adam introduced Amber. They started working on their letters and such. Adam let Sarah go home for the day. Adam walked over to the sofa and pulled out one of many medical books and started reading them. She tried to keep the boys quiet while she was teaching them, so they wouldn't disturb Adam, but it was hard. They were very rambunctious. By the time she was ready to leave, Blake could write half of his name, and he was so excited. Mark was trying to sing the alphabet song and was getting pretty close to mastering it. Adam had been watching all along. He was impressed with Amber's ability to take control and teach the boys so easily. It was as if she was born to teach. Adam walked into the kitchen and told the boys it was time to start cooking supper. Amber looked at Adam and asked, "Do you need some help?" Adam smiled.

"No, I think we got it. You should be getting home."

"Okay. Bye, boys. I'll see you on Thursday."

"Amber, can I talk to you for a minute?" Adam asked.

"Sure."

"I just wanted to thank you and say I'm really impressed with your teaching skills." Amber laughed, "Thanks, my true calling is teaching someone to sing the alphabet song."

"It's more than that. You reached them and made them want to learn. Thank you."

"No problem. I'll see you on Thursday," she said as she walked out the door.

Chapter Twenty-Seven

Bailey knew it was time for her mother to wake up soon, so they had moved her down into the dungeon and placed her in the steel cage. Kingston, Ashton and Bailey all stood alert, waiting for her to wake up and make her first move. Bailey could taste the emotions in the room pouring off Kingston and Ashton. She wanted to yell at both of them to get control because it was making her a little dizzy. That is when she heard the snarls coming from the steel cage. Her eyes locked onto her mother's face, and her mother wasn't there anymore. Joey was watching all three of them, as if trying to find the weakest link to take first. Ashton looked at Bailey, and she knew what he was thinking.

Something is wrong. She is not the same as the other vampires. Whatever Elizabeth is made her different. Elizabeth is truly evil. Bailey, I have no idea how to help her now. I don't think we can put Kingston in there with her, Ashton thought.

We have to do something, Bailey thought. Then Kingston spoke.

"Joey, my Joey. I'm so sorry. Look at what has happened to you." Joey continued to stare at Kingston while snarls escaped her lips. She was constantly scanning the room, looking for a way out. Bailey could hear her thoughts now, and it scared her so bad that she didn't know what to do. *Blood, I need blood. Human blood. All of these here are humans. I shall kill them all and drain every ounce of blood from their bodies—every single drop,* Joey thought.

"No, I will not allow that, Joanne. You are not going to kill anyone. You are my mother, and Kingston is your soul mate. You have loved him always."

Joey hissed, "I have no soul, so I can't have a soul mate. He is dinner...and so are you."

"We can do this the easy way or the hard way, but you're not hurting anyone. I have the power to kill you, and I will use it."

"Hah, I'm your mother. You said so yourself. You are not going to kill me, Bailey."

"I don't want to, but I will."

"So, you expect me to live in this cage while you feed me...what exactly?"

"We will get you blood, but right now we need to trust each other."

"I see," Joey said. Joey lunged for the door so fast that Bailey didn't see it happen. She tore the door from its hinges and threw it across the room. She then leaped onto Ashton. Bailey blasted Joey with a ray of white light, and she fell back in pain. The white light seemed to affect her differently than the others. It had burned her skin where it touched, and Bailey had barely used any of the light. She used just enough to throw her off of Ashton. Ashton leaped to his feet, fully aware at how dangerous this situation was. Joey eyed Bailey with a look of disgust and then lunged at her. Bailey shot her again with the white light, blasting her full on the chest. She fell back and cried out in pain. Kingston stepped in and placed himself right in front of Joey.

"You're hurting her...Stop!"

"Kingston, get out of the way. That is not Joey anymore," Ashton said.

"I will not. Joey, you need blood. Take mine."

"NO!" Bailey yelled. "She will not have the desire to stop."

"She needs me now, and I will not walk away," Kingston said.

"Its suicide if you go to her now," Bailey said.

"I'm already dead without her," he said. He ran to Joey, and she lunged for him, biting into his neck. Kingston moaned out in pain, but didn't attempt to move. Bailey was screaming for Joey to stop. She was caught between a rock and a hard place. She could save her dad by killing her mother, or she could let her mother continue to drink her father's blood, and he would surely die. Just as Bailey made the decision to vanquish her mother, her mother pushed Kingston away.

Light started flowing through her every pore. Joey was radiating such an intense light from within that Bailey had to look away. Then Joey started screaming and thrashing about. When the other vampires transformed back to humans, they didn't cry out in pain. She could tell her mother was clearly in pain. Bailey didn't know what to do, but she needed to check on Kingston.

Bailey walked to Kingston, and the blood vessel in his neck was still streaming with blood. She took her right hand and pulled from her core the power of healing. Bailey touched her palm to Kingston's neck, and she felt the healing powers flow from her body to his. Kingston raised his head and smiled.

Bailey walked over to her mother, who was still thrashing about, to see if she could take the pain from her. She touched her palms together and started thinking about pulling the pain from her mother. She then placed both palms on each side of her mother's face. Bailey felt the struggle within her mother, and she pulled with the white light as hard as she could. Bailey fell to the floor as the intensity of the pain crashed through her entire body. Within minutes, Bailey heard her mother's voice, and she knew she was human again, but something was happening to Bailey. The darkness she had pulled from her mother was fighting to gain control of Bailey. Bailey raised her head and looked into Ashton's eyes. He was horrified. Her eyes were pitch black and hollow. Ashton ran to her and picked her up into his arms.

"Bailey, fight it, honey. Resist the darkness. You can resist. Don't let it take you away from me. You promised. I love you. Please!" He watched as Bailey pushed the blackness away from herself with the white light, only to have it snap back into her like a rubber band. She pushed it away again and still the same thing. Ashton cupped her face in his hands and looked directly into her eyes. He then kissed her and the longing she felt for him gave her the strength to push the blackness from her mind. They saw it hover above her head, and Bailey had the feeling it was going to leap into Ashton. She blasted it with the white light and it vanished. They both sat for a while, holding each other. Joey was now at Kingston's side, holding his head in her lap and stroking his hair. Bailey and Ashton sat in silence, both feeling the need to hold each other and say nothing.

Joey looked into Kingston's eyes and said, "Kingston, I'm so sorry. I could have killed you."

"But you didn't. You stopped. I'll be fine," Kingston said.

"I love you so much, Kingston."

"I love you, Joey, and that is all that matters. Now don't give it another thought. It was not your fault. You didn't have any control over your own actions."

"How did you stop it?" she asked.

"We are truly soul mates, and that is why you're human again. Bailey is the reason you were able to let go of the darkness. Otherwise, I fear it would have driven you mad." Joey didn't say anything. She just clung to Kingston, and he held her tighter.

Amber waited until midnight on the third night before she started trying to call Bailey. The suspense of not knowing whether her mother was a vampire was killing her. Bailey and Ashton had gone back to the loft. They had to be back at Perfidia's first thing in the morning to see if there were any signs that Elizabeth had been back at the house. They had to find her and destroy her. Bailey and Ashton were both completely exhausted from everything that had taken place, so they didn't hear the phone ring over and over again throughout the night.

Amber was in panic mode now. She had been up all night going crazy—wondering if her entire family had been wiped out and if Elizabeth would soon come for her. She decided she would make her way to Perfidia's house. She figured she could find it again. She remembered it was off the 101, so it shouldn't be too hard to find. Besides, she couldn't sit around and wait to hear from Bailey. She knew she promised Bailey that she would not come around; that she would wait for her to call, but Bailey didn't understand what it was like not knowing if the people she loved were dead. She got in her car and took off toward Perfidia's.

Traffic was crazy, but that was the usual in Los Angeles. It could take an hour to go ten miles in certain places. Even though traffic was moving at a turtle's pace, it was moving. She rolled down her windows. The sun shined brightly today, and she could feel the heat warm her skin. Amber loved living in California. She had heard a lot of people say it was home to the fruits and nuts of the world, but she just knew it as a place where everyone could feel like they belonged—a true melting pot of culture mixed in with a freedom that is like no other place in the world.

Amber pulled off the 101 freeway to look for a few landmarks to remind her of where she was, but nothing seemed that familiar. Then she saw the shopping center that she had passed on her way out, and she knew immediately which way to go from there. She would be at the house in less than ten minutes. Good or bad, she would find out if her family was okay.

Elizabeth had decided the only way to kill Bailey would be to take her by surprise, so she was biding her time and waiting for the perfect moment to swoop in and destroy Bailey's world. She was watching as Bailey and Ashton pulled into the driveway. She wanted to get them inside the house before she attacked either one of them. Elizabeth knew she was different now. At first, she thought she was going to be able to love again, but the darkness was too much. She realized that one can't love without a soul, and she knew that she was truly the living dead, made up of dark magic. Her shell was the same, but she was not the same on the inside. She imagined that if she cut herself to see if blood would spurt from her veins, that blackness would ooze out instead. The only thing she knew now was the darkness controlled her, and this was the life she was given. She wanted to live, so she would do what the darkness commanded of her.

Ashton and Bailey wearily made their way inside the house. They had checked all the rooms, but didn't find any sign that Elizabeth had been back. They walked outside into the backyard to see if there were any signs of her out there. That is when Bailey heard the car door slam and knew someone was there. She ran to the side fence and was upset to see her sister cautiously, but anxiously, making her way toward the house. Bailey motioned for her not to go inside and yelled, but Amber didn't see or hear her. She had one thing on her mind right now and that was finding out what happened to her family. There was no side gate, so Bailey couldn't reach her sister before she made her way inside. She wished for once that she had locked the front door. She ran back to get inside, but Elizabeth's cloudy form billowed down from the exterior of the house and materialized right before Bailey and Ashton. Her eyes were hollow and filled with death. They looked sadistic, and they glared a devil's glare at Bailey. The only thing Bailey could think about was Amber and Ashton. How was she going to protect two humans—two humans she couldn't live without? Elizabeth spoke then.

"You will die today, Bailey."

"No! You will, Elizabeth!"

"Hah, you're going to try and vanquish me like you did Perfidia? Good luck with that."

"I don't need luck. I have the powers to destroy you. You had choices here, and you chose the wrong path. You cannot be allowed to live."

"I think you're mistaken as to what you're up against this time, Bailey. As evil as Perfidia was, she still had a glimmer of humanity in her, and that is why you were able to destroy her. I have no such *glimmer*. I have no light of life at all. You will not beat me. You will die. Don't worry, I'll take care of Ashton." Bailey's eyes raged with fury. The powers within her boiled, and she was ready to duel.

"I'm ready when you are. Give me your best shot," Bailey said. Elizabeth smiled a deathly grimace and said, "As you wish." She shot a look at Ashton and started speaking the vampire transformation spell. "*Vomica cruor phantom ex lux lucis, vas of obscurum, forever a lamia.*"

Elizabeth raised her hand to cast the spell toward Ashton. Just as Elizabeth released the spell toward Ashton, Bailey shot a blast of white light toward the spell, diverting its path. Bailey looked up just in time to see Amber come outside as the spell hit her, knocking Amber to her knees.

"What have I done?" Bailey moaned. "Amber, NO!" The fury rolled through her like a million stampeding elephants, and she faced Elizabeth with a new vengeance. When Elizabeth locked her eyes on Bailey, the eyes staring back at her let her know that Bailey had darkness within her, too. This fight might be more equal than she had thought possible. Tendrils of light expanded from every inch of Bailey's body. They were inching their way toward Elizabeth like snakes slithering down a path. Elizabeth's eyes narrowed and she hissed out a sound of alarm. She tried to run from the light, but she couldn't. She cast her own dark light toward Bailey, but the rays shining from her acted as a shield and the black light bounced right off. The tendrils continued to snake their way up Elizabeth's body, searing her skin at the touch. Bailey continued to project the light onto Elizabeth until every inch of her body was covered. Elizabeth was trying to resist the light by casting her own darkness from within, but it was no match to the powers that Bailey held.

Elizabeth struggled, snarling out a ragged breath. Then, one by one, the tendrils climbed up her neck to her mouth and slid down her throat, slowly suffocating her. She gurgled out a scream, but couldn't fight it. Then the black light spewed out from her mouth, and Elizabeth's body fell to the ground like a hollow log. Bailey pulled from her core once more every ounce of love she could imagine, along with the white light, and blasted the black light out of existence. With Elizabeth's lifeless body lying on the ground, Bailey leaped over her and ran to Amber. Ashton was already holding Amber, and they didn't know whether she would become a vampire or not.

Printed in the United States
by Baker & Taylor Publisher Services